The Vanishing of Margaret Small

Praise for Neil Alexander

'Calling all fans of uplit! A tender, thought-provoking and totally gripping novel . . . from a wonderful storyteller . . . deserves to be a huge hit.'
Matt Cain

'A beautiful story of human spirit and its power to thrive against the odds. I'm so glad that I read it and got to meet Margaret.'
Anstey Harris

'A fantastic, feel-good story . . . rich in nostalgia and a joy to read. A book that will keep you smiling long after you finish.'
Matson Taylor

'Beautifully observed and poignant. An outstanding debut.'
Alex Brown

'A captivating and charming story. Margaret will warm the cockles of your heart.'
Imogen Clark

The Vanishing of Margaret Small

Neil Alexander

First published in Great Britain in 2022 by

Bonnier Books UK Limited

4th Floor, Victoria House, Bloomsbury Square, London, WC1B 4DA

Owned by Bonnier Books

Sveavägen 56, Stockholm, Sweden

A CIP catalogue record for this book is available from the British Library.

ISBN: 9781471414510

This book is typeset using Atomik ePublisher

Printed and bound in Great Britain by Clays Ltd, Elcograf S.p.A.

Embla Books is an imprint of Bonnier Books UK

www.bonnierbooks.co.uk

Prologue

5 NOVEMBER 1947

I was seven years old when they vanished me. The Rat Catcher done it. He stole me from Grandma. In the beginning, you see, I lived with Grandma, for Mother had died soon after I was born.

On days when I was naughty, Grandma told me I was cursed. She said my red hair was the work of the Devil; that I was a changeling, swapped by the fairies, all for what my mother had done. What my mother had done, she wouldn't say. I learned very quickly not to ask. If I did, God help me, she'd get angry, give my legs a good hiding with the belt.

There was this man, you see. His name was Mr Grey, but everyone on our street called him the Rat Catcher. Oh, he was a sneak! Tall and crooked, with a long silver ponytail that snaked all the way down his back. He worked for the Board of Control – them lot who put you away for good. His job was to nick children from their houses, take them up St Mary's in Canterbury. Not just any children, mind – only the ones like me, what was different.

The day they vanished me was a black day. Grandma was cooking in the kitchen. She put me in the sink, so I could watch the fireworks from the window. Part of the window was boarded up with wood, where the glass had been blown off during the war, but I could still make out the Catherine wheels and the Roman candles, the loud noises and bright lights, flashing up in the sky.

When the knock at the door came, I thought it was more fireworks going off, but it got louder and louder until Grandma put down her knife and went to answer it. It was him. Mr Grey. I'd met him once before, when Grandma took me to see him in his big office. He done all these tests on me, asked me lots of questions that I didn't know the answers to. Things like: 'Where is London?' I said to him, it's near where Grandma comes from, which is true, for she's from a place called Lewisham. It ain't far from there, I'm sure of it. But Mr Grey said I was wrong. He said, 'Margaret, I'm afraid you'll need looking after all the time.'

Grandma must have known he was coming, for she had my suitcase all ready. She handed it over to Mr Grey. Then she gave me my favourite doll, the broken one with only one eye. Grabbing its little arm, I carried it towards the front door. I stopped, turned to look at Grandma.

'You come, too,' I said, holding out my hand.

She stayed where she was.

She said, 'You'd better get going, Margaret. You don't want to keep the nice gentleman here waiting.'

I looked at Mr Grey and shook my head.

'I don't want to.'

'You do as you're told,' she said, her voice colder this time.

Fireworks was still going off outside. The coalman's cart went rattling past, a group of lads hanging off the back. Laughing and shouting they was, chucking penny bangers on the street. The night smelled of burning wood. Mr Grey put me in the car, slamming the door shut. I climbed up on the seat, looking out the back window. Grandma was standing by the front gate, hugging her coat. She was smoking a cigarette and waving. I waved back at her. Mr Grey started up the engine and I watched her go inside. It was the last time I saw her. She never came to visit me after that – not once. Never had me home for the holidays, neither. Not even a birthday nor Christmas card.

1

'C'

I'm watching you from a coffee shop on Whitstable High Street, dragging your battered tartan shopping trolley with its slightly wonky wheel. Everything about you looks wonky: the clear-framed glasses, held together with sticking plaster, which slip down your nose every so often, the fingerless pink gloves, and the white trainers with their purple shoelaces undone. Head low, eyes down, you shuffle along with a slight limp. You're smaller than I thought you would be now – much smaller – but I can't help smiling. Like the town itself, there's something charming about you. A little rough round the edges, perhaps, eccentric, even! You blend in well here. This really is the perfect place for you.

Stopping at the flashing yellow light, you look both ways before crossing the street, slowly, towards the cafe. You pause on the pavement outside, directly in front of where I'm sitting. Peering in, you squint at the cafe's cosy interior: the wooden counter with its coffee machine and display of home-made cakes, the chalkboard sandwich menu and the magazine stand. I cradle my latte in both hands. It's as if you're looking through me – a ghost.

Your glasses have slipped to the end of your nose and your head is tilted back, neck stretched, mouth wide open, flecks of briny white spit forming threads at the sides. You stare straight ahead, your grey hair clinging tightly to your forehead in wet ringlets. Part of me wants to wave. Part of me wants you to recognise me, but you don't. Leaning in closer, you mutter something to yourself. I can't make out the words – bloody something-or-other – then you turn around, drag your trolley off in the direction of the harbour, its wheels clattering along the pavement. I'm tempted to run after you, to stop you in the street to say hello, but I don't want to rush in too soon – it might upset you. By now, you will have received the gift I sent you. It was just a little something to let you know I'm here, watching out for you. Did you like it?

As you disappear from view, I sit for a minute, deliberating over whether to follow you or not. In the end, my curiosity gets the better of me. I can't help myself. Taking a deep breath, I leave my coffee unfinished, pay the woman behind the counter. Pushing open the door, I step outside and follow you down the High Street.

2

8 AUGUST 2015

Like a lot of old folk, I live on my own. It suits me fine. When I was younger – in my twenties and what have you – I used to long for a husband, but I'm 75 now. If I had a husband, he'd likely be dead as a doorknob. I'm no better off.

In my whole life, nobody ever asked me if I wanted a man. Nobody said, 'Why don't you marry?' They think it's impossible, you see. They think people like me don't have feelings. Humph. I could teach *them* a thing or two about feelings. If I could have any man in the world, it would be the singer, Michael Bolton. What I wouldn't give to run my fingers through his lovely permed hair.

'Lots of people live on their own. There's no need to be frightened, Margaret.'

This is what Frances, the social worker, said when they moved me into the flats on Cromwell Road in the eighties. You'd think it would be easy for someone like me, living alone, for I never had no family or nothing. I still ain't got used to the peace and quiet, though, not really. When you've been in a hospital most of your life, moving into the community feels strange. It takes a long time to get used to. Not that I'd ever want to go back to the hospital. Life is OK now. Things could be better, yes, but they could also be a lot worse.

I've lived in Whitstable for thirty-odd years. The town's changed loads in my time. It used to be mostly pubs, pound shops and charity shops. Like a lot of places in Kent, though, Whitstable's gone to the snobs. They have a Costa Coffee now, and what Wayne, my support worker, calls 'shabby chic' shops. I call them 'rip-off' shops myself – they charge a fortune for repainted furniture, and old cups and saucers that don't even match. You won't catch me buying any of that rubbish. Some people have more money than sense. There are more tourists coming here now, too. You can hardly move for them in summer. I don't like it. It's hard to wheel my trolley down the High Street when there's a group of Japanese people in the way. Some things ain't changed, though. V. C. Jones, the fish and chip shop, is still there, and Peter Cushion's seat. Peter Cushion was a famous actor who done vampire films. He used to live in Whitstable, but he's dead now. At least I think he is, for I've never seen him on his seat. It's on the beach, next to the car park in Island Wall. On Fridays, I like to get a small cod and chips and sit there looking out over the bay.

An odd thing happened this morning. An envelope came in the post with fifty quid and a letter inside. Apart from catalogues, coupons for pizzas, and bills, I don't normally get letters, so this stood out: the words on the envelope was written in black ink, long and twisty, like liquorice laces. It made no sense to me. Wayne usually reads my post, but it's his day off. I kept looking at it, over and over again. Who would want to send me fifty quid? It ain't my birthday until April, and I'm far too old for Valentines. I ain't got many friends, neither. God knows who it's from. I put the money in my purse, and the note in my pocket for safekeeping. Maybe I'll ask one of the staff in Sainsbury's to read it to me.

I go to Sainsbury's every day, except when they close it for the holidays. My favourite part is the beginning, when you go through the sliding doors. As soon as they swish open, you get a big whiff of all the fresh food. It's like being on *Blind Date* when the screen goes back. I don't get people who shop for things on the computer. Don't they want to touch what they're buying first?

The vegetable aisle is quiet today. I hate it when it gets busy. I avoid coming then. Mornings after nine is good because most people are at work. I don't feel so rushed. I can take my time, talk to the staff, or whatever. I like to spend a good hour choosing what I'm going to have to eat. Today's Saturday so I'm making soup for lunch and corned beef hash for tea. I'm a good cook. If I learned one thing at St Mary's, it was cooking. And cleaning, of course. My flat is always spotless.

I tear off a plastic bag and squish it open at the top. I fill it with four tomatoes, making sure I've rolled each one slowly around in my hand first, carefully sniffing it for freshness. I then spend twenty minutes or so picking through all the lettuces. I choose the one I like the look of most and put it in my basket.

'Corned beef, is it?' says Gail on the meat counter.

She's always so happy, Gail. And her make-up is lovely. To look at her, you'd never guess her husband ran off with a tart. Another reason I don't get involved with men. They're more trouble than they're worth. I watch Gail cut four slices of meat and weigh them on the scales.

'One pound and three pence,' she says, wrapping the meat in plastic and printing off a sticker.

She pats the sticker gently on the side of the package,

handing it to me. I hold it for a moment. It feels soft to the touch, light and clingy, like a baby's blanket.

I reach for my purse, clicking it open and taking out the folded fifty-pound note. I'd forgotten I put it there.

'You pay at the till, love,' says Gail. 'Remember?'

'Of course.' I nod, putting the money back in my purse. 'Only someone posted this to me this morning. I've no idea who sent it, though.'

Gail smiles. 'I wish someone would send me a bit of extra cash. I'm working my fingers to the bone saving for a fortnight in Fuengirola. It's expensive now with the euro, and there's no money in sliced meat.'

I want to ask Gail to read my letter, but a small queue has formed behind me. When I go to hand it to her, I hear the man behind me mutter 'stupid cow' under his breath. There's no need for that sort of language in Sainsbury's, so I move on.

There are so many soups to choose from. Sometimes it feels like they're all calling out to me from the shelves like the men on *Blind Date*: 'pick me, pick me'. As I make my choices, I hear Cilla's voice in my head: 'Soup Number One! What's your name and where do you come from?' I can't help laughing; it's nice to be the centre of attention for a change. The words on the labels make no sense to me, so I go by the photos. I take a Heinz tomato and a Campbell's cream of chicken. I then whisper an apology to all the soups I'm not taking home. I hope they won't be too upset. Before going to pay, I nip over to the drinks aisle and grab a can of cider, placing it in the basket next to my other shopping.

The new checkouts confuse me, so I join the long queue for cigarettes, even though I don't smoke.

'This till is card only, love,' shouts the woman behind the counter when she sees me standing at the end.

I don't carry a card, so I panic. A young ginger-haired boy in a Sainsbury's uniform comes over and asks me if I'd like to use the self-service checkouts.

'I don't know how,' I say.

The boy smiles. He says his name is David and he's here to help. As I reach into my coat pocket for my purse, I remember the envelope that came in the post this morning.

'David, love,' I say, handing it to him. 'Can you tell me what this says? My eyesight is terrible.'

This ain't a complete lie, but I'd rather David think of me as just old, rather than old *and* stupid.

David nods and smiles, reading out the words: 'Margaret Small, Cromwell Road, Whitstable.'

'That's me,' I say. 'What about inside?'

David opens the envelope, takes out the note and unfolds it.

'What's it about, then?'

'"Dear Margaret . . ."' He reads the words slowly, like he's having trouble understanding them himself. '"A little something to brighten your day. Love C x".'

He turns it over, to check there is nothing written on the back.

'What does that mean?'

'I guess it means that this *C* person doesn't want you to know who they are.' He grins. 'Maybe you have a secret admirer.'

'Fat chance,' I say, snatching the note back off him, my face growing hot. 'Can you help me scan my groceries now, please?'

After I leave Sainsbury's, I wander over to the bakery and buy two iced fingers to have later with my cup of tea. As I turn to drag my trolley up the High Street, it starts to rain. A summer shower. I stop in the middle of the pavement and tip my head back. Closing my eyes, I stick out my tongue, try to catch the warm, spattering droplets. This puts me in the mood for a hot drink. There's a cafe over the road: Tea and Times. They do nice cakes and sandwiches. Normally it's a bit out of my budget, but maybe I could use some of this money to treat myself to a hot chocolate. I cross the road and peer in the window. My glasses are wet and steamy and slipping down my nose, so it's hard to see. Inside, the cafe looks packed.

'Bloody tourists,' I say out loud. 'Nowhere to sit with them lot taking up all the room.'

The rain is easing off now, so I head towards the seashore.

Taking a seat on Peter Cushion's bench, I get my mini CD player out of my bag. It was Wayne who got me into audiobooks. He took me to the library one day. I'd never been there before. I never saw the point, but they had a whole section full of CDs. For someone who can't read, it's a miracle. It means I get to hear stories. I've only been doing it a year, but, so far, I've got through all the Hobbit books and Rod Stewart's autobiography. This past week or so, I've been listening non-stop to Cilla Black's life story, *What's It All About?* I listen to it every day. I even put it on in bed, for it helps me sleep.

I press play. Straight away, Cilla starts speaking to me. I know it sounds silly, but I find it comforting. Her voice is soft and gentle. It's like listening to an old friend. She's telling me about how she coped after her husband Bobby's death. She says she went into automatic pilot. Her words are soothing. It's like she's sat next to me on the bench. For a moment I forget she's no longer here.

A little something to brighten your day.

I think of your words, as I look out over the seafront. The tide is in. I open my can of cider as the sun blazes in a blue sky. The same words go round and round in my head, like seagulls circling the bay. In the distance, a family are paddling in the water. A red-haired girl in a bikini is holding her father's hand. She reminds me a bit of you, Cilla, when you was younger.

It's been a week since she passed away. A whole week. I could hardly believe it when I saw it on the news. I stayed in bed and didn't eat for three days. On the fourth day, Wayne came over and made me spaghetti hoops.

'You need to keep your strength up, Margaret,' he says. 'Cilla wouldn't want to see you in this state.'

Well, if only he knew. He read me her obituary in the papers – it was beautiful. I made him cut it out for me, even though I couldn't read it myself. It's on my fridge.

Monday 3rd August, 2015

Daily Observer

Cilla Black obituary

Cilla Black, who has died at her home in Marbella, Spain, aged 72, first shot to fame in the early 1960s, emerging as one of the decade's most successful pop singers.

In an era dominated by male guitar bands, Black was part of a new wave of young female singing stars, which included Dusty Springfield, Lulu and Sandie Shaw. Black's profile received a significant boost through her association with fellow Liverpool musicians the Beatles, with whom she shared a manager, Brian Epstein. John Lennon and Paul McCartney penned several of her biggest hits, including "Love Of The Loved" and "Step Inside Love".

Born Priscilla Maria Veronica White on the 27th May 1943 (Cilla Black was her stage name, suggested by Epstein), Black rose from her humble beginnings as the third child of a Liverpool dock worker, and a mother who sold clothing on a market stall, to become one of the biggest stars of the Swinging Sixties. In 1964 she topped the UK charts with "You're My World". Further hits followed with "You've Lost That Lovin' Feeling" – later covered by the Righteous Brothers – and "Anyone Who Had A Heart" by Burt Bacharach and Hal David. The latter was originally written with Shirley Bassey in mind.

In 1966, she had several more chart successes, including "Alfie", composed by Bacharach especially for Black. The song was used to promote the film of the same name, which starred Michael Caine.

In later years, Black's career focus shifted from singing to presenting. A run of successful shows throughout the 1980s and 1990s – including *Blind Date* and *Surprise, Surprise* – made her one of the wealthiest women in British television.

Black's husband, Bobby Willis, died in 1999. She is survived by three sons, Robert, Ben and Jack; she also had a daughter, who died at birth in 1975.

Cilla Black, born 27th May 1943; died 1st August 2015.

Me and Wayne sat down together afterwards and listened to one of her records: *Cilla Sings a Rainbow*. It's my favourite. Wayne tried to get me to sing along, but I was too choked up. When someone has been a part of your life for so long and they pass . . . It's been many years since I've felt loss like that. It sounds odd, I know, but you was like family to me, Cilla. It was comforting to me just knowing you was still alive, still out there.

Taking a sip of cider, I look out to sea, listening to the jangle of the masts, the sound of seagulls squawking. On holiday in Spain, they said. A stroke. A tear runs down my cheek. Pulling an old tissue from my coat pocket, I wipe under my nose.

'You was taken far too soon, Cilla,' I whisper to myself. 'You and me, we should have had more time together.'

Just like magic then, the memories come pouring back: years and years of memories. They flood my mind like flying birds, flapping everywhere. Closing my eyes, I sense the beat of white wings, the red glow of a sunset. I put my hand in my pocket, feel the light tickle of paper against my fingertips. This can only mean one thing.

Cilla is trying to contact me, I think. *Cilla is coming back*.

3

5 NOVEMBER 1947

From inside Mr Grey's car, I wondered what it was at first, this giant mansion hidden behind dark trees, with a tall fence and an iron gate and a long, swirling drive coming down. I rubbed the steam off the window with my hand, peering out. Lit up by the moon, the house looked haunted.

Mr Grey pulled up in the driveway in front and switched off his engine. He opened the door and stepped outside. Already you could hear the racket: people screaming and shouting. Like a madhouse, it was.

The noises frightened me. Not just the screaming, but the sound of Mr Grey's boots on the gravel – crunch, crunch, crunch – as he came round the back of the car to fetch me. Through the window, I saw him strike a match, light up his pipe. He opened the door.

The cold air hit me, the smell of smoke. Mr Grey's face was red, like the Devil. I hugged my knees to my chest and bunched my fists. I shut my eyes, hoping they would all just vanish.

'Come here, Margaret,' he says. 'You're home now.'

His gloved hands reached across the back seat for me. The Rat Catcher.

I had on my favourite dress that day, the one I wore to

church on Sundays: it was mauve with a frilly white collar. No doubt Grandma put me in it for show, so I looked good for the nurses, but she needn't have bothered. On the way up in the car, I wet myself. The dress was soaked through. The backs of my legs felt cold and damp against the leather car seat.

Mr Grey grabbed my feet then and started pulling. His hands felt hot and sweaty on my ankles, like when a boy gives you Chinese burns. I held onto the door with all my might, but it was no use. He yanked me out of the car feet first, *whoosh*, lifted me right up, so I was swinging in the air. The whole sky went rolling over like a cartwheel; everything was upside down. I was terrified. There was only one thing for it. I elbowed him on his you-know-what, hard as I could.

'Jesus effing Christ!' he says. 'What do you think you're doing?'

'Do you need help, Mr Grey?'

First a woman's voice, then more crunching on the gravel, quicker this time – crunch, crunch, crunch, crunch, crunch. This was Violet Cunningham, Chief Ward Supervisor at St Mary's. She was a short, fat lady with a pink face. She was wearing an apron and a pointy white hat, like a cone. All of the nurses wore those funny-looking things.

'This little cretin just punched me in the privates,' says Mr Grey. 'Almost winded me.'

By this point, I was screaming out loud, kicking my legs all over the shop.

'Alice!' Nurse Cunningham says. 'Alice! We need an extra pair of hands here!'

A younger woman came running out of the house into the driveway. This was Nurse Fitts. She was as tall as Nurse Cunningham was short, taller than Mr Grey, even, and as lanky as you like.

16

'We'll need to restrain her,' says Nurse Cunningham. 'She's just this minute assaulted Mr Grey.'

Nurse Fitts nodded. She ran back inside.

All the blood was rushing to my head. Things was starting to blur. Nurse Cunningham took my arms and shoulders. Together, she and Mr Grey lifted me down slowly to the ground. I lay there for ages, just rocking from side to side.

As soon as Nurse Fitts came back, she knelt down, started wrapping a bandage around my mouth. I could feel her bony fingers digging into my chin, then into the back of my skull, as she done the cloth in a knot, tying it tight from behind. Stones was sticking to my cheeks. If I looked to the side, all I could see was my face reflected in the toe of Nurse Cunningham's shiny black boot.

Then everything went blank.

The next thing I knew, I was on a wooden stool, being stripped of all my clothes.

'What a dirty little girl,' says a voice.

I realised slowly, for I was still half asleep, that this was Nurse Cunningham.

'Will you look here, Alice,' she says, pulling my Sunday dress over my head. 'These knickers are soaked through with piss.'

The room smelled of bleach. And something else. It wasn't pleasant.

'Straight for the bin, this garment,' says Nurse Cunningham, after she was done inspecting my dress. 'There's no saving it. Shame. I might've had it for one of my own girls.'

'Oh, but the stench, Violet,' says Nurse Fitts. 'Goes straight to the pit of my stomach.' She made a noise like she was being sick.

'Get her in the bath,' says Nurse Cunningham. 'We can't

put her in the villa in this state. It'll set the others off.' She started pulling at my knickers. 'Oh please, for the life of me! Would you look here, Alice? I think she might have shit herself as well.'

'Oh, don't say that,' Nurse Fitts says. 'My stomach's queasy enough as it is. You'll be cleaning me up and all.'

'Well, I'm fed up with it, Alice,' says Nurse Cunningham. 'The mess.'

'Speaking of mess,' says Nurse Fitts. 'I was told they're planning on fitting a few of those new urinal things in the men's wards. That'll make a huge difference, won't it?'

'I very much doubt it,' says Nurse Cunningham. 'The way some of these defectives aim, it'll just mean more piss for us to mop up at the end of the day. I was saying to Dr Firmin last week – twelve wards and we've only six basins to wash our hands with. It's an absolute disgrace. And they wonder why we've had so many deaths this year. It's hygiene, I tell you. Oh, and it makes my blood boil the way they expect us to be all la-di-dah when the inspectors come round, filling the vases with fresh flowers and all that nonsense. The amount of bleach we got through last time. No, Alice, you mark my words. Next time we get a visit from the board, we should tell it like it is. That'll show them.'

Nurse Cunningham turned on the tap. Water started gushing out.

'Oh, and what a surprise! We're out of hot water again! Well, she'll just have to cope with it freezing cold. I can't put her to bed like this. Pass me the jug. I'll need a hand lifting her, too.'

Taking an end each, they picked me up and dropped me into the bath. What they done next nearly killed me, the shock of it. They poured a jug of ice-cold water over my head.

'That'll teach you not to wet yourself,' says Nurse

18

Cunningham. 'Alice, hand me the soap and the loofah. She needs a bloody good rub down.'

She started scrubbing me all over with a stiff brush.

Afterwards, Nurse Fitts put a towel over my head, patting it hard to dry off my hair. Neither of them took any notice of my crying.

The admissions ward was where they put all the new children who arrived at St Mary's. It was a big room with bars on all the windows, like a prison. There was loads of beds, twenty on either side, all squashed together in a row. Nurse Fitts threw my suitcase onto a bed and undone the straps. She lifted the lid. Inside was all my clothes, toys and a few picture books. I watched her hold one of my dresses up to the window, like the washing powder ladies in the magazine adverts, as if she was checking to see if it was clean.

Nurse Cunningham came into the room carrying a huge empty sack.

'Just drop the lot in here, Alice,' she says, holding it open on the floor.

'What are you doing with my clothes?' I says.

'Never you mind,' she says. 'We've had enough of your cheek already.'

'Some nice things in here, Violet,' says Nurse Fitts, lifting my suitcase and turning it upside down. 'I might get them out again later and have a proper look.'

All my skirts, petticoats, socks and knickers went tumbling into the sack. After she was done filling it, Nurse Cunningham hauled the sack up onto the bed, tying it at the top with string. She pointed at a big cupboard which had piles of clothes in it. Not nice clothes, but old rags, things a beggar might wear.

'You'll find plenty of dresses and undergarments in here,'

she says. 'They get shared out between the girls. Everyone gets treated the same.'

She started fumbling around inside the cupboard then, rummaging through a load of rags. She pulled out this tatty old thing.

'Look at this one, Alice,' she says. 'Full of holes. Some of these dresses are falling apart.'

'I'll get my sewing girls to fix a pile of them next week,' says Nurse Fitts, who was sat on the bed, fiddling with Dolly, the only thing they'd let me keep from my suitcase.

'Fix?' says Nurse Cunningham. 'We could do with getting some new ones. These are beyond fixing!'

'The board sent us a note last week,' says Miss Fitts. 'We're not allowed to throw anything out until it's past repair. I reckon a lot of these can still be salvaged.'

'This place is going to the dogs, I swear,' says Nurse Cunningham. She turned to me. 'Give me your towel.'

I shrugged the towel off my shoulders, handing it to her.

'Hold up your arms!'

I did as I was told. She forced the dress over my head, pulling it down to my waist and knees. If I was a stouter girl, and a few years older, it might've fitted me, but this thing was enormous: baggy, like a sack. You didn't get to pick your size. You got what you was given. The dress smelled funny, of moth's balls, dead people's stuff like you find in the jumble sales. It was covered in patches and the material was rough and itchy. Oh, it made my skin crawl! I felt dirty wearing it. The shoes they gave me was awful, too. Ugly old clodhoppers. Black leather boots with laces right up to the knees. When you walked in them, you felt like you was being weighed down. And they didn't half give you blisters.

Worst of all, though, was the knickers: they was bloody

old-fashioned with stripes, like the deckchairs on Margate beach. They made you look like something out of the circus. We wasn't allowed our own knickers, we shared them, so you was lucky if you got a pair that wasn't stained with piss, or worse. That was one of the awful things about St Mary's – not being able to wear your own clothes, having to wear other people's. Everything you put on – the frocks, the shoes, the stockings, even those wretched knickers – had the name of the hospital sewn onto them. They did that so you couldn't run away. If you did, they would find you. And then God help you, you'd be punished.

That was the last day I saw my stuff: all my nice clothes and shoes, vanished! It ain't a nice thing to say, I know, but looking back, I think Nurse Cunningham might've nicked them to give to her own children. Not that it mattered. I was 41 years old when I left St Mary's.

Those dresses would've been far too small for me by then.

4

'C'

I follow you down the High Street, making sure I keep a few steps behind. You walk slowly, talking out loud to yourself, stopping every so often to look in the shop windows. You take a left at the charity shop, heading towards Island Wall. Apart from a pair of angry seagulls fighting over a discarded box of fish and chips, Whitstable is quiet tonight. Most of the day trippers have gone home. Pausing by the entrance to the empty car park, I watch you wheel your trolley up the ramp and take a seat by Cushing's View. There are some steps further along the seafront. I climb them, cautiously, and sit on one of the benches a few metres down from you. The sun is still blazing over the estuary, the view of the Isle of Sheppey and Southend-on-Sea clear as a photograph. You take a portable CD player from a plastic carrier bag, resting it on your lap. You put your headphones on, then lift out a can of cider, flicking the tab open, tipping it into your mouth. You stare out to sea, then you close your eyes, like you're lost in some memory. Seeing you alone like this makes me feel guilty about the way things turned out. You missed out on so much, through no fault of your own, and I want to make that up to you, I really do. We may not be able to change what happened in the past, but we can change the future, Margaret. You and I, we deserve a second chance – especially you. God knows you've had to put up with a lot.

I've made up my mind. When I get home tonight, I'm going to send you another gift. I hope you use it to treat yourself to something nice. Like I said, you deserve it.

5

18 August 2015

Why are you writing to me, Cilla? Have you got something important to tell me? Some news? It's Tuesday morning and I'm on my way to Sainsbury's. You sent me another envelope this morning. Inside was a fifty-pound note, and a postcard of the Royal Albert Hall. The postcard had the same black liquorice writing on the back. I'm hoping David is working today; he'll be able to read it to me. I thought about showing it to Wayne, but I don't want to tell him about you – not yet. He's had enough of me talking about Cilla. He gets annoyed if I so much as say your name.

'You need to try and get over what happened, Margaret,' he says.

It's hard, though.

Cilla whispers in my ear. She's talking about Bobby's death, how it took her a long time to get over him. She got through the pain by sticking to her normal routine and making cups of tea. And when things got really bad, she went to Barbados.

I can't afford Barbados on my disability benefits, so Sainsbury's will have to do.

As soon as I get to the supermarket, I make my way to the dairy aisle to pick up a tub of cheese triangles. With my headphones on, it feels like Cilla is walking beside me, chatting to me while I do my grocery shopping. It's nice to have company for a change.

'Dairylea or Laughing Cow?' I say to Cilla.

A girl standing next to me, wearing a tight white T-shirt and denim shorts, gives me a funny look and I realise I'm shouting. She mouths something at me, but I can't hear what she's saying, so I take my headphones off.

'Are you asking me?' she says.

'No, love,' I say. 'I'm talking to my friend, Cilla.' I realise how stupid this makes me sound. 'On my mobile, I mean. It's amazing what these phones can do nowadays. What do they call it? Hands-free?'

The girl stares at my headphones, which are plugged into the CD player in my hand. She nods and then, picking up a packet of cheese strings, throws them in her basket and walks off.

I put my headphones back on and stand there, gazing at the cheeses for a while longer. I don't like to rush things when I'm in Sainsbury's.

Moving on to the next aisle, I catch sight of the lovely David. He's on his knees, stacking the biscuit shelves. I'm after a packet of cream crackers to spread my cheese triangles on, so it gives me an excuse to talk.

It's a while before he notices me standing behind him. Cilla is telling me about the time she played a stripper in the musical *Gypsy* and wore fairy lights on her bum. The thought of it makes me laugh out loud. David stops what he is doing and turns around to see me chuckling to myself. He must think I'm mad.

I take my headphones off.

'David, can you tell me where the cream crackers are, please? I'm having trouble finding them.'

David stands up and smiles. 'Why don't I grab you a packet? Just the one?'

I nod. He's such a kind and helpful young man.

'Oh – and David,' I say, as he's putting the crackers in my basket. 'Would you mind reading this letter for me? I've forgotten my glasses again.'

I fumble around in my purse and hand him the envelope with the postcard in it. I try to lip-read, watching his mouth move slowly along with the words.

'What does it say?'

He scratches his head. 'Nothing, really. I'm guessing the sender is from London, though, judging by the postmark and the photo. Have you ever been to the Royal Albert Hall?'

'Only once,' I say. 'To see Cilla. It was years ago.'

'Cilla?'

'Cilla Black. My favourite singer.'

David nods. 'I remember Cilla, yeah. My nan loves her.'

'The postcard,' I say, my heart beating faster. 'Can you read it to me?'

David leans in closer. He's wearing a lovely aftershave. I can't help having a sniff, even though I'm old enough to be his grandmother.

'"Dear Margaret",' he says. '"Here's another little something for you to treat yourself with. Love C x." Maybe C is for Cilla,' he laughs. 'What do you think?'

I know he's only joking, but I can feel a tiny flip in my stomach. I whisper 'Thank you' and, taking the postcard, slip it back into my carrier bag. Right now, the supermarket feels too bright.

I need to get out of here, I think, making my way to the exit.

A blast of warm air hits me as the sliding doors burst open

on to the High Street. In my rush to leave, I almost trip over a small dog tied to a railing outside, waiting for its owner. It starts barking at me, wagging its tail with excitement.

'It *is* you, ain't it, Cilla?' I say out loud.

I take a deep breath, for I can hardly believe it. Of all the things to happen, Cilla. Really, what are the chances?

6

1947

They kept me in admissions for two weeks. For the first few
days, I hardly slept. I cried all through the night. When I
did manage to drift off, I'd wake up not knowing where I
was, thinking it was just a dream.

'Where's Grandma?' I'd say to the nurses. 'When's she
coming back?'

I asked them the same question, over and over. One time,
Nurse Cunningham got so sick of it, she threw a bucket
of cold water over my head. I screamed, lashing out in all
directions. She called for Nurse Fitts, who came running over.

'Don't stand there gawping, Alice!' snapped Nurse
Cunningham. 'This is how we teach the little devils their
place.'

She told Nurse Fitts to pin me down while she tied straps
round my wrists and ankles, tightly, so I couldn't move. The
straps was like big men's belts, black leather, with metal
buckles. They left bruises and red marks on your wrists if
you tried to wriggle out of them.

I did my best to put up a fight, but it was no good. I was
no match for the nurses, they was stronger than me. So I
lay there, frozen, as Nurse Cunningham leaned in, her face
close to mine.

'There's no point crying,' she says. 'Your grandmother can't hear you. She isn't coming back.'

I could feel the heat coming from her cheeks. Her breath smelled like gone-off milk.

'St Mary's is your home now,' she says. 'Screaming and kicking will only make things worse.'

I stopped crying then, for what was the point? Who would've helped me? Besides, I was afraid of her. The look on her face was pure evil.

They cut off my hair. My lovely long hair, which used to touch my shoulders, got chopped into a pudding bowl. Nurse Cunningham did it. She wasn't a blooming hairdresser, even I knew that. It was awful. When she held up the mirror, to show me how I looked, I cried. Straight away Nurse Fitts was on hand with a big box of hair clips.

'Look at these. Aren't they pretty?' She wasn't lying. 'Pick one, Margaret. Pick your favourite colour.'

I asked her if I could have one of each, in all the colours of the rainbow: *red, yellow, pink, green, purple, orange, blue.*

But Nurse Fitts told me I could only have one. It was the rules, she said. So I chose blue, for it matched the dress I had on that day. It was a navy dress, old-fashioned-looking, with a white apron. We wore them on Sundays.

I got given a pair of glasses, too. This was after Dr Firmin done an eye test on me and said I was short-sighted. I hated wearing them at first, these great round things, with thick lenses, like the bottom of a milk bottle. After a while, though, I didn't mind them so much. I could see the sky better when we was outside. Even Nurse Cunningham said they suited me. She said they made my eyes look bigger.

After two weeks, they moved me out of admissions and into a new ward. It was just like the old one, only more crowded. There was about seventy-five of us in there, all girls.

Imagine the noise we made! It was dreadful, like Bedlam. Worst of the lot was Grace. Vile, she was. She used to throw her chamber pot up and down the ward. Her urine would go all over the place. Dora wasn't much better. A big, stout thing, she used to sit on the bed, banging her feet against the metal frame. Oh, she was violent. She went for the staff. Even they was frightened of her. If you upset her, she'd grab your throat, rattle you like a collection tin. Then there was Bernadette, an older lady. She'd lost her daughter in the war and it drove her potty. Some nights you'd see her sleepwalking with no clothes on, the floorboards creaking as she walked up and down crying out her name. One night I woke up to find her standing at the end of my bed, tapping my feet with her fingers, whispering, 'Sally, Sally, is that you down there in the hole? It's Mummy. Can you hear me, baby? It's cold up here, so cold.' She kept saying the same thing.

At first I thought she was a ghost, for I'd overheard Nurse Cunningham tell a group of girls caught talking after bedtime that St Mary's was haunted.

'If you lot don't shut up,' she said, 'you'll get a visit from the White Lady!'

Bernadette shouldn't have been in our ward, though, not really, for we was all children. They must've had nowhere else to put her.

7

18 AUGUST 2015

Back in my flat, I try to remember what Sainsbury's David told me. *Here's a little something to treat yourself with.* Is that what you wrote, Cilla? Looking at the letter again, I try to make sense of the words, but they wobble around the page too much. They won't stay still. The only thing I recognise is *C*, so it must be you, Cilla, for who else would be trying to contact me?

Folding the postcard in two, I slip it into my cardigan pocket and pull out my headphones. I untangle the wires and put them in my ears. Taking a deep breath, I press play. As soon as I hear Cilla's voice, I feel calmer. It's like she understands what I'm going through, as if she's trying to reassure me. Cilla tells me that, whenever she had something that was bothering her, she used to ask Bobby. I think about the people I could speak to, but – apart from Wayne – there is nobody.

I sit at the kitchen table for a while, staring at Cilla's obituary on the fridge, listening to her talking about the time she got a standing ovation. It's raining outside. The patter on the shed roof sounds like people clapping.

'Is everything all right, Margaret?' I look up to see Wayne standing in my hallway, soaking wet and folding up an umbrella. He's a big bear of a man, tall with a brown beard. He's wearing a bright blue raincoat. 'I hope you don't mind, but I let myself in. I was ringing the doorbell for ages.'

'Give me a minute, Cilla,' I whisper, taking my headphones off, placing them on the kitchen table.

Wayne looks confused as he unzips his raincoat and hangs it over the back of a chair to dry.

'Who were you talking to just now?'

'No one,' I say, pressing pause on my CD. 'I was just muttering to myself.'

Wayne nods, but I can tell he thinks something ain't right.

'Have you forgotten about our lunch date?'

What day is it today? Tuesday.

Of course. Wayne said he would take me to the pub for lunch. He said it would be good for me to have a treat after my loss. I'd completely forgotten.

'Wayne,' I say, 'I'm ever so sorry.'

'You can't sit around the house all day moping and listening to Cilla. I keep telling you, Margaret. You need to get out and about.' He picks up my CD player. 'This,' he says, 'is not good for your mental health.'

I stare down at the table, feeling like a child who's been told off for something that ain't their fault.

Wayne's voice softens. 'Lunch is on me today, OK? My treat.'

It's then I remember the fifty-quid note in my bag. I feel guilty. It should be me paying for lunch. Wayne has been so kind to me, especially these past few weeks. He don't get paid a lot. I owe it to him. The thing is, I'm frightened he'll start asking questions. He looks after all my money, you see, so I'll only end up having to explain to him about Cilla and where the money came from, how she's been trying to contact me. Now ain't the right time to tell him.

'I'll go and get ready, then,' I say.

Before I leave for the bathroom, I make sure I take the postcard from my cardigan pocket and put it in my bag.

8

1947

The girl in the bed next to me was reading a book. She had the blanket pulled all the way up to her waist. I couldn't help noticing how pretty she was: pale skin, curly blonde hair and a button nose. She reminded me of the actress Shirley Temple, who Grandma took me to see in the cinema once. It was the film where she sings 'On The Good Ship Lollipop'. Afterwards, I would sing that song all the time – until, one day, Grandma got so sick of it she told me to shut up.

'Margaret,' she says, 'you've got a voice that would wake the dead.'

Well, I never sang in front of her again after that. Not once. I was too scared to. In case of the dead, you see.

The girl looked up from her book.

'I'm Joan Chance,' she says. 'I'm not like the others here. I can read and write.'

I lifted a corner of my blanket and put it in my mouth. Joan stared at me, her eyes wide open.

'Well . . . can't you speak then?'

She said this very quietly, for the nurses didn't like us talking before bedtime. If they heard you making too much noise, they'd scare you with stories about the White Lady – or, worse, you'd be punished.

'My name's Margaret.'

'Do you read, Margaret?'

I shook my head, letting the blanket drop. I'd never met anyone who spoke like Joan before. She was posh, like one of those hoity-toity BBC ladies off the wireless. *How now, brown cow*: that sort of voice.

'What a surprise!' She yawned. 'Most of the others in here can't read either.' She picked up her book again.

'Grandma used to read to me sometimes, though,' I say. 'Story books and that. Fairy tales. I asked her to come with me, but she wouldn't.'

'Where do you live?'

'Gordon Road.'

'Is that in London?'

'It's on the corner. Over that way.' I point at nowhere in particular.

'What age are you?'

'Seven.'

Joan turned her head to check she wasn't being watched by the nurses, then sat up straight in bed, pushing her shoulders back.

'I'm older than you, then,' she whispered. 'I shall be ten in March.'

'Ten?' I say, in amazement.

I'd never met anyone who was ten before. I started counting to ten with my fingers, trying to imagine what it would be like to be that old. *One, two, three, four . . .* I stopped when I got to seven. I couldn't remember what number came next.

'It's my birthday in April,' I say.

'Oh', she says, sounding bored.

I watched her turn over a page in her book. It had a picture on the cover, of a boy and girl sat on a flying red chair.

'What's the book?' I asked her.

'Enid Blyton,' she says. '*The Adventures of the Wishing-Chair.*'

'Can it fly up to the sky?' I pointed up at the tall bars on the windows. 'Away, away!'

Joan put a finger over her mouth to warn me to shush.

'It can go anywhere. France, Italy . . . Australia.'

'Even to Gordon Road?'

Joan nodded.

'Wish?' I say, pointing at a row of chairs in the corner with wheels on them. *Wish* was my new favourite word.

Joan shook her head. 'Those are wheelchairs,' she says. 'To help girls like me get around.'

She put her book down and lifted the blanket, so I could see underneath. Her poor legs was bruised and twisted.

'Polio,' she says, pulling the covers back up. 'I wouldn't be in this place otherwise. He only sent me here to recover.'

'Who did? The Rat Catcher?'

'The Rat Catcher?' Joan screwed up her nose like it was the stupidest thing she'd ever heard. 'No. *Daddy*! I overheard him talking to the doctor about it, how it was best if they sent me away. Daddy would deny it, of course, but it's true.'

She looked like she was about to cry then. I rubbed my eyes, not sure if I should start crying, too.

'Anyway . . .' Joan tossed her head back. 'Mummy says lots of talented people suffer from diseases. Keats had tuberculosis and Rupert Brooke died from a mosquito bite, it's very romantic. I'll bet neither of them lived anywhere as awful as St Mary's, though. It's full of nincompoops!'

'Nincompoops, nincompoops!'

I didn't know any of the people Joan was talking about, but what a funny word! I kept saying it, over and over again. It was the first time I'd laughed since I came to the hospital. Joan told me to be quiet.

'You'll get us both in trouble,' she says.

Still laughing, I clambered across the bed and sat next to her. I snuggled up, enjoying the warmth of her body against mine.

'Will you read to me?'

She stiffened at first, but then she relaxed, letting me in. Opening her book, she began telling me all about the adventures of Molly, Peter and the pixie, in the Land of Dreams.

Like me, I suppose, she was glad, at long last, to have found a friend.

9

The Peter Cushion is a Wetherspoon pub. It used to be the old bingo hall, but they've done it up. I like going there because it feels as if you're stepping back in time. And the food is cheap. They do a small meals range, which suits me fine. I don't eat much these days.

We take our usual seat in the corner, next to the bar and the slot machines. Wayne goes to get the drinks. A Diet Coke for him and half a Strongbow for me. It's early, so there aren't many people, apart from a woman sat on her own in the corner, reading a magazine, and a few men in caps. One of the men puts down his drink and stares right at me. It makes me feel uncomfortable. I reach for my bag. The letter you sent me is still safe inside. I'm keeping it secret, for now, at least. Besides, what would be the use in telling anyone about you, Cilla? Wayne already thinks I'm going soft in the head.

I watch Wayne pay at the bar with his card and feel guilty again. I should be buying lunch. Looking around the pub, there are old black and white pictures of Peter Cushion everywhere. Peter Cushion in *Dracula*. Peter Cushion in *Sherlock Holmes*. Peter Cushion in *Frankenstein*. Peter's eyes follow me around the room.

38

Does he know my secret?

I clasp my bag shut, just as Wayne arrives with the drinks. 'I've ordered you a small cod and chips,' he says, setting the glasses down on the table.

I try to focus on something else, something other than your letters. I notice Wayne is wearing a new T-shirt. It's bright red with white writing all over the front.

'What does your T-shirt say?' I ask him, taking a sip of cider.

'Do you like it?' Wayne stands up to show me. 'I had it delivered this morning.' He reads out the words: SOME PEOPLE ARE GAY, GET OVER IT.

The two men in caps are staring again. One of them coughs. They must think we make an odd couple.

'It's very nice,' I say. 'Maybe they could do T-shirts like that for people with disabilities, too.'

'Now there's an idea. I'll drink to that, as Rihanna would say.' Wayne raises his Diet Coke and we do cheers. 'Shall I be dad and fetch the sauces?'

Wayne has been my support worker for nearly six years now. When he first told me he was gay, it came as a shock. I wasn't happy about it. I told him as much. I even said to him, 'It ain't natural. Two men. It ain't right. I don't like it.'

Wayne was really upset.

He said, 'I'm very fond of you, Margaret, but I don't think I can carry on being your support worker if you won't accept me for who I am.'

I told him I needed to think about it. He left my flat. I went to my bedroom and cried for a few hours, listening to Michael Bolton on repeat.

The next day, Wayne called me on my mobile.

'Well,' he says, 'have you thought about it?'

'I still ain't sure.'

'Put it this way. What would Cilla do?'

'What's Cilla got to do with anything?'

'Cilla has lots of gay friends.'

'Cilla has gay friends? Like who?'

'Dale Winton. Paul O'Grady.'

'Paul O'Gravy's gay?'

'Yes, of course! And Christopher Biggins.'

'Biggins is gay?'

Silence.

I told Wayne I would ring him back and I put the phone down. My head was spinning like a disco ball. It seemed like everyone in the whole world was gay.

'Please don't tell me Michael Bolton is gay, too,' I said, staring at the photograph of him stuck to my fridge door. 'Let there be one man left for me.'

And then I thought, *this ain't about you, Margaret.*

I could hear Cilla's voice in my head, just like it sounds on the TV, telling me off for being so stubborn.

'Come on, chuck. You're being a bit selfish here. Wayne's who he is. Just as you're who you are. Neither of you can do anything to change that. He's a good friend, yes? He looks after you and treats you kindly. You have a lorra, lorra laughs together. Why would you let a good friend like that go?'

Tears flooded my eyes, making the Michael Bolton picture on the fridge door wobble. Fishing my mobile out of my handbag, I sat down at the kitchen table and pressed on Wayne's number. A photo flashed on my phone screen, of me and Wayne, raising our plastic beer glasses outside the Old Neptune pub, the sea behind us. The phone started ringing. Click. A voice at the other end. It was Wayne.

'Wayne, love,' I said. 'I'm ever so sorry for what I done. It was stupid of me. Are you still my friend?'

* * *

The food arrives. I jab a piece of bright orange batter off
the cod with my fork and dip it in a blob of tomato sauce,
chewing it slowly. I chew everything sixty times. Joan told
me to do that. Good for the stomach, she used to say. Ain't
it funny how the past seems more real than the present?
We're going back nearly seventy years.

My memory was a lot clearer then than it is now.

10

1947

Over the next few weeks, I started to get more used to life at the hospital – the rules and the routines. Me and Joan became good friends. She read me stories every night, Enid Blyton, mostly. She made me laugh, especially when she did the different voices. It was like having an older sister. I don't know how I would've coped without her. St Mary's was a frightening place, you felt like you was being watched the whole time, but Joan made it better somehow. She looked after me, made me feel safer. Every moment I spent with her was special: I would have done anything for her. So, when Nurse Fitts says to me one morning, 'You're a strong girl. You can help us look after Joan if you like,' I was over the moon. That was how I became Joan's helper. I was one of the more able patients in the ward, you see.

Every morning, at half past six, Joan would shuffle to the end of her bed and wait for me. Then Nurse Fitts, or one of the other staff, would help me to lift her into her wheelchair. It wasn't easy, learning how to push a wheelchair. I was only small. The handles just about reached my head, so it was hard to see in front. The first time I tried to steer it, I was pushing it across the floor when something hit one of the wheels. Putting the brake on, I went round the front of the chair to have a look. There was a chamber pot, upside down on the floor, everything spilling out: a big yellow puddle, with bits floating in it. I screamed. Nurse Fitts came running over.

'That's it, Margaret,' she says, placing my fingers over the handles. 'Now move forward.'

Nurse Fitts was nice. She calmed me down. Once I learned how, I used to enjoy wheeling Joan around.

While it was far from perfect, life at St Mary's was better in the old days. As children, we didn't have to work, you see. And we liked the routine. Every day, after breakfast, me and Joan would go and sit in the day room, where we'd stay until lunch, then we'd go back and spend the rest of the afternoon playing with toys or listening to stories. Dinner was at five and afterwards we'd go to the day room again for recreation hour. You was allowed to run around then, play games before bedtime. Bedtime was always seven.

It was nice and bright in the day room, with its high windows and polished wood floor. It was just as well, really, for we spent most of our time there. There was loads of chairs and tables, and all of the tables had little vases on them, which we used to help the nurses fill up with dried flowers. At one end of the room was a fire. It had a big metal guard round it. There was a wireless as well, so you could listen to the shows, and a games box with playing cards, Snakes and Ladders, jumping jacks and so on. There was no television, though. We didn't get a television until the Queen's Coronation in 1953. One of the charities gave it to us. They was forever giving us stuff. I don't want to sound ungrateful, but a lot of it was rubbish: holey knickers with threads hanging off them, books with no pictures (no use to the ones who wasn't able to read), pots of jam, half eaten and full of crumbs. I even got given a balaclava once.

'It'll keep you warm, stop you getting a chill,' says Nurse Cunningham, pulling it over my head and laughing.

Time seemed to go more slowly when I was younger. Even though I'd only been at St Mary's a few weeks, I felt like I'd known Joan all my life. I could never imagine being without her: we went everywhere together. I thought our friendship would last forever. Joan's life outside the hospital was a lot different from mine, though. She had family, you see, real family who still cared for her. Not that Joan seemed bothered.

It was coming up to Christmas. We'd spent the earlier part of the day making paper chains out of old newspaper to hang around the doors and windows in the day room. It was still the afternoon, but already it was starting to get dark. Joan and me was playing a game of tiddlywinks, but she looked miserable. Most of the time, she was staring out of the window, not talking to me. I had to keep reminding her it was her turn. I was beginning to wonder if I'd done something wrong when she finally came out with it.

'I'm going home for the holidays.'

Just hearing the word 'home' made my stomach leap. I flipped a green counter, missing the jar. In my panic, I started asking Joan lots of questions.

'When are you going home? How long for? Who will read me stories?'

'Calm down, Margaret,' she says, taking my hand. 'I'll only be gone for a few weeks.'

I breathed a sigh of relief.

Not many of the patients got to leave St Mary's at Christmas. Joan was one of the lucky ones. She got to go home a couple of times a year. 'Parole', they called it. Her parents was allowed to see her on Visitors' Day, too. The hospital allowed that once a month. You used to see children queuing up by the dining hall, waiting for their mums and dads.

'Don't you mind, Margaret?' Joan would ask when nobody came to visit me.

'Not really,' I used to say. 'I ain't bothered.'

I was lying, though.

One of the reasons Joan's parents could visit any time they liked was because they was rich. They lived in a big house in London. Her father was a famous actor, Desmond Chance. Nurse Cunningham was a big fan. Joan used to reckon she had a soft spot for him, as she was always making us listen to his plays on the wireless.

'I do love a bit of Noël Coward,' she'd say, taking a racket from the games box and swinging it from side to side. 'Anyone for tennis?'

'Does he play tennis, then?' I remember saying to Joan. 'Your father.'

'Not in real life!' Joan leaned over to check Nurse Cunningham wasn't listening. 'Don't breathe a word of this to anyone, especially her,' she whispered, 'but Daddy says the plays he's in are a load of old rot. He only does them for the money.'

'Will I ever get to meet them?' I says. 'Your parents.'

'I should think so. Really, though, they're not that interesting.'

As soon as Joan was better, she said she was going to be a Hollywood actress. She told me about her part in *The Little Mermaid*, the hospital pantomime she was doing in a couple of weeks.

'I have the main role, of course,' she says, 'but then I did write the script myself.'

I asked her if I could be in the pantomime, too.

'I don't see why not,' she says.

I could hardly believe my luck. I put a yellow tiddlywink on the table and flipped it.

This time, it landed in the jar.

11

'C'

I usually avoid Wetherspoons, but I'm enjoying watching you make use of the money I gave you. The fish and chips don't look too bad, actually. Maybe we can have lunch together one day?

By the way, I'm the one sat in the corner on my own, by the stairs, near the fruit machine.

For a moment there, I thought I saw you looking at me. Do I look familiar?

12

18 AUGUST 2015

'Are you OK, Margaret? You look like you've seen a ghost.'

Wayne's voice pulls me out of my memories.

'You've barely eaten a thing.'

'I was chewing,' I say, putting down my knife and fork. 'My good friend Joan used to say I should chew everything sixty times.'

A young girl in a Wetherspoons uniform comes over to collect our plates.

'Everything all right with the food?' She says each word slowly, her voice raised, like she's speaking to a child.

'Yes, love,' I say. 'It was nice. I only have a small stomach, though. I didn't have room for the peas. I hope you don't mind.'

The waitress hovers at the end of the table. She's staring at me, smiling. The way people do when they reckon I'm a bit simple. You'd think I'd be used to it, but it's even worse now I'm older. I half expect her to pat me on the head. I start clearing away the things on the table, to show her I'm as capable as anyone. I lift Wayne's plate. Scraping the scraps off, I slip it underneath mine, placing the cutlery on top.

'Do you stack, or are you gentry?' I say, handing the pile over to the waitress.

47

'I beg your pardon?'

'You're like me,' I say. 'You stack, you see. My friend Joan, who I knew at St Mary's, she never stacked, she was gentry. Not many of them left nowadays.'

The girl looks at me as if I ain't the full ticket and walks off.

I wonder if now is a good time to tell Wayne about the letters. All morning, thoughts about Cilla have been going round and round in my head, like a big black dog chasing its tail. This is what happens when I worry about something, you see. The worry takes over, I get obsessed, and then I can't think straight. I can't think of anything else. It makes me so tired. When it happens, I just want to go to bed and sleep. It's the only way to stop my mind racing. It's the only way to get some peace.

Wayne takes a sip of his Diet Coke.

'I've had an idea, Margaret, about these stories you have of your time at St Mary's. Why don't we make an audiobook about your experiences?'

I ain't listening at first. I'm too caught up in my thoughts. I stare at a picture of Peter Cushion on the wall.

'I'll help you record it,' he says. 'You just talk into the microphone.' Wayne pauses. 'Is everything OK, Margaret? I mean, it's just an idea. You don't have to . . .'

I drain the rest of my Strongbow in one gulp. The cider is making me feel more relaxed. My mind flicks back to the conversation.

'An audiobook? Do you mean like what Cilla done?'

'Like that, yes. A sort of oral autobiography.'

'Would it have my name on the cover?'

Wayne nods.

I open my bag and take out Cilla's CD, *What's It All About?* I look at the picture of her, thinking how glamorous she is in her black suit, with her hair and make-up done.

How lovely it would be to have my own audiobook, I think, *with my own name and picture on the cover.*

I remember the fifty quid in my purse and your message: *Here's another little something for you to treat yourself with.*

I have an idea then.

'If I'm doing an audiobook,' I say, 'I'll need to get my hair done, put make-up on. I can't go on a book cover looking like this.'

Wayne laughs. 'Stop putting yourself down, Margaret. You're absolutely gorgeous, inside and out. Never let anyone tell you otherwise.'

'Can I get my hair done, though?'

'I can book you an appointment, if you like.'

'Yes, please.' I says. 'At that place in Canterbury you told me about.'

'Razzle Dazzle?'

'That's the one.' I nod.

Wayne's best friend Gary has his own salon, so Wayne gets a discount. I've wanted to go there for ages because I like the name of it. It sounds posh.

Wayne picks up his phone to call the number.

'What day?'

'Friday.' I pause for a second. 'Tell him I want it coloured. Red, the same as Cilla.'

Wayne raises an eyebrow.

'What's wrong with red?' I say. 'I used to have red hair, back in the day. I wasn't always grey, you know.'

'If you're sure that's what you want, Margaret.'

He dials the number, putting his mobile to his ear. In all the excitement, and giddy with cider, I almost blurt out my secret.

49

Guess what! Cilla's written me a letter. She's coming back!
Something stops me, though. Now ain't the right time.
Wayne will only think I'm a looney tune.
No. I'll tell him when I'm ready.

13

1947

'What in heaven's name have they done to you, Joanie? You look like a ragamuffin.'

Mrs Chance crouched down on the ward floor, so she was facing Joan in her wheelchair. She didn't notice me at first, for I was stood behind. I couldn't understand why she was so upset: that day I'd helped one of the nurses put Joan in this navy-blue sailor suit to wear back to London. We'd dressed her ever so smart.

'For pity's sake, dear, look at the state of you,' says Mrs Chance, taking a comb out of her handbag and dragging it through Joan's hair. 'I've never seen so many knots!'

'Ouch, Mummy!' says Joan, pushing her away. 'You're hurting me!'

Mrs Chance sighed, putting the comb back in her bag. Next, she pulled out a handkerchief, licked it, started rubbing it all over Joan's face. Joan screamed.

'Please don't do that, Mummy! I hate it, you know I do. Your breath smells!'

She tried turning her head away, but Mrs Chance had hold of her chin.

'It's for your own good, darling,' she says, scrubbing round Joan's mouth.

51

Mrs Chance was even posher than Joan, which is saying something. She wore red lipstick and her hair was blonde, like Marilyn Monroe, tied up at the back in a giant green bow. She had on a massive fur coat, like a yeti, and the highest heels I'd ever seen. I couldn't take my eyes off her.

'Daddy won't be long, dear,' she says, stuffing the handkerchief back in her handbag and taking out a silver cigarette case. 'He's paying our driver. We had a terrible journey. The roads were shocking.'

She tapped her cigarette on the handle of Joan's wheelchair, then put it in her mouth and lit it.

'Oh, for goodness' sake, where has your father got to? Desmond, dear? Desmond!'

The smoke from her cigarette blew into my face and I sneezed.

'Goodness gracious.' She turned to face me. 'Who's this?'

'This is my friend Margaret, Mummy,' says Joan.

Mrs Chance flicked the ash from her cigarette on the floor and glared at her.

'Where's she from?'

'Why don't you ask her?' says Joan. 'Margaret can talk, you know.'

'I'm from Gordon Road,' I say, pointing to one of the windows. 'I lived there with Grandma before they vanished me.'

'Vanished you?' says Mrs Chance. She turned to Joan. 'Why, your little friend here has a charming way with words. I hope you're not picking up her rather proletarian vernacular.'

She bent down and whispered something in Joan's ear.

'Don't be beastly, Mummy,' Joan says, pushing her away. 'Margaret has been a huge help to me.'

I couldn't help noticing the sleeping animal Mrs Chance had hanging round her neck. It was long and thin, like a kitten that had been stretched through a mangle. I was fascinated by it; it looked ever so peaceful, lying on her shoulder, its little eyes shut. I asked her if I could touch it.

'Go on then,' she says, taking another quick puff on her cigarette. 'If you must.'

She leaned towards me, the fur on her coat brushing my cheek. It tickled. She smelled of lavender water and smoke. As I stroked the sleeping pet, she told me his name was Bertie.

'Isn't he just adorable?' she says. 'He's a stole.'

'Stole?' I says, pulling my hand away in a panic.

So Mrs Chance was a thief? Footsteps and loud voices was coming from down the corridor. For a second, I thought it must be the police coming to arrest Mrs Chance for stealing poor Bertie, but it was only Nurse Cunningham. She had a man behind her. A tall man in a hat and a bright blue suit and a yellow tie. He was carrying an umbrella.

'Why, Mr Chance,' she was saying, 'it's so lovely to have you back at St Mary's again. The children will be thrilled.'

'Daddy!' Joan screamed.

Mr Chance gave his umbrella to Nurse Cunningham. He ran towards Joan, falling to his knees and throwing his arms around her.

'Joanie, darling! How lovely to see you,' he says, taking off his hat and plonking it on Joan's head, where it dropped down over her eyes and nose. Joan frowned, tipping her head back.

'Why didn't you visit sooner, Daddy?'

'I'm dreadfully sorry, sweetheart,' he says, 'but Daddy's been ever so busy. Showbiz, you know how it is. I was on tour for six months with *Private Lives*. Took me all over the country, even the North. I haven't had a moment to myself. If it's any consolation, Mummy's barely seen me either. I'll make it up to you both, darling, I swear.'

Joan stuck out her bottom lip. He pinched her on the cheek.

'Chin up, dear,' he says. 'Why, I was saying to Mummy in the car just now how much I'm looking forward to the pantomime.'

'The girls have been practising really hard,' says Nurse Cunningham, who was still holding Mr Chance's wet umbrella.

'That's terrific!' says Mr Chance, standing up and brushing down his trouser legs with his hands. 'God loves a trier, eh, Joanie?'

He took his hat off Joan's head, ruffling her hair. Joan pulled a face.

'He really does,' says Nurse Cunningham. 'But it pains me to say this – it's been a real challenge for us this year.'

'A challenge?' Mr Chance looked concerned.

Nurse Cunningham stood wringing her hands.

'Well, what with the facilities at St Mary's being so poor, we really could do with a bigger space to perform. There was talk of us building a recreation hall. The church gets so overcrowded, you see. And the roof leaks where we had that bomb damage. It's still not been fixed. Of course, the main problem is money.'

Mr Chance raised his hand. 'Stop there, my dear woman! I absolutely won't hear of this. There's bound to be something we can do. Isn't that right, Bunty, darling?'

'Oh, of course,' says Mrs Chance. She dropped her cigarette on the floor, stubbing it out with the toe of her shoe. 'Actually, Desmond, I've just had a rather splendid idea. What about the tombola we organised last summer?'

'Ah, yes!' says Mr Chance. 'Now that was super successful. We raised huge amounts of money for them. I say, what charity was it again, darling? Legends Help the Lame?'

'No,' says Mrs Chance, rolling her eyes. 'We did the raffle for Legends. The tombola was for The Children's Society.'

'*That's* it!' says Mr Chance, turning to face Nurse Cunningham. 'A wonderful charity! Very worthy cause, but then they all are, you know. As I was saying to our driver on the way here this evening, it's good to give something back because, let's face it, we are all very fortunate.'

Mrs Chance nodded. 'We like to do our bit, don't we, Desmond? For the children.'

'Ah, the *children*,' says Mr Chance.

Nurse Cunningham smiled. 'That's ever so kind of you, Mr Chance. Really, anything you can do to help the hospital raise funds is greatly appreciated.'

'My pleasure, dear,' he says, suddenly looking very serious. 'Tell me now, are the press here this evening?'

'You know, I didn't even think to invite them,' said Nurse Cunningham.

'My dear woman,' says Mr Chance, 'you missed a trick. It's not just about the money, you know. Get a photographer to take a snapshot of me with a few children from the pantomime, and hey presto! Instant publicity for your new recreation hall. The donations will come rolling in. I have a few editorial contacts at *The Times*, which I can pass on to you if you like?'

'Oh, I see,' says Nurse Cunningham, blushing. 'That would be very helpful, Mr Chance. If you don't mind. Only I didn't think—'

'Of course you didn't think, dear. But I must apologise. I have this dreadful knack of forgetting that not everyone is as *au fait* with the national papers as we are.' He turned to Mrs Chance, raising his eyebrows. 'Darling, will you remind me next time we're down here to give Ralph Trowbridge a call? He always gets a decent shot.'

Mrs Chance nodded. She took a notebook from her bag and scribbled something down.

'Right,' he says. 'Let's not beat about the bush. We've got a lot to get on with, especially this one, who, more importantly, has a show tonight.'

He leaned over, kissing Joan on the cheek.

'We'd better get ready, Margaret,' says Joan.

'I say, who's your little friend here, Joanie?'

Mr Chance patted me on the head.

'I'm Margaret,' I says.

'Tell me, Margaret, what role are you playing in the panto-mime tonight?'

I covered my eyes with my hands. I wasn't used to men talking to me.

'Go on, Margaret,' says Joan. 'Tell Daddy about your part in the chorus.'

I shook my head.

'Timid little thing, isn't she?' he says, kneeling down and taking my hand. 'I hope you're not going to be too shy on stage. This is your opportunity to shine, Margaret, to show everyone what a talented girl you are!'

He turned to his wife then.

'Why, this is exactly the sort of child we need for the publicity photograph. Perfect, in fact. I say, Bunty, darling, we definitely need to get a photographer down here next time, eh?'

14

On Friday I catch the bus into Canterbury. I'm taking your advice, Cilla. I'm going to treat myself to a new hairstyle with the money you gave me. If I bump into you in Whitstable, I want to look my best.

The bus is quiet today, which is a relief. I take one of the priority seats near the driver. I feel safer sitting at the front. Even now, you see, I get scared on the bus. It's teenagers, mostly, who frighten me. They can be ever so rude. It happened to me just a few months ago, on my way back from Herne Bay. The bus was packed, there was no seats at the front, so I had to sit at the back. I was terrified. A couple of stops later, two girls got on. Teenagers. They was dressed in bikini tops and short shorts, screaming at each other the whole time.

'Oh my God, Summer, you look sick in that photo! I'm gonna send it to you.'

They was playing awful music on their phones.

One of the girls kept shouting: 'My pussy, my pussy.'

Why does she need to tell everyone on the bus about her stupid cat? I ain't interested, that's for sure.

They sat down opposite me, which made me feel a bit sick. I pretended to look out of the window but, every so often, I would glance over and catch them staring at me. They was sniggering and pulling horrible faces, sticking their tongues out and chanting 'My pussy, my pussy' over and over again. My whole body was shaking and my heart felt like it was about to explode. All I wanted to do was get off the bus and walk home. One of them called me a horrible word I'd never use myself. I didn't cry, or say anything, though. I didn't want them to see I was upset. Nobody on the bus tried to stop them; all the people just sat there. When things like that happen, I hide. I don't want to go out of the house. Because really, who wants to put up with that? Not me.

It took me ages to learn to go on the bus by myself. *Years.* Jean used to come with me. Jean was my support worker before Wayne. Then before Jean there was Gloria. Oh, she was posh! Ever so old-fashioned, Gloria was.

'Button up your coat, Margaret!' she used to say. 'You don't want to look like a vagabond.'

As if I would want to look like a vagabond. I don't even know what one of them is.

Jean was one of my favourite carers. She had her moods, though. She used to have a collie called Lassie. One day we took Lassie to Brighton. We got the bus all the way there. It was my first-ever time on the bus. It took ages, but I wasn't scared because Jean talked to me about stuff and made me feel safe, and we sang ABBA and 'Summer Holiday' by Cliff Richard. Jean used to say that one day she would marry Cliff, but when I said this to May, Jean's best friend who's dead now, May says, 'What nonsense, Margaret! Cliff would never have been interested in a woman like Jean.'

'Why not?'

May just laughed. 'Jean's not Cliff's type,' she says.

Brighton was beautiful. Oh, it was gorgeous! One of the nicest places I've ever been. Jean bought ice creams and we walked along the pier. I walk slowly because of my hip, but I don't mind doing it for a bit. It was a really hot day; even Lassie was panting. I remember Jean saying to me, 'Take Lassie's lead, Margaret. Go on. Take her walkies.' So I did. But there was these boys throwing stones in the sea, who made me frightened, so I let go of the lead. Lassie ran off into the water and got wet, then she jumped up on Jean's skirt, her new skirt from Dorothy Perkins!

'This has ruined my day,' Jean says, marching Lassie and me back to the bus. She told us both to sit down and be quiet. 'I have the most awful headache,' she says.

She hardly spoke a word to me all the way back to Whitstable. Not one word. It was like she'd sent me to Conventry.

As soon as I sit down on the bus, I take my CD player out of my Tesco carrier bag, put my headphones on and press play. Straight away Cilla starts telling me about her friend Brian. He was her manager in the sixties. He died young, when he was 33, and it hit Cilla hard.

'When somebody close to you dies,' she says, her voice a whisper, 'memories float in and out of the mind at the most unexpected, inappropriate times.'

I know what she means. Ever since Cilla died, I've been thinking about the past a lot. I can't focus on anything. Even when I'm watching *EastEnders* or *Corrie*, my mind drifts and I start thinking about all of the people I used to know. Most of them are no longer here. Being old can be ever so lonely. *Only the lonely*. Ain't that the name of a song? I try to remember how it goes. Outside the bus window, the houses, trees and cars rush past. Backwards, they go, flashing fast in front of my eyes.

15

1947

Nurse Fitts poked her head between the red curtains.

'How is everything backstage, girls? Are we all in our positions?'

There was a lot of coughing and shuffling.

'Take your fingers out of your nose, Janet,' she says. 'Octopuses don't have fingers.'

Janet was one of the girls from my ward. She had Down's syndrome, as did a lot of other children at St Mary's. She was performing in the chorus with me and her costume was amazing. To make it, the nurses had got some old pairs of stockings and stuffed them with rags and newspaper, then hung them round her neck to look like arms. I was jealous.

'What about me?' I says.

I had a bit of a sulk, so they dressed me up as a crab. They made me a mask out of an old porridge box and gave me a pair of oven gloves for claws. Joan's mermaid costume was the best, though. The nurses put her in this beautiful long blonde wig and made her a tail from two old pillowcases, which they stitched together and covered with milk bottle tops. Earlier that week, a group of boys had helped build a massive rock out of papier mâché. We put it around Joan's wheelchair to hide it. On the night, it really did look like she was sitting on a rock. Even the nurses thought so.

'It's a full house,' Nurse Fitts says to us. 'Remember to smile, like I told you. Good luck!'

Her head disappeared, just as the twinkly music started playing. Somebody coughed. A few people went *Shhh!* Then the curtains opened.

The lights was blinding, but I could just make out Mr and Mrs Chance. They was sat in the front row with Nurse Cunningham next to them. I half hoped Grandma might be there, too, but she wasn't, of course.

Bernadette was the first to speak. She was playing a lump of seaweed. She spoke quietly, her voice shaking.

> *A long time ago, in a land far away*
> *There lived an old sea king*
> *Whose daughter was gay*
> *And pretty and kind, and all of those things.*

Grace was the sea king. She stood at the front of the stage, wearing a cardboard crown and holding a garden fork with green tinsel on it. It was her turn to speak next.

> *My wife has been dead now for many a year*
> *This ocean too small*
> *To hold all my tears*
> *And those of my daughters, my favourite of all.*

Grace had barely finished speaking when Joan, who had been sat on a rock, combing her hair, burst in.

> *That is me! Daddy's favourite. The Little Mermaid!*
> *For I am the youngest of six.*

61

I long to be older, so I can escape,
Riding high on the waves like a phoenix!
But I must stay down here, under the sea
Until I am fifteen years old.
Just the thought of that day makes my heart burst
with glee
For at last, I'll escape from the cold.

While I waited my turn, I stood watching the pantomime from the side. It was magical, it had everything in it: singing penguins, dancing dolphins and hula-hooping mermaids. The time flew by and before long it was my turn to go on stage with the rest of the chorus for the grand finale. All of us was dressed as sea creatures: eels, winkles, clams, cockles and mussels. Janet, the octopus, was leading the way. We'd been told to follow her in a straight line. I was stood at the back, my knees knocking. The music started: 'I'm Forever Blowing Bubbles'. This was our signal to move, but as soon as I started walking, my crab mask slipped down my face, meaning I couldn't see properly. While the others formed a circle around Joan's rock, I ended up getting lost and wandering back off stage. Luckily, Nurse Fitts was waiting in the wings. She grabbed me, swung me round in the right direction, so I could join the others. At the end of the show, Joan sang a solo – ('There'll Be Bluebirds Over) The White Cliffs Of Dover' – and we all took a bow. I couldn't wait to take my mask off, so I could see again.

The audience loved it. They got up on their feet, clapping and cheering. Afterwards, Mr and Mrs Chance came backstage to congratulate us all. Mr Chance said it was one of the best things he'd ever seen in the theatre. He signed my mask for me. I've still got it, even to this day, and I can remember what he wrote:

20th December 1947

Dear Margaret,
    Congratulations on your starring role as 'crab' in
"The Little Mermaid". My wife and I thoroughly
enjoyed your performance!
    All best wishes for Christmas and the
New Year.
    Desmond Chance

The next morning, Mr and Mrs Chance came to take Joan home for Christmas. As I wheeled her over to the main entrance to meet them, I heard Mrs Chance yelling at Nurse Cunningham.

'Never again!' she says. 'We found a cockroach scuttling about in the lavatory, and there was enough hair in the bathtub to coat the abominable snowman. Why, the sheets were as stained as your apron, Nurse Cunningham and, as for the slattern manning reception . . . Well, I'm sorry, but next time, we're staying in a hotel. We both said that, didn't we, Desmond?'

'Yes, dear,' says Mr Chance, who was standing behind her with Mrs Chance's coat hanging over his arm like a dead dog. 'Not to mention being continually poked in the rib by a broken bedspring. At one point I thought I'd cracked something. Shocking place, honestly. I'm not exaggerating when I say they were hospitality illiterate.'

'I'm so sorry,' Nurse Cunningham says to them. 'Only I've had family stay there before. They said it was fine. I wouldn't have recommended it to you otherwise.'

'Not to worry, dear,' says Mr Chance, sighing. 'We London folk are a fussy lot. I'm not saying I expected to find the equivalent of the Savoy here in Canterbury, but certainly not something quite as squalid as that place.'

'It's a shame, really,' says Mrs Chance. 'I mean, we had such a lovely evening watching the girls do their pantomime . . .'

'That's enough now, Bunty,' says Mr Chance, lifting up his wife's coat and putting it round her shoulders. 'Let's not bang on about it. I'm sure Nurse Cunningham has infinitely more pressing things to deal with.' He knelt to speak to Joan. 'Are we all set for home then, Joanie? Bags packed?'

Joan nodded. She put her arms around Mr Chance's shoulders for support as he lifted her out of her chair.

'Don't forget to say cheerio to Nurse Cunningham and Margaret,' he says, carrying her towards the main doors.

Joan waved at us from over his shoulder.

'Bye, Margaret,' she says. 'Happy Christmas.'

'Happy Christmas, Joan.'

I waved back, trying my best not to look upset.

Nurse Cunningham says, 'Thank you so much for coming. I'm ever so sorry about the lodgings. Only I'm not used to staying in expensive places myself. I should've suggested you stay somewhere a bit more civilised.'

'Oh, nonsense, dear. Ignore us!' says Mrs Chance. 'We're a couple of old fusspots. At any rate, we shall sleep well in our own beds tonight. Tally-ho then, we'd best get going. We've kept our driver waiting long enough. It was nice to see you, Nurse Cunningham, as always.'

'Don't forget what I said to you about funding,' says Nurse Cunningham, lifting her dress and curtseying like they was the King and Queen of England.

'Why, of course not, dear!' says Mrs Chance, rushing towards the door. 'It shall be top of our list of priorities for the New Year. Have a good Christmas now. You too, Margaret. Toodle-pip!'

16

1947

To begin with, Christmas was miserable without Joan. We'd only known each other a month or so, but she was my best friend and I missed taking her everywhere. One time, I got Dolly out of bed and put her in a wheelchair. I pushed her around, talking to her, but it wasn't the same.

Christmas Day was a special occasion. They gave us bacon and eggs for breakfast, much nicer than the usual porridge. Then after we'd eaten, the nurses took us to the day room, where all our presents was laid out under a big tree. The presents was from the government. That year, I got crayons and a book for drawing in. I remember drawing a picture of a house with me and Joan inside. The house was grey, with a square garden and a tall fence around it.

On Christmas night they let the boys come over to the girls' wing. They did that every year. The boys went round the wards, singing carols, and the nurses invited them in. I wasn't used to seeing boys. I felt shy at first, but once they started singing, I relaxed a bit and joined in. The nurses put food out for us, too. It wasn't the normal food they gave you at mealtimes, it was different: thick slices of corned beef, hard-boiled eggs, cakes and mince pies, jelly and ice cream. They had other staff on at Christmas, too; it wasn't the usual nurses. They was a lot nicer.

After the boys left, we had a party. They put records on the gramophone and the girls danced together. Janet was my partner. We'd got to know each other during the pantomime, and she was good fun. We drank fizzy pop and she taught me how to rhumba.

Once Christmas was over, though, the days dragged on. I missed talking to Joan. She was probably only gone a few weeks, but it felt like forever. I got bored of just drawing and staring out of the window all the time. Besides, who else did I have who could read me stories?

One day, after New Year, the nurses took a group of us down to the pictures in Canterbury to see *The Wizard of Oz*. We hardly ever got to leave the hospital, so this was a treat. Janet and me sat next to each other on posh red chairs. We ate popcorn and drank cola through straws. The first time the witch appeared, we grabbed each other, screaming. Nurse Cunningham, who was sat behind us, leaned over and pinched us both hard in the back of the neck.

'People have paid good money to see this film,' she says. 'The last thing they want to hear is you two howling like a pair of flying monkeys.'

Later, Janet whispered to me that Nurse Cunningham was just like the Wicked Witch of the West, which made me laugh and spit my drink out. After the film was over, we whispered, 'Lions and tigers and bears, oh my!' all the way back to the ward.

We used to enjoy getting outside the hospital. For us, it was a change of scenery. As a child, I felt like I had a bit more freedom at St Mary's. That all changed, though, once they built the recreation hall in the 1950s. We was no longer allowed out into the community. We watched the pictures at St Mary's instead. They was mostly cowboy films, which I hated. Bloody rubbish, if you ask me.

It was Mr Chance who helped to raise the money for the recreation hall, through his charity work.

'Isn't this better?' the nurses said to us. 'You don't need to go all the way to the cinema now. You can stay here and watch the films instead.'

I didn't think it was better. Things was worse, if anything. After they built the recreation hall, we never got to go anywhere, you see. They kept us indoors all the time, like bloody prisoners.

17

Razzle Dazzle is only a short walk from the bus stop, on the other side of the Westgate Towers. I find it easy enough. From the outside, it looks posh, exactly the sort of place Cilla would go if she was having her hair done. The glass door makes a ringing sound when I push it open. Inside, everything is black and white and sparkling clean. The floor looks like a chessboard and there's a Whitney Houston song playing on the radio. Clutching my plastic carrier bag, I shuffle my way across the black and white squares to the reception desk. The blonde girl sitting behind it is flicking through a wedding magazine. She's wearing white jeans, a black jumper and earrings big as hoopla hoops. She looks up at me, smiling, her eyes and mouth wide open.

'Welcome to Razzle Dazzle,' she says. 'My name is Bree. How can I help you today?'

Bree don't sound English. Her voice reminds me of somebody off *Neighbours*. I can't think who. Reaching into my plastic bag, I pull out my copy of Cilla's CD *What's It All About?* and put it on the reception desk.

'I want my hair to look like this,' I say. 'Same colour, same style.'

There's a long pause as Bree stares down at the photo on the CD in front of her, and then at me.

'Interesting,' she says. 'Would you like me to make you an appointment?'

'I've already got one,' I say, grabbing the CD back and putting it in my bag. 'At one o'clock.'

Bree nods. 'Lovely. What's the name?'

'Gary,' I say.

'Gary?' Bree stares at me for a moment. 'Your name's Gary?'

'Of course my name ain't Gary,' I snap at her. 'I ain't a man, if that's what you was thinking. My name's Small. Margaret Small.'

'Oh God, I'm so sorry,' says Bree, tapping my name into the computer. 'Let me just have a quick look for you.'

Another girl comes wandering over. She's tall and carrying a black clipboard. She gawps at me.

'Do you need a hand, Bree?'

'Would you be so kind as to take care of Miss Small, Destiny? She is booked in with Gary at one p.m.'

'Sure thing.' Destiny looks at me and smiles. 'Come this way, Miss Small.'

Destiny asks me to sit down on a black leather sofa.

'Gary won't be long,' she says. 'Can I get you a tea or coffee?'

'I'll have tea, love. If you don't mind.'

'How do you take it?'

'Milk. Only make sure it's full-fat.'

Destiny nods. 'Sugar?'

'Three, please.'

'Of course. Would you like to read a magazine while you wait, Miss Small?'

'No thank you, love. I've got my audiobook for company.'

As soon as Destiny goes off to make tea, I get my headphones out of my bag and put them on. Pressing play, I sit back and listen to Cilla talking about the time she had her hair done for the cover of her album *Sher-oo!* They styled it in a perm, she says, with big curls – like sausages. It looked awful on her. I'm laughing so loudly at this that Bree from reception comes over to ask if I'm all right.

'I'm fine, love,' I says. 'Don't worry about me. I was just talking to my friend, Cilla. She was telling me about a bad haircut she had once. I hope your Gary does a better job with mine.'

18

1948

'Get up off the floor, dear,' says Nurse Cunningham. 'We don't crawl here, we walk!'

Poor Joan. Ever since she came back to St Mary's after the holidays, she'd been learning to walk in calipers. They was a Christmas present from her parents and she hated wearing them. It didn't stop her trying. Determined, she was. After a couple of weeks of practice, though, she could still only manage a few steps, then she'd fall over again.

'Can you help me up, Margaret?' she says. 'It's these wretched things.'

I reached down and gave her my hand. She stood up slowly, grabbing me for support.

'I've got a good mind to report you to Daddy,' she says, glaring at Nurse Cunningham. 'I'm sure he wouldn't like to hear you speaking to his daughter like that.'

Nurse Cunningham laughed. 'Listen to Little Lady Fauntleroy,' she says. 'Someone's starting to get ideas above their station'.

'It's true,' says Joan. 'Daddy told me all about his plans for the St Mary's Summer Fete. I've a good mind to tell him what a rotten old witch you are. Then we'll see how much money you manage to raise for the hospital!'

I'd never heard Joan speak to Nurse Cunningham that way. I was shocked. I hid myself in a corner, behind Joan's wheelchair.

'That's enough of your cheek,' says Nurse Cunningham. 'One of these days I'm going to lock you in the punishment room. That'll teach you.'

'You wouldn't dare,' says Joan. 'You know I'll only tell—'

Nurse Cunningham snorted like a pig. 'Do you really think your father will believe your story over mine, dear? Don't be so ridiculous, child.'

'I'm not a child. I'm nearly eleven. Practically an adult.'

'Well, start behaving like one, then,' says Nurse Cunningham. 'Your father knows only too well what a spoiled brat you can be. He even told me so himself.'

'He did not!' Joan screamed. 'You're a liar!'

Nurse Cunningham laughed. 'Liar?' she says. 'The very first day he left you at St Mary's, he said to me, "Don't take any nonsense from this one. She can be a bit of a handful."'

'You're making it up! You horrible woman. I won't stand for it! Daddy wouldn't say such a thing.'

Nurse Cunningham grabbed Joan by the wrists, dragging her off her feet and lifting her up, so they was face to face.

'On the contrary,' she says, 'those were his exact words. Now, unless you want to spend a whole week in the punishment room, you'd better learn to keep your mouth shut. Am I making myself clear?'

Joan nodded. Nurse Cunningham let go of her wrists and Joan slumped back to the floor.

'Now if you don't mind,' she says, 'there are other patients in this hospital who need my help this morning.'

She turned to me then.

'See to it that she keeps practising, Margaret. Having spoken to Mr Chance on the telephone last week, I know he's keen for her to make progress by his next visit. Judging from today's lesson, he's going to be very disappointed. Am I right, Joan?'

Joan was a fighter – I'll give her that. She put on a brave face. It was only after Nurse Cunningham left that I noticed she was crying.

Every June, they held the annual sports day at St Mary's. It was a big event and everyone looked forward to it. Even if you was bad at sports, you could still win something, for they did all kinds of races: races for those who could run fast, and races for the children like me, who was slow.

By spring, Joan was able to get around in her calipers. She still preferred her wheelchair, but she was determined not to give up on them. Most mornings, after breakfast, me and one of the nurses would help her practise in the day room. In the beginning, she would cry with frustration, saying her arms hurt. She'd tell us there was no point – that she wanted to give up. But it wasn't long before she got the hang of it and, to cheer her up, Nurse Fitts suggested that she take part in the sports day.

As soon as it became a competition, Joan was desperate to win. When the actual day arrived, though, we was both in for a shock. It turned out they had put the two of us down for the same race: the slowest walker.

The rules for the slowest walker was different from a normal race; you had to go as slowly as you could. The winner was the person who came last. I forgot about that, though. As soon as Nurse Fitts said, 'On your marks, get set, go,' Joan screamed at me, 'Faster, Margaret, faster!'

I went as fast as I could. So fast, I was the first one to cross the finish line.

'I've won,' I says. 'I've won!'

'No you haven't,' says Joan, who was about half a mile behind me. 'I've won!'

Joan could be crafty sometimes.

I did the three-legged race that year, too. Joan couldn't do that one, so Janet was my partner. As soon as Nurse Cunningham tied us both together at the ankles with a pair of her old stockings, we fell over. She only did it to spite us, for I saw her pointing and laughing with one of the other nurses.

I said to Janet, 'Never again. You won't get me doing that, no way.'

Janet agreed with me. They could be bloody horrible sometimes, those nurses.

I liked the blind boxing, though. It was funny. Only the boys was allowed to do it. They used to have to run around in a blindfold, trying to hit each other, dodging the punches. The girls would stand round in a circle, cheering the boys on. They stopped doing it the year one of the nurses got punched in the face by accident and was rushed to hospital. I still remember her eye when she came out. All swollen and black. She had to wear an eyepatch for weeks. It made her look like a pirate. She wasn't happy.

Sports day was good fun, though. At the end of the event, the nurses always gave you prizes; everyone got sweets and chocolate, even those who didn't win. I've still got the certificate they gave me for coming last in the egg and spoon race. It's up in the loft in Cromwell Road somewhere.

19

Gary seats me in front of a big mirror with bright white light bulbs all around it. I look at my reflection and my heart sinks. My hair is a grey mess, and my white cardigan has got a big ketchup stain on it from the fish finger sandwich I had at lunch. To hide it, I take off my cardigan, turn it inside out and put it back on again. The label is sticking out the back and you can still see the stain, but at least it ain't as obvious as it was before. Imagine if Cilla saw me now. It's bad enough Gary seeing me in this state. He's a handsome man, just like Michael Bolton when he had longer hair: tall with white jeans and a black shirt, open at the neck to show off his smooth chest. I never knew Wayne had such good-looking friends.

'Where did you meet Wayne, then?' I ask.

'On an app,' says Gary, pressing a lever to raise my chair higher.

'A nap? What, you met while you was having forty winks together?'

Gary laughs. 'Not quite. Well, come to think about it, it *was* a bit like that. How can I describe it? It was through a phone app, like Facebook.'

'Don't you mean Grindr?' says the skinny man with dreadlocks cutting hair next to me. 'Or was it Scruff?'

75

'Shut it, Sean,' Gary says to him. 'Or I won't let you borrow my clippers again.'

'I ain't on Facebook,' I say.

'Very wise, Margaret,' says Gary. 'You're not missing much. Just a bunch of sad, lonely people posting fake versions of their lives.'

I ain't got any friends, I think to myself, *apart from Wayne. And he ain't going to want to be friends with me much longer if I keep hiding things.*

I decide I'm going to tell him about Cilla tomorrow. I can't keep her a secret any longer. It's time. He'll think I'm mad, but there's no avoiding it. Wayne must know the truth.

'What look are we aiming for today?'

Gary runs his fingers through my hair, gently stroking my head. All of a sudden, I feel shy and nervous.

'I have a photograph,' I say, rummaging in my plastic bag for my Cilla CD and handing it to him. 'I want my hair like that.'

Gary takes the CD and looks at it closely.

'Oh God, wasn't it awful about Cilla?' he says. 'I couldn't believe it when I heard it on the news. Another icon gone. She was a legend. A legend with fabulous hair. Not to mention that voice.'

'Do you reckon I could have hair like Cilla?'

Gary moves my head from side to side and looks closely at my reflection in the mirror.

'If you want my honest opinion, I think the colour will suit you fine. It would be a real shame to lose these lovely curls, though.'

'Just colour it then, you mean?'

I'm enjoying all this attention from gorgeous Gary.

'Yeah, I'll cut it, give it a bit of shape. And texture, too, of course. Once I've put the colour in, I'll get Destiny to give you a wash and shampoo, OK?'

I nod and say, 'Yes, it sounds brilliant.'

Right now, I'm in the mood to do anything Gary tells me.

After Gary has finished painting my hair, he wraps it in tinfoil and shines a big lamp on my head. He leaves me sitting on my own for a while. This part is boring. To pass the time, I play a game where I try and remember the names of as many Cilla songs as possible: 'Something Tells Me (Something's Gonna Happen Tonight)', 'Anyone Who Had A Heart', 'Don't Answer Me'. Every so often, I catch my reflection in the mirror and I can't help chuckling to myself; with the silver squares in my hair, I look just like the Tin Man from *The Wizard of Oz*. This would have been a good costume for the fetes they used to dress us up for as children at St Mary's.

After what seems like ages, Destiny comes to collect me. She asks me to follow her through a pair of beaded curtains into a tiny room, which has a couple of basins for washing hair.

'Take a seat,' she says. 'Can I take your bag for you now?'

'I'd rather keep hold of it, love, if you don't mind,' I say, sitting down on a chair and resting the bag on my lap. 'You can't be too careful these days. There's a lot of thieves about.'

Destiny shrugs.

'Fine by me.' She strips the tinfoil off my hair, throwing it in a bin next to the sink. 'Sit forward, then,' she says, putting a towel behind my neck. 'Now lean back.'

I do as I'm told.

'You're a bit stiff, Miss Small. Try and relax.'

It feels a bit uncomfortable at first, but I follow Destiny's instructions and close my eyes, lying back on the towel. She turns on the taps and I hear the trickle of water.

'Is the temperature OK for you?' she says, as she starts to wet my hair.

'It's fine, love.' I chuckle to myself. 'Not like when they used to wash me in the old days. The water was bloody freezing then.'

Destiny ignores me. I hear her squeezing a blob of shampoo out of a bottle and rubbing it into her hands. There's a lovely smell, like Mint Imperials, as she lathers my hair. My scalp is tingling. Her fingers are soft and light, slipping and slopping around my head. My whole body shivers as she starts rinsing off the suds, the soap and warm water lapping over my ears, down the side of my face. And then the strangest thing happens. I start crying. I don't know why, because this is so lovely, but it's as if all the sadness is pouring out of my head, mixing with the warm water, vanishing down the sink. Destiny runs her hands through my hair one last time to squeeze the water out. It makes a squeaking sound. She asks me to sit up while she dries me off with a towel. She's a lot gentler than Nurse Cunningham used to be, that's for sure.

'Have you worked here a long time, love?' I say, although what I really want to ask her is if she'll wash my hair all over again. It felt so nice.

'Only since the start of the summer,' she says. 'I'm doing my A levels, so I only work half-day Friday, and Saturday.'

Destiny finishes patting me dry with the towel. I'm enjoying this, being pampered.

'I would've liked to have done A levels,' I say. 'But they wouldn't let me.'

'Why not?' she asks. 'Did you do badly in your GCSEs?'

'GCSEs?' I laugh. 'If only. There was no GCSEs in my day.'

'What did you have instead?'

'Not a lot,' I say. 'Good luck with the hairdressing, though. I think you'll be good at it.'

Destiny takes me back to Gary, and I watch as he takes

78

out his scissors. He starts trimming my hair. At first, I'm not sure if I like it or not. I look like a wet ferret. The colour's too dark, more brown than red, but Gary says it'll look more like Cilla's when it's dry. The blow-drying takes ages, but I don't mind. As far as I'm concerned, Gary can take as long as he likes. When he's finished, he holds up a mirror, so I can see my hair from the front and back.

'What do you think?' he says. 'Is it how you wanted it?'

I can't believe I'm staring at my own reflection. I look completely different.

'You've vanished the grey, Gary,' I says. 'All of it, completely vanished.'

Gary grins. 'Surprise, surprise, Margaret,' he says. 'You look fabulous! Cilla would be proud.'

'Would she?' I says, tears welling up in my eyes. 'Do you really think so? My Cilla?'

'Absolutely,' says Gary, plumping my hair with his hands.

Even Destiny, who has brought me over another cup of tea, agrees with him.

'You look beautiful, Miss Small,' she says. 'I can't believe the transformation.'

'It's incredible, isn't it?' Gary says. 'I hope our Wayne doesn't think you've made all this extra effort for his sake?'

'What do you mean?' I says.

'It's his birthday next week, isn't it? A group of us are going up to London together. I've even got myself a special outfit for the occasion. It's this all-in-one—'

'Spare us the gory details, Gary,' says Sean, the skinny man with the dreadlocks. 'There are ladies present. Speaking of which, you look amazing, Miss Small. That colour has knocked years off you.'

Bree, the receptionist, comes over to have a look at my hair, too. Everyone is telling me how nice I look. Their words go in one ear and out the other, though: I'm too busy thinking about Wayne's birthday, you see. My mind's been so caught up with Cilla lately, I'd completely forgotten about it.

What sort of a friend am I?

20

'C'

I saw you get off the bus today, just as I was coming out of the estate agent's on the High Street. I've been looking at properties down here for a while now. My dream has always been to have a little house by the sea, with a white picket fence and wild flowers in the garden. I'd love to have you over if I do eventually find somewhere. You look amazing, by the way! I can't believe what they've done to your hair. What a transformation, it really suits you. I was tempted to pop to the florist's and buy you a nice bouquet, to congratulate you on your new look, but I thought that might be a bit much. I don't want to overwhelm you. Another time, perhaps?

21

1948

In the summer of 1948, they held the Fete and Flower Show at St Mary's to raise money for the new recreation hall. Mr and Mrs Chance both helped organise it. They came down from London especially for the day.

When they arrived, I was in the day room with Joan, getting ready for the decorated wheelchair and fancy dress parade. Joan said she wanted to look the best out of everyone, so earlier that morning, Nurse Fitts had helped me tie balloons to her chair. We pegged flowers to the wheels: a mixture of daisy chains, buttercups and hyacinths, which the nurses had let us pick from the hospital garden. Normally girls wasn't allowed in the garden, because the male patients worked there, but sometimes the nurses took us out for a treat. I used to love pressing my nose into the roses, smelling the perfume, feeling their soft petals brush against my mouth and cheeks.

Joan wore a beautiful pink frock with matching ribbons in her hair. One of the nurses gave her a lovely purple umbrella, too, with a white lace frill. She looked ever so nice. They dressed me up as the rag-and-bone man. I wore torn trousers, with a frying pan strapped to my back. The nurses rubbed coal dust all over my face and gave me a potato sack filled with old rubbish to carry about. Nurse Fitts said it was one of the best costumes she'd ever seen.

'Why, darling,' says Mrs Chance, kneeling down and hugging Joan. 'You look fabulous! Doesn't she look fabulous, Desmond?'

'Not wearing your calipers today, Joanie?' says Mr Chance.

Joan pulled a face, like she was sulking. He turned to me then and started laughing.

'I say, your friend Margaret here is as black as my boot.' He made a noise like a donkey. *Haw haw haw.*

'I think I've found it, Mr Chance,' says Nurse Cunningham, coming into the ward carrying a brown parcel.

'Thank heavens,' says Mrs Chance. 'I thought we might have left it at home. Do you want to open it, dear? I do hope it's useful. You'd be surprised how much money these things raise.'

'Indeed,' says Mr Chance, still laughing. 'People will buy any old tat!'

'It's hardly tat,' says Mrs Chance.

'Oh, of course not, dear. I was just thinking about the time at the Dorchester, when that poor chap bid his life savings on one of my old cravats.'

Mrs Chance tutted. 'It wasn't his life savings, Desmond. Don't exaggerate.'

Nurse Cunningham put the box down on the table. She took a pair of scissors from her apron pocket and cut the string.

'Be careful, dear!' says Mrs Chance. 'The material's very delicate.'

Nurse Cunningham undone the flaps and reached inside. She lifted this hat-type thing out of the box; it was purple, with a long feather on top.

'Why . . . thank you, Mrs Chance,' she says.

She held it up to the ceiling, turning it around to get a better look.

'Do you like it?' says Mrs Chance. 'I made it myself.'

Nurse Cunningham looked confused. 'Forgive me if I sound ignorant, Mrs Chance – I'm not very good with fashion, but what is it, exactly?'

Mrs Chance frowned, taking the hat off her.

'Don't worry, dear,' she says, looking Nurse Cunningham up and down. 'That's perfectly understandable. Have you got a pen? You'll want to make a note of this if you're planning on selling it as a raffle prize.'

'Oh, of course,' says Nurse Cunningham. She put her hand in her apron pocket and took out a pen and a bit of paper. Leaning over the table, she licked the nib. 'What would you like me to write?'

Mrs Chance put her hand on her chin. 'Hmm. Let me think,' she says. 'How about "especially handmade"? No, don't say "handmade", that makes it sound cheap . . . What about "designed"? Yes, that's it . . . "Especially *designed* by actress Bunty Chance for this year's Fete and Flower Show is this fabulously . . ." No, wait, let's call it "exclusive" . . . Yes . . . that's it . . . "This fabulously *exclusive* long-quilled cap in mauve velveteen and yellow moss crêpe".'

Nurse Cunningham was scribbling fast on a bit of paper. She kept crossing things out and writing them over again. When she was finished, she handed it to Mrs Chance.

'Very nice,' says Mrs Chance. 'But there's only one *n* in Bunty, dear.'

'What time do things generally kick off, then?' says Mr Chance, who was sat at the table, reading his paper.

'Quarter past two,' says Nurse Cunningham. 'We have military music from the Guards' depot, then it's the decorated wheelchair parade.'

'And you remembered to book the photographer this time?'

'Oh yes, Mr Chance, you'll be ever so proud of me. Mr Trowbridge is arriving at one o'clock.'

'Marvellous! Ralph is a super photographer, one of the best in the business. I've always thought he's rather wasted out here in the sticks.' Mr Chance rolled up his paper. 'And don't let me forget, Nurse Cunningham, we need to get several shots of the recipe book.'

'Oh,' she says. 'I'd forgotten all about the recipe book. How exciting.'

'I thought of the title, of course,' says Mr Chance. 'Bunty thinks it's genius.'

'What's it called?' says Nurse Cunningham.

'*Simple Suppers. Easy recipes that even a fool can manage.*'

'Aren't you clever, Mr Chance?' she says.

Nurse Cunningham wasn't half as nice as pork pies in front of Joan's parents. Oh, I hated her sometimes.

'It was a hell of a lot of work, my dear,' says Mr Chance. 'But these things often are. I find myself agreeing to do something for a good cause and before I know it, I'm working flat out, opening my address book, badgering all my theatre chums for tombola prizes and so on. I did well this time, though, didn't I, Bunty?'

'*Exceptionally* well, Desmond,' says Mrs Chance. 'You are very fortunate, Nurse Cunningham. We've got the cream of the acting profession in this book.'

Mr Chance laughed. 'The *cream* of the acting profession! Dammit, darling, why didn't I think of that? We could've used it in the foreword. *La crème de la crème.*'

Mrs Chance put her hand on his shoulder and gave him a little peck on the cheek.

'Too late now, dear. Let's save it for the reprint. It's bound to sell out.'

Mr Chance coughed. 'Why don't you fetch a few copies from the car, Bunty? I'm sure Nurse Cunningham would like to see them.'

After Mrs Chance left the room, Nurse Cunningham went and sat down next to Mr Chance at the table.

'Who's in the book?' she says, sounding excited. 'Anyone I know?'

'My dear girl, I should jolly well think so!' says Mr Chance. 'Who haven't we got? There's a simple syllabub from John Mills. Alec Guinness has given us his apricot fool, Vera Lynn's donated her Spam goulash and my dear friend Fanny Cradock has loaned us not one, but two recipes – baked hedgehog, and Escoffier's pêches Melba. Admittedly the latter is quite complicated, but she's a novelist and a rising culinary star. I wasn't going to argue. Huge draw, huge draw.'

'I'm so impressed,' says Nurse Cunningham. 'How much are we going to sell them for?'

'Four shillings and sixpence a copy,' he says. 'The hospital gets any profit we make. I've got several hundred books, in boxes, in the boot of the car. I'll leave it with you to tally up the numbers, but it should amount to a reasonable sum. I'm happy to sign a few copies, too, which will of course raise the value even more.'

'Why, it's so generous of you to do all this for the hospital,' says Nurse Cunningham. 'Really, we're so grateful.'

'It's the least I can do, dear. Honestly. Please don't make a fuss.'

Joan made a noise, as if she was clearing her throat.

'We must be getting on, Daddy,' she says. 'Margaret and I have still got lots of preparation to do for the parade.'

'Very well, dear,' says Mr Chance. 'I can tell when we're not needed.'

He winked at Nurse Cunningham. Her face went as red as tomato sauce.

'Why don't I take you through and give you a tour of the kitchen, Mr Chance?' she says. 'I can ask one of the patients to make tea. It'll give us a chance to have a proper chat about fundraising and our plans for the new recreation hall.'

'Why, that sounds like an excellent idea,' he says.

After they had left, I noticed Joan was upset. She looked pretty as a princess, but her eyes was all teary.

'Are you OK, Joan?'

'I'll tell you later,' she says.

22

22 AUGUST 2015

I don't know why I bothered getting a clock. I can't tell the time, so what's the point in having one? Some people like the ticking sound, they find it relaxing. Not me. It makes me panic. It makes me think what little time I have left, like those quizzes on TV, where everything is against the clock.

It feels like I've been listening to the ticking of the kitchen clock all morning while I wait for Wayne to pick me up in the car. We're going to Dreamland in Margate for part of his birthday celebrations, even though his actual birthday ain't until next week. In my day, you had one birthday and that was it. You was lucky if you got a card and a mandarin orange. Young people nowadays don't know they're living.

I thought Margate might be a good place to tell Wayne about the letters, but right now, all I can think about is that bloody clock ticking. The doorbell rings, making me jump. Wayne is standing outside. I tell him to come in. I tell him I need to talk to him about something important.

'Can't it wait?' Wayne looks at his watch. 'I told Charisma we'd be at her house for quarter past. I'm already running a bit late.'

'Charisma?' My heart sinks. 'You never said *she* was coming.'

88

Charisma is one of the other people Wayne supports.

'Didn't I?' Wayne bites his lip. 'I could've sworn I told you the other day over lunch. Sorry! Your hair looks amazing, by the way. Gary's done a great job!'

I shake my head. At this rate, I'll never get the chance to tell Wayne about my letters.

Charisma lives in shared accommodation just off the Thanet Way. Near the drive-through McDonald's. Wayne parks outside her house and toots the horn.

'I wonder what ailment Charisma's going to be suffering from today?'

'Ailment?'

I push Cilla's latest letter deeper into my plastic carrier bag, under the box of Pop-Tarts and can of Lilt I've brought for the journey. I'm still annoyed it's not just me and Wayne going to Dreamland. Why did he have to invite bloody Charisma?

'She's what you might call a hypochondriac,' says Wayne.

'What's that?'

He laughs. 'Shush, I'll tell you later. Here she is.'

Charisma is having trouble getting into the car. The lock is on. Wayne reaches over and flicks the button. She opens the back door, throws her *Doctor Who* rucksack onto the seat and squeezes in. She's wearing a Meat Loaf T-shirt, a pleated skirt, pink trainers and white sports socks pulled all the way up to her knees. She's out of breath, puffing and panting.

'Bert's really ill,' she says, slipping the seat belt over her large breasts. 'Not being funny, but I don't think he's going to last the night. It's very touch-and-go.'

Wayne turns the key to start up the engine.

'Who's Bert?' I say. 'Do I know him?'

'Just a minute.' Charisma unzips the front pocket of her backpack and takes out her blue asthma inhaler. She presses it twice, breathing in. 'You know Roz? Lives in a mobile home in Seasalter.'

'Oh, *her*,' I say. I do know Roz, but we ain't friends. A few years ago, we had a massive row in Herne Bay, over a game of crazy golf. I saw her kick the ball into the hole when she thought I wasn't looking. She ain't spoken to me since.

'So who's this Bert, then?' Wayne asks.

Charisma takes another puff of her inhaler.

'Bert is Roz's pet rat. She has two, you see. Bert and Ernie. Not being funny, but if Bert goes, Ernie's going to get depression. It's the way with rats. You need more than one, otherwise they get lonely, they get depressed.'

'Aww, I hope he gets better soon,' says Wayne, fiddling with the car radio. 'I'd love another pet – a dog, ideally – but I just can't cope with the thought of them dying. I was in absolute bits when I lost Whigfield and Gina G, my guinea pig girls. They break your heart when they go, animals.'

I watch Charisma pull a small cushion from her rucksack and push it under her bottom. She shuffles around on it, like she's trying to get comfortable.

'I brought my own seat,' she says. 'It's these piles, they're killing me. Not being funny, but I'm dreading going to the toilet. She leans over the seat, whispers in my ear. 'Here, do you have piles? They're bleeding awful.'

'No I do not!' I say, crossing my arms.

And even if I did, I think, I wouldn't tell you.

Graham Norton is on the radio talking about Alma Cogan and the big frocks she used to wear. He plays 'Never Do A Tango With An Eskimo'. Wayne starts singing along, but I ain't in the mood to join in. And neither is Charisma. She stares out of the window, watching all the rubbish people have dumped by the roadside go flying past. Don't get me wrong,

I like Charisma, but in the two or three years I've known her, I've only seen her smile once. This was when Wayne took us for a ride on the Romney, Hythe and Dymchurch miniature railway. The whole journey she had a massive grin on her face; all the way to Dungeness and back, she never stopped smiling. It was the loveliest thing.

'What sort of music are you into, Charisma?' says Wayne.

Charisma pulls at her T-shirt, stretching it over her chest. 'Meat Loaf.'

'What about Michael Bolton?' he says. 'Margaret's a big fan – aren't you, Margaret?'

'He's handsome, ain't he?' I say, trying to be social even though I don't feel like it.

Charisma looks at me like I've just farted.

'I like rock,' she says. 'Meat Loaf. Bon Jovi. T'Pau. Proper music.'

'Oooh, back in the day, I used to love a bit of T'Pau,' laughs Wayne. "China in your haaaand." Carol Decker, eh?'

'Didn't she have red hair?' I say. 'Like Cilla.'

'Yeah,' says Wayne. 'I'm sure I read somewhere, years ago, maybe in *Smash Hits*, that she's a Scouser, too. What is it with Liverpool and ginger singers? Cilla, Carol Decker . . . Sonia.'

'Cilla has the best voice, though,' I say, very loud. I look out of the car window, up at the sky, hoping you can hear me, wherever you are. Squeezing the bottom of my carrier bag, I feel for the edges of your letter. I need to check it's still there. If I get the chance today, I'm going to tell Wayne about you.

Wayne points out the road sign for Margate.

'Not long now,' he says. 'Another half hour and we'll be on the scenic railway.'

There's a retching sound. Charisma, who looks as pale as

a jellyfish, leans over on her cushion, and taps Wayne on the shoulder.

'Not being funny,' she says, 'but can you stop the car? It's my guts. I think I'm going to be sick.'

23

1948

The Fete and Flower Show was one of the best days of my life. Me and Joan won two awards in the parade: Best Fancy Dress and Best Decorated Wheelchair. Mr Chance was the judge. He made us both come on stage and take a bow, then he gave us a chocolate bar and a certificate as a prize. I was ever so proud; I'd never won anything in my life before. A man from the paper came and took a photograph of us. We had to stand in front of the swings and roundabouts. Mr Chance put his arms around us and we held up copies of the recipe book he'd done. Even though I couldn't read, I could tell it was good, for it was full of pictures of famous people from the films and magazines.

'Well done, girls,' says Mr Chance. 'Look at the camera and say *Simple Suppers*!'

After we had our photos taken, me and Joan went round the fete together. They had all sorts of things: a patients' trampolining display and Skee-Ball; rings and darts, a horse race game and a coconut shy. It was a beautiful day, not a cloud in the sky. We watched a Punch and Judy show, then cheered and clapped at the Boy Scouts playing their bugles. There was a man with an accordion and a monkey on his shoulder, which he let us take turns at holding. He was my favourite. We had a go on the hoopla, too. I was rubbish at it, but Joan was brilliant. She won a bag of fruit drops, which she shared out between us. It was a magical day. I was so happy, I didn't want it to end.

Later on, though, Joan said she had something to tell me. She made me promise not to get upset. We was sitting on the grass opposite the playing fields, drinking lemonade. The sun was shining so bright, I had to cover my eyes with my hand. I was sweating, too. It was boiling hot in that rag-and-bone man costume.

Joan put her hand on the frying pan on my back, patting it.

'I'm leaving,' she says. 'I'm leaving St Mary's.'

My bottle of lemonade fell over, spilling out into a puddle on the grass.

'Look what I've done!' I cried.

'Here, clumsy, you can have mine.' Joan handed me her bottle.

'What do you mean, you're leaving?' I says, my voice shaking. 'Are you going on holiday again? Christmas is ages away.'

'I'm leaving for good this time.'

'I don't understand.'

'They're sending me to boarding school, Margaret. They said it's no good me being here.'

'But I thought you liked it at St Mary's? You're my best friend. What will I do?'

Joan bit her bottom lip. 'You'll be all right, won't you?'

'When are you going?'

'Tomorrow morning. I wanted to tell you sooner, but Daddy said to leave it until after the parade. I didn't want it to spoil your day.' She reached over and took my hand. 'It was a good day, though, wasn't it? We had fun.'

First Grandma, now Joan. Why did the people in my life always leave me?

The next morning, Joan was waiting for me by the main door. I put my arms around her.

'I'm going to miss you,' I says.

'You won't even notice I'm gone,' she says. 'I'm going to write to you at least once a week.'

'But Joan, I . . .'

'I'm sure one of the nurses will read it for you. They might even help you write a reply.'

No they won't, I thought, my eyes filling up with tears.

Mr Chance came into reception with Mrs Chance and Nurse Cunningham.

'I say, ladies, that was a rather successful fundraiser, eh?'

'Amazing!' says Nurse Cunningham. 'We've not counted all the money yet, but we sold most of the recipe books, and Mr Trowbridge said the paper will make a sizeable donation towards the appeal. Not to mention any money that comes in as a result of the publicity. I can't thank you enough, Mr Chance.'

'Nonsense, dear, it was the least I could do. You've done a marvellous job looking after Joan over the past few years. It was a terrible time for us. At one point it was really touch-and-go with her illness, so thank you.'

'You'll keep in contact with us?' says Nurse Cunningham.

'Absolutely. Anything you need, just give Mrs Chance here a call. She organises my diary.'

'We need to get a move on, Desmond,' says Mrs Chance. 'You have an event at the Rotary Club later this afternoon.'

Mr Chance laughed. 'See what I mean, Nurse Cunningham? I'd be absolutely lost without her.'

He turned Joan's chair around and started wheeling her towards the doors.

'Come on, darling, let's get you back home where you belong.'

24

'How can anyone eat candyfloss gracefully? I mean, look at me!' Wayne points at the shiny pink beard on his chin. 'Thank goodness for Wet Wipes! I look like a gay garden gnome.'

He pats down his face, sticky with sugar. Out of the three of us, he's the only one laughing, though. All morning, I ain't been able to think of anything but the letters in my bag, and when I'm going to tell Wayne about Cilla. Normally I like funfairs, but today my nerves have got the better of me. I panicked when I got lost in the hall of mirrors and couldn't find my way out. Then, later on, I dropped my purse on the dodgems and the coins went everywhere. The scenic railway was OK, I suppose, but Charisma enjoyed it more than me. The whole ride, she was beaming from ear to ear. As soon as it was over, though, she went back to being her usual grumpy self.

We finish off our packed lunches on one of the picnic benches. Charisma sits opposite me. Her eyes dart around the funfair, as if she's looking for something, then she leans over and whispers she has an issue 'down there'.

'I might be a while,' she says. 'Not being funny, but it's these piles. They don't half make a mess.'

She wanders off to find a toilet.

I down the last dregs of my can of Lilt and let out a loud burp. Wayne gives me one of his looks.

'Do you want to help me clear up this rubbish?' he says.

I panic when I see he's holding my plastic bag, the one with your letters in it. I snatch it off him.

'Oi!' I shout. 'I have a few things in there. Women's bits and pieces.'

Wayne looks surprised. He takes a step back. We gather up the crisp bags and empty cans, stuffing them in the bins. He asks me if I want to go on the Big Wheel with him, while we're waiting for Charisma. I nod, clutching my bag close to me. Maybe this is my chance to talk to him about Cilla.

Dreamland is loud, even louder than the wards at St Mary's. The noises confuse me. Music pumping out of big speakers. Children laughing as they rattle up and down on the Beehive Coaster. The Waltzer whooshing and whirring, spinning round, and round, and round. I feel dizzy just looking at it. When we get to the Big Wheel, Wayne goes to buy the tickets. I wait for him to come back, staring up at the big circle of cars painted in different colours. I decide then it's time to tell him my secret.

'Happy birthday to me,' sings Wayne, after we've taken our seats on the ride. 'Have you had a good day, Margaret?'

I nod as the Big Wheel moves slowly forward, my stomach lurching.

'I need to talk to you about something, Wayne. Something private.'

'Hold on a second,' he says, as we're lifted into the sky. 'Perfect selfie opportunity, don't you think?'

He turns his phone towards us both. I try my best to smile, but it's hard.

'Isn't this amazing?' he says. 'Look, you can see all over Margate. There's the pub which does the cider we like!'

As he points, the car swings in the wind, making my legs feel funny.

The words fall out of my mouth.

'It's Cilla,' I say. 'She's been trying to get in touch with me. She's coming back.'

As soon as I say these words, our car stops at the top of the Big Wheel. We sit in silence, as it rocks back and forth in the breeze.

When Wayne finally speaks, his voice is soft, like he's talking to a child.

'I thought you were over this, Margaret. People don't come back from the dead. Life isn't like *Dallas*, you know. Cilla's not going to suddenly reappear in the shower, like Bobby Ewing.'

I stare at him. 'I know she ain't,' I say, my eyes wide and watery. I lower my head, wishing he would take things a bit more seriously sometimes. 'Ignore me. I'm being silly.'

Wayne takes a deep breath and sighs. 'You're not being silly. You're grieving, Margaret, and sometimes grief can make people do silly things.'

A seagull swoops past, dropping something from its beak. I watch it spiral downwards, spinning in the wind like a dead leaf. I cling to my carrier bag, frightened it might blow away.

'Would you like me to speak to someone?' says Wayne, quietly. 'There are people who can help.'

My voice trembles. 'What type of people?'

'Professional people,' he says. 'You know . . . doctors.'

Doctors? I knew it! He thinks I'm ill. He thinks I'm going mad, senile. If I ain't careful, they'll lock me away again, vanish me, just like they did before.

'Leave it,' I say, close to tears. 'Just leave it. It don't matter.'

We spend the rest of the ride in silence. As the car moves slowly towards the ground, Wayne points out Charisma, standing on her own by the kiosk, looking small and lost. He takes out his phone to ring her. My fingers twist around the carrier bag with your letter in it. Wayne might think I'm a fool, but the proof is right here, in this envelope, ain't it? I know it's you writing to me, Cilla. Who else could it be?

25

The card shop on the High Street is quiet today. A young blonde girl is standing behind the till, but she's too busy looking at her mobile phone to notice me when I walk in. This makes me nervous, because I need help finding a card for Wayne's birthday. I need support with choosing the right one. I can't always tell from the pictures what type of card it is. Last year, I got him one congratulating him on his retirement. Wayne laughed when I gave it to him.

'I'm only 38,' he says. 'Not quite ready to give up working yet.'

I only picked it because it had a picture of a small dog on the front and Wayne likes dogs. I was so embarrassed.

I try to get the blonde girl's attention by waving my hand, but she ignores me. The card shop is bright. There are shiny silver and gold heart-shaped balloons sticking to the ceiling, and rows and rows of cards, none of which I can read, along the walls. The carpet is filthy and looks like it could do with a good hoovering. I can't help feeling cross. The girl behind the counter clearly don't care; she's obviously more interested in her phone. If that was me, I'd be grateful to have a job. I'd keep the place spotless. Some people don't know how lucky they are.

I head towards a row of pink cards with pictures of baby girls, teddies and love hearts. I know I'm in the wrong section, but I can't help stopping to have a look. They're ever so pretty. I pick up a card with a cute elephant and a little mouse hugging each other. I laugh out loud, thinking to myself how it would never happen in real life.

'Can I help you?'

The girl has come out from behind the counter and stands next to me, staring. She's chewing gum, a habit I've never liked.

'What's your badge say, love?' I ask. 'My eyesight ain't so good.'

'What? This?' she says, pointing at the name badge on her boob. To look at her, you'd think I'd asked her what her bra size was. 'Tiffany. Why?'

'I'm looking for a card, Tiffany.' Tiffany is only half paying attention. She's typing a message into her phone. 'It's for my friend Wayne.'

She takes the card from me and looks at it.

'Has he had a baby girl?' she says.

'He's gay.'

'Well, that doesn't matter these days, does it? Look at Elton John. He has children and he's gay.' Tiffany's eyes go all misty. 'What about Tom Daley, though? I used to have such a crush on him before I found out. A waste of a good man, if you ask me.'

'A waste?'

'Don't get me wrong, I love the gays. Graham Norton, Dale Winton . . . They're funny, aren't they, gay men? Not like lesbians. I should know. My sister's one and she's miserable.'

I think to myself, *if I had a sister like Tiffany, I'd be miserable, too*, but I don't say nothing.

'So what kind of gay is your friend, then?'

'What kind?' I say. I shrug. 'The normal kind, I suppose.'

'Does he like drag?' Tiffany picks up a card. 'This RuPaul design is very popular with our gay customers.'

'Drag?' What was she saying about Wayne? 'Wayne's just Wayne,' I say. 'He likes dogs.'

Tiffany sounds disappointed. 'Dogs?'

'What wrong with liking dogs?'

'Oh, nothing, it's just . . . Well . . . it's a bit boring, isn't it?' I point at a card with a dog wearing a superhero costume. 'What about that one?'

'Is Wayne your uncle, then?' Tiffany asks.

'Don't be daft. I'm old enough to be his mother.'

'That card is for uncles. Let's try again, shall we?' Tiffany rummages through some more cards, then hands me one with a pug on the front. 'I bet he'll love this.'

'Can you read it for me?'

'Happy birthday. Pugs and kisses.'

'That's funny,' I say, chuckling at the joke. 'Perfect. I'll take it.'

I follow her to the counter to pay, handing her the money.

'By the way,' she says, 'I've put a pink envelope in the bag for your friend. Gays love pink.'

As she gives me my change back, I can't help but notice her hands. Pale and smooth. They remind me of Eva, a girl I once knew at St Mary's.

'Anything else I can help you with?'

'There is one thing,' I say. 'Can you write a message on the card for me?'

26

1969

'This place is mad, Margaret. How do you stick it?'

This was Eva. Eva Finch. She was the new girl; she only came to St Mary's in the late sixties, which was long after Joan had left. They brought her over from another hospital. She had bad nerves, you see. Ever since she was young, she'd suffered from them. She was well into her thirties now.

I was 28.

That morning, they'd sent us round the back of the villa to fetch the coal together. Them buckets was as heavy as lead. It took two of you to carry one.

'Mad?' I lifted up the lid to the big concrete bunker. 'What do you mean?'

'Don't you find it a bit odd?'

'Odd?'

Eva blinked. 'That we can't talk to the fellas?'

I laughed, for I certainly didn't find it odd. By then I'd been living at St Mary's more than twenty-one years, and it was just how it was. They forbid you from mixing with the men. Everybody knew that. Even on Saturdays, when they used to put on the dances for us in the recreation hall, they kept us separate: women on one side, men on the other, with the nurses standing in the middle, watching you like bleedin' hawks the whole time, making sure you didn't cross the line. The women used to dance with each other while the men looked on from the sides.

'It don't bother me,' I says, picking up a shovel and sticking it in the coal. 'Boys are a bunch of idiots.'

'Is that what you really think, though? Haven't you ever been with a fella?'

She was attractive, Eva: ever so skinny, but pretty, like a little bird. She had lovely green eyes with long sticky-out lashes. Her hair was blonde, like Twiggy, and cut into a pudding bowl like mine. It suited her, though. Even those wretched dresses was OK on Eva. Somehow she managed to look all right in them.

'Been with a fella?' I says. 'No, I bloody well ain't! You don't mix with men here. It's the rules. Men is trouble, anyway. I heard one of the nurses say it. They ain't worth the bother.'

I scooped up a pile of coal, dropping it into the bucket. Eva gasped. 'My God! Look how black your hands are, Margaret!' She was leaning against the wall, her arms crossed, staring at me. 'They're filthy. Like a man's!'

I threw my shovel on the ground.

'Yours would be filthy and all if you bothered to do any work.' I bent over, grabbing one of the bucket handles. 'Here. Take the other one.'

Eva made a face. She pulled the sleeve of her dress down over her hand and slowly lifted the handle. To look at her, you'd think I'd asked her to pick up dog shit.

'You'll get used to it here,' I says, slamming the bunker lid shut with my other hand. 'I know I did.'

At St Mary's, Eva and me was what they called the 'working girls'. Once you was a certain age, if you was able enough, they gave you jobs to do. Nothing fancy, mind. It was mostly cleaning, or cooking. During the day, we both worked in the laundry room. It was this huge barn, with beams across the ceiling and a concrete floor, which was always soaking wet from the suds. In the middle of the room was two rows of stone troughs for hand-washing the linen. That was my job. Oh, but them garments used to get mucky! You had to scrub them in hot water until they was spotless. Took hours sometimes. By the end of a shift, your fingers was wrinkled and your feet ached from standing up all day. It was hard work, but I loved it. I took pride in what I done, even though I never got paid, not one flipping penny. In them days, none of the women did. If you was lucky, the nurses might give you a chocolate bar, or a bag of boiled sweets, but that was it. The men, however, they got paid in cash. Sixpence a week. It was a right cheek, if you ask me.

Eva's job in laundry was different from mine. She was clever. Like Joan, she could read and write, so they put her in charge of all the paperwork. Me and the other laundry girls used to give her our baskets, filled with whatever garments we'd spent all day washing and pressing, and Eva would write down who they belonged to and the numbers of the different wards.

Monday to Friday we was in the laundry from half past eight until half past five, then afterwards we went to the kitchen to help make the suppers. We worked there until about half past seven at night. The patients did most of the cooking, with a bit of help from the nurses. I liked working. It kept me busy, stopped me from sitting around all day doing nothing, like the 'lower grade' patients, poor things. Eva hated it, though. Oh, she couldn't bear it. Eva wasn't like me, you see. She'd had a life on the outside. Before all that business with her nerves, she'd gone to school and learned stuff. She'd been able to go where she wanted, do as she pleased. She wasn't used to rules, having nurses gawp at you all the time, like you was a goldfish in a bowl.

I remember the first shift we done together in the kitchen. I was on potato duty and Eva was prepping parsnips for a mutton stew. She hated anything to do with mud or dirt, so peeling vegetables was her worst nightmare; she couldn't even stand to touch them. She was blinking and her head was twitching. She done that when she was stressed.

'I've nearly cut my finger twice with this knife, Margaret,' she says, putting it down on the chopping board. 'It's dangerous, you know. I shouldn't have to do it.' She was whispering. She knew if the nurses heard her complaining, they would have a go at her.

'Do you want me to do it for you?' I says, scooping a sprout out of a potato.

She paused. 'Would you really?'

'I don't mind.'

'You're good at peeling, though.'

Eva smiled. Picking up her huge sack of parsnips, she put them down on the counter in front of me. She shook her apron out. A few loose vegetable scraps fell to the floor. She ran her hands under the tap, flicking them dry. Crossing her arms, she leaned against the sink. She stood like that for ages, just staring at me, watching me work.

After a while, she says, 'I don't half envy you, Margaret.'

I stopped what I was doing and looked up at her, surprised. 'You envy *me*?'

She nodded. 'Yes, of course. I can't peel parsnips to save my life.'

'I can teach you if you like,' I says, pleased as Punch that she thought I was good at something. 'It ain't hard, you know.'

She laughed. 'I appreciate the offer, but don't waste your time. Women like me aren't cut out for manual labour.'

Eva looked down at her feet then, her head twitching. She had a sliver of parsnip peel stuck to her boot. She shuddered, scraping it off with the heel of her other foot.

'Manual?' I says. 'What do you mean?'

Eva ran her hands up and down her arms, like she was cold. 'Working with your hands, cleaning and cooking. You're really good at it.'

'Thank you, Eva.'

'No need to thank me, darling. It's the truth. I've been watching you. You're much better than me.'

'It's only because I've had more practice.'

'Don't put yourself down. You're a natural.'

It was hard not to smile, for Eva was being so kind to me. I wasn't used to the attention. I looked down at my hands, which was rough and dirty from cooking.

'I tell you one thing, though, Eva. I ain't pretty like you.'

For some reason, saying this made me feel embarrassed. I covered my face with my hand, turning away.

'You're too kind, Margaret.' Eva laughed.

I looked round, smiling at her.

'It's true, though, ain't it?'

Eva smiled back. She had lovely white teeth, not like mine. She stretched her fingers out, examining her nails. I carried on quietly with my work, looking up every so often, noticing how clean and smooth her hands was.

It rained all week; the heavens tipped it down. Everywhere you looked in St Mary's, there was puddles of muddy water: on the corridor floors, in the dining room, even in some of the villas, where the gutters and roofs was leaking. One night, me and some of the others had to help move a bunch of the low-grade patients out of Villa 13, for part of the ceiling had caved in. We didn't even have time to finish eating our supper. They told us we had to carry the patients and bring them next door. It wasn't right; there was already too many people in there. Poor little mites. It got ever so crowded. The laundry room got flooded, too. It had a tin roof. When it rained, the noise in there was deafening, like gunshots going off. Along with Nurse Cunningham and Nurse Fitts, we had to put down sacks, to soak up the water. We was used to the floor in there being wet, with suds and things, but not like that! Our feet was drowned, right up to our ankles.

'Can you do me a favour, Margaret?' Eva says to me one afternoon that week. 'I'm meant to be dropping these sheets off at Manor House. Would you mind taking them for me?'

Eva said she had a bit of a cold coming on. To be fair, she didn't look her usual self. Still, I wasn't sure. I didn't have permission to go up Manor House; that was Eva's job. She told me not to worry, though. She said she would cover for me if anyone asked.

'Besides,' she says, 'who's going to know?'

'I ain't been down that way,' I says. 'What if I get lost?'

'You won't get lost, you daft sod. You only need to go in a straight line. It's not far. I'd do it myself, Margaret, but it's this chill. I feel awful. You're all right with that, aren't you?'

I nodded. It was easier than saying no. Eva had this way of getting me to do things for her. She put her hand in her pocket and took out a brown envelope.

'Just knock on the door when you get to Manor House and give this letter to Mrs Dingley, along with the laundry. It's an invoice.'

'I don't understand, though.'

'Like a bill?'

'Do I need to collect any money?'

I was starting to panic. I get like that when I have to do things with money, even now.

Eva told me to calm down. She said Mrs Dingley would sort out the payments later. I just had to give her the basket and the envelope.

'It's very simple,' she says.

'I ain't sure—'

'It'll take you fifteen minutes at the most.' She looked at me and smiled.

'Oh, give it here, then,' I says, taking the basket off her.

And that was how I met Alfie.

27

24 August 2015

After the card shop, I drag my trolley down the High Street to Rock Bottom Records, one of my favourite places in Whitstable. It's just across the road from Peter Cushion's tea rooms. It's been there years and years and I pop in at least twice a week. I can spend hours looking at all the records. There are hundreds of them; plastic crates everywhere, filled with all sorts – pop, disco, jazz, country – you name it. They don't just have records; they have tapes, too. And CDs. I prefer records, but I like buying CDs for my Discman so I can listen to music when I'm walking around the shops: ABBA, Cilla, Michael Bolton. I might be in my seventies, but I still have modern tastes.

Sid, the owner, is standing behind the counter reading the paper. He's wearing a straw hat and a Kate Bush T-shirt. I've never been a fan of Kate Bush myself. Too much weeping and wailing for my liking, but Wayne loves her. Would you believe he paid over a hundred pounds to see her in concert last year? A hundred pounds! I can think of far better things to spend my money on than Kate bloody Bush. Sid smiles when he sees me coming in.

'All right, Margaret? What are you after today?'

'Actually, you might be able to help. I'm looking for a birthday present for my friend, Wayne,' I say. 'He's gay.'

111

Sid laughs. 'Is he now? And how old is this friend of yours?'

'He's 38.'

Sid puts down his paper and comes out from behind the counter.

'Do you know what type of music he's into?'

I think about it for a minute.

'Same as me, really. He likes all sorts. Madonna, Diana Ross, Queen.' I look at Sid's T-shirt. 'Oh – and Kate Bush.'

'A man with impeccable taste then.' Sid laughs and starts rummaging through one of the crates. He pulls out a record and hands it to me.

'How about this one? Recognise the band?'

I hold the record in both hands, staring closely at the photograph. There's a cowboy, a policeman, a sailor, a builder, a Red Indian and a man in a leather cap with a black moustache. I'm not sure what the man in the leather cap with the black moustache is meant to be, but the others look familiar. A song is coming into my head, but I can't quite place it.

'Not ringing any bells? You do surprise me, Margaret. Let me put it on for you. Trust me. You'll know it when you hear it.'

Sid takes the record behind the counter. He slides it from its sleeve and sets it on the player. He lifts the needle, placing it carefully on the record. The record crackles, then the music starts. Drums, trumpets, clapping. A voice singing 'Young man . . .'

'I know it,' I says, my hand tapping the side of one of the crates. 'What's it called?'

'Wait for the chorus,' laughs Sid.

'I've got it!' I shout out the answer like I'm on a quiz show. 'It's "Y.M.C.A."!'

For a moment, I'm lost in my own thoughts. Ain't it funny

how music can take you back, make you think of people and places you hadn't thought of for a long time? We used to dance to this record at St Mary's. It would've been the late seventies. I remember the nurses teaching us how to make the shapes of the letters with our hands.

Sid's voice brings me back down to earth.

'What do you think? Would your friend like it?'

'I ain't sure,' I say, the memories still running through my head. 'Have you got any Madonna?'

Sid wanders over to one of the crates by the shop window and starts flicking through more LPs. He pulls one out and holds the cover up for me to have a look.

'This is the only one I've got at the moment.'

Madonna is in a black car. She's wearing a fur coat, and there's a handsome man in a yellow hat and coat sat next to her.

'*Dick Tracy* soundtrack,' says Sid, '1990. Never saw the film myself. Not one of her better-known records, to be honest, but your friend might appreciate it if he's a fan.'

'Go on then,' I say. 'I'll take it.'

'Yours for £4.99, my love. And, seeing as you're one of my most loyal customers, I'll throw in this Phil Collins mug, completely free of charge.'

'Thank you, Sid. You are kind,' I say.

Sid lifts the mug from the shelf and hands it to me. I stare at the black and white photo on the side.

'Don't Phil Collins look young? He was a bit of a looker in his day, you know.'

Sid laughs. 'Not a patch on Michael Bolton, though, I'll bet. Now, before I forget, I've got something else you might be interested in.'

He opens a drawer behind the counter and lifts out a small brown paper bag.

113

'Came in last Friday. Seven-inch single. 1966. A real find. Not many vinyls from those sixties girl singers around these days. They're very rare.'

He takes out the record. It has a plain cover, no pictures. Dark green, with some writing on the top and white swirls around the label.

'What is it?' I say.

He puts the record on the player and places the needle on it.

'See if you can guess.'

I freeze on the spot as Cilla's voice drifts out of the speakers. She sounds hurt and upset, like she's crying. She's asking what's life about? What's the point of it all? She's singing about fools and kindness and Heaven, and how – without love – we are nothing. We just exist.

And Alfie. She's singing about Alfie.

A lump rises slowly in my throat.

For it's then that I realise: Cilla's not only singing about her Alfie, she's singing about my Alfie, too.

28

'C'

You didn't notice me earlier. I was hidden away in a corner, flicking through a crate of jazz records, pretending to focus on the pictures on the sleeves, occasionally lifting one out – Billie Holiday's Lady Sings the Blues, *Ella Fitzgerald and Louis Armstrong's* Ella and Louis *– and glancing at the back cover, before returning it to its place. My mind wasn't on the records, though; it was on you and your conversation with the man behind the counter. You were looking for a record for your friend's birthday, you said. You came across as so kind and caring. It was so touching, the way you spoke to him. You're such a lovely soul, Margaret. It really breaks my heart to think about what they did to you all those years ago. You didn't deserve to be treated like that, to be locked away. You aren't mad or a criminal. You're a beautiful woman with a heart of gold.*

The man behind the counter played a record for you. Cilla Black's 'Alfie'. As soon as you heard the music, you stopped what you were doing and stood still – frozen – on the shop floor. And when Cilla started singing, you smiled. Your lips began mouthing the words to the song. At first it came out as a breath, a whisper, then your voice got gradually louder, and louder, until you were singing along to the record in unison with Cilla, your eyes wide, gazing up at the ceiling, your arms

115

outstretched, like you were standing under a spotlight, facing an imaginary audience. You looked so happy, in rapture even, but your eyes told me a different story. There was sadness there. And joy. And something I couldn't quite put my finger on. Something which made me want to rush over, give you a huge hug and tell you that everything is going to be OK, that you have people watching over you, but – of course – I couldn't.

Isn't it funny how certain songs can trigger such strong emotions? It's happened to me lots of times, usually when I'm driving. 'Bright Eyes' by Art Garfunkel always does it. I've had to pull over and stop the car. What was it about 'Alfie' that moved you so much, Margaret? Maybe one day, you'll tell me.

29

1969

When I look back on that day, I think about how all our lives was to change forever. The day I met Alfie.

Manor House was in the hospital grounds. Annie Dingley lived there. Annie was one of the staff in charge at St Mary's. Some of the work we done, like the laundry, or growing vegetables on the farm, was for the people in the village outside; they used to pay the hospital for our services. Not that we saw any of the money, mind. Annie took care of that side of things.

When you was in the laundry room, you always knew if you was doing a job for the outside world because the nurses would ask you to take extra special care. They'd say, 'Those sheets are for the baronet', or 'That tablecloth belongs to Lord So-and-so'. At first I used to get nervous doing jobs for the rich folk, but once I learned they was happy with my work, it got easier. I took pride in what I done.

It was the first dry day we'd had in a while, and the sun was shining when I left the laundry room. The basket was heavy, so I'd put it on top of my head to make it easier to carry. This turned out to be a bad idea, for the path was still muddy from the rain. About halfway there, my ankle got

117

caught and I lost my balance. I fell to the ground face first. The basket, filled with clean white sheets, toppled into the mud. Cursing myself, I clambered to my feet, put everything back in the basket and carried on walking.

It didn't take me long to reach Manor House. It was more of a cottage than a manor. The door was wide open. The air smelled of fresh paint. Someone had the wireless on and there was singing coming from inside: a man's voice, something about fools falling in love. Putting the basket down on the front step, I knocked on the door. There was no answer. I knocked again. No answer. The man carried on singing. Fed up of waiting, I banged even louder.

The music stopped.

'I'm coming, I'm coming,' says a voice from inside.

A man appeared. He looked cross, but his eyes was a lovely shade of blue, like the dried flowers in the day room. He stared at me, then at the door.

'What the fuck? I've just painted that. Didn't you read the fucking sign?'

I looked at my hand. My knuckles was bright red, and there was a messy smudge on the door where I'd been knocking.

'I'm sorry,' I says. 'I was told to bring this washing for Annie. Only I dropped it and it ain't clean no more.'

The man continued to look me up and down. I lowered my head to escape his staring.

'You better come in, then,' he says, his voice friendlier. 'You can give your hands a wash. I'm Alfie, by the way.'

I stayed put.

'Margaret,' I says. 'Only I ain't allowed to make friends with boys.'

'Who said I was your friend?'

He winked, put his hand on my shoulder and led me into

the hallway. Picking up the laundry basket from the front step, he brought it in.

'You should've got someone from St Mary's to give me a ring,' he says. 'I could always have come down and collected the basket for you.'

'Will Annie be cross with me?' I says. 'I didn't mean no harm. I—'

'Annie, get cross? Have you met Annie? She's soft as butter. Wouldn't harm a fly.'

'Where is she, then?'

'You just missed her. She went into the village to buy a few groceries.'

'Only I was just doing Eva a favour.'

'Eva?'

'My friend at the hospital.'

'Ah . . .' says Alfie. 'I recognise the name.'

'She won't be in trouble, will she?'

'Relax. Why would she be?'

There was something soothing about his voice, like he didn't care about anything. It calmed me down.

'If you're worried, I can always tell Annie there's been a delay. I can sneak the basket down later for you, save you carrying it back yourself. You can give the sheets another wash then.'

'Can you do that?'

'Sure, leave it with me. Like I said, Annie's soft. She's not like some of those nurses down at the hospital. Mean old bitches.'

'How do you know the nurses?'

'I'm a patient at the hospital myself. Been here a few months.'

I should've known by the way he was dressed, of course, but still, he looked different from the rest of us. In the same way Eva was different.

'What are you in here for, then?' I says. 'You don't look handicapped.'

'Handicapped?' He laughed. 'Jesus Christ, no. Good question, though. Why am I here?' He scratched his head. 'Got myself in a bit of trouble. Nothing big. I didn't murder anyone, if that's what you're thinking.'

'Murder?'

'I'm joking,' he says. 'It's a joke.'

Alfie told me how he'd been helping Annie out during the daytime. Doing odd jobs around the house for her.

'As my old da used to say, "If you can work with your hands, you don't need your brain."'

'I do the laundry.'

'So I see.' Alfie pointed at the basket full of muddy sheets. 'Bloody good job you're doing there, too.' He laughed again. 'I'm only kidding, Margaret. I can't help it. It's just my sense of humour.'

'I work in the kitchen as well,' I says. 'I peel the vegetables and do the cooking.'

'A woman of many talents. You'll make someone a good little wife one day.'

Alfie pinched me on the cheek. I turned my head away, blushing. Me, a wife? What was he thinking? I was surprised he would even say such a thing.

'You know I ain't going to get married,' I says. 'It don't happen to people like me. They don't allow it.'

Alfie smiled. 'Don't be such a pessimist. You never know. One day your Prince Charming might ride into St Mary's on a white horse and whisk you off your feet.'

'What's a pissimist? Is that something to do with the rain?'

Alfie laughed. 'No. Well, kind of, I suppose. A *pessimist* is someone who always thinks the worst is going to happen.'

'That sounds like me, then,' I says, nodding. 'It's true,

though, ain't it? I'm never going to get married. We ain't even allowed to talk to the men here.'

'How come you're talking to me, then?' Alfie grinned.

I was starting to like this Alfie. He was different from how I had imagined boys to be. He seemed to understand me. I felt a strange sensation then, like a frog hopping around in the bottom of my stomach. It was like nothing I'd ever felt before. I wasn't sure if it was good or bad.

'I'd best be getting back,' I say.

'Stay,' he says. 'Annie will be another couple of hours. I'll make you a cup of tea. You need to relax.'

'Are you sure?'

I was only meant to be gone half an hour. What if Nurse Cunningham or Nurse Fitts realised I was missing? I'd be in trouble.

'Take a seat,' he says. 'Actually, wait a second! I need to fetch something from upstairs.'

As he left the room, I looked around me.

This must be how other people live, I thought. *Normal people, who have families and what have you.*

I tried to remember what life had been like at Grandma's, but it made me sad thinking about the past.

The living room was small, much smaller than the rooms at St Mary's, but it didn't feel crowded. There was two armchairs, facing the fireplace, a gramophone, and a small table with a telephone. The cream carpet fascinated me. I'd never seen carpet before. I leaned down and brushed it with my fingers, making sure I didn't stain it with paint. It was soft, not like the bare wooden floors we had at the hospital. Everything in the room was spotless, too. It smelled of polish, not bleach. And I remember thinking how quiet it was: no noise, no screaming. It was the sort of place I could only dream of living in.

121

Just at that moment, I caught my reflection in the mirror. I was a mess. My hair was all over the place, my face brown and covered in mud. Alfie came back into the room carrying a cream towel.

'I brought you this,' he says, laying it out over one of the armchairs. 'Go upstairs and wash your hands before you get comfy.'

How gentlemanly of Alfie to put a towel down for me – like a red carpet, almost. I felt like the queen. As I made my way upstairs to the bathroom, I could hear him whistling the song that was playing earlier on the radio, the one about fools falling in love.

When I came back down, Alfie was waiting for me in the living room. He'd laid out a tray with two mugs and a plate of biscuits.

'Help yourself to Annie's garibaldi,' he says. 'I'm not keen on them myself.'

He pushed the plate towards me. I took a biscuit, shoving it in my mouth in one go. Then I reached for another.

'Jesus.' He laughed. 'Anyone would think you were starving.'

'These biscuits are lovely, though,' I says, my mouth full. 'What was that song you was singing earlier?'

'"Why Do Fools Fall In Love?" One of my mum's favourites. She used to say it was about her and my dad. That was before she died.'

I put the garibaldi I'd just lifted back on the plate.

'I'm sorry to hear that, Alfie,' I says.

'Cancer. You know how it is.' Alfie paused, then, leaning over, he whispered, 'Do you fancy a dance?'

The frog in my stomach started leaping around again. I put my hands on the sides of the armchair and went to stand up.

'I'd better go.'

Alfie reached over and touched my leg.

'Don't be daft. You want to stay. I know you do.'

I moved my leg away.

'I don't d-dance with men,' I stammered. 'We ain't allowed. It's the rules.'

Before I could say anything else, Alfie grabbed my hand and pulled me up from the seat.

'We're alone. Who can see us?'

I looked around to check if anyone was looking, but Alfie was right. It was just the two of us.

Alfie let go of me and walked over to the gramophone. Pulling a record out of its sleeve, he put it on the player and set the needle on it. The record began to crackle, then a voice I'd not heard before:

'Dum dum dum, dumby doo-wah, ooh yeah, yeah yea-ah. Only the lonely.'

Taking my hand again, he led me into the middle of the room. He grabbed my waist and we began swaying in time to the music. He leaned into my ear, his lips brushing my neck.

'Have you ever been with a man before?' he whispered.

I shook my head, a tiny shiver creeping up my spine.

'Kiss me,' he says.

So I did.

30

1969

When I got back to the laundry room, Eva was sitting on top of the counter, reading a magazine. She didn't look up. I walked straight past her, into the store cupboard. I closed the door, stripped off my muddy clothes and stuffed them into a basket. I tiptoed to the sink and quietly turned on the taps. Picking up a bar of soap, I started washing my hands. My knuckles was still filthy, caked with red paint. I scrubbed and scrubbed at them with a brush, then I took a flannel, rubbing my face clean.

I could hear Eva talking from outside.

'You took your time,' she says.

Ignoring her, I wrung out the flannel, watching the water – reddish brown, like sarsaparilla – swirl round and down the plughole. I dried myself, then I put on a clean overall and an apron from one of the baskets. As I came back into the laundry room, Eva looked up from her magazine.

'Didn't you hear me?' she says. 'I was asking what took you so long?'

'I got lost,' I says, yawning.

'Did you speak to Annie, then?'

I ain't proud of what I did next, but I lied to her. I lied to Eva. I told her I'd seen Annie: that she'd invited me into

124

her house and made me a cup of tea. She was a nice lady, I said. All the while, I was hoping Eva wouldn't ask too many questions. Lucky for me, she seemed more interested in reading. I admitted about the dirty washing, though. I said Annie was sending someone back down with it later, to have it washed again. Eva seemed all right with that.

'Changing the subject,' says Eva, picking up her magazine, 'shall we play our favourite game?'

To stop us getting bored in the laundry room, Eva had invented this game, Fab Or Flake Off? The rules was that she would show me pictures of boys, sometimes girls, and then we would say 'Fab' or 'Flake Off', depending on how good-looking we thought they was. This time, she showed me a photo of Cliff Richard standing in a field. He was wearing a red shirt, his hair slicked back.

Eva's eyes twitched. Licking her finger, she ran it down Cliff's chest.

'I wouldn't mind meeting him down a dark alley. Definitely Fab. Don't you think?'

'He's all right, I suppose,' I says. 'For a man.'

Eva laughed. 'Just all right? Is that why your face has gone as red as Cliff's shirt, then?'

I put my hands on my cheeks. They was boiling hot. It wasn't Cliff I was thinking of, though.

Later that afternoon, Eva came over to my sink to tell me there was a man come to see me.

'He's not bad-looking,' she says.

Alfie, true to his word, was waiting by the counter. As soon as he saw me, he took his cap off.

'I thought I'd drop this down to you sooner rather than later.' He grinned as he set the dirty laundry basket on the counter. 'I didn't want you getting into trouble.'

'Thank you,' I says, taking the basket from him.

I waited for him to leave, but he just stood there, smiling at me.

'You need to go, Alfie,' I whispered. 'You shouldn't be in here. It's against the rules. If you get caught—'

'So I get caught.'

He shrugged, leaning his elbows on the counter. Picking up Eva's magazine, he started flicking through it.

Eva, who was hovering behind me, cleared her throat and took the liberty of introducing herself.

'I'm Eva,' she says to him. 'I'm in charge of laundry.'

Alfie looked up from the magazine and smiled. He held out his hand. Eva shook it.

'Nice to meet you, Eva,' he says. 'I've heard a lot about you.'

Eva laughed. 'All good, I hope?' she says. 'How do you know Margaret, then?'

'We met earlier,' he says. 'Up at Manor House.'

Eva folded her arms. She gave me a look, as if to say *you never told me anything about this.*

'I'm doing a few odd jobs for Annie,' Alfie says.

'Really?' says Eva. 'I go up there a lot. I've not seen you there.'

'Only started last week,' he says. 'I was working in the cripple mat shop before that, but I got bored and started messing about, so they sent me up to Annie.' Alfie put his hand in his pocket and took out a packet of cigarettes. 'Smoke?'

I shook my head. 'You need to leave, Alfie. We'll get in trouble.'

'No we won't,' says Eva. 'I'm in charge while the nurses are on lunch. It's one of the perks of being a high-grade.' She turned to Alfie. 'I'd love a cigarette,' she says.

'Why don't we share one?' he says, lighting one and passing it to her.

Eva inhaled, giving it back to him.

'I didn't know you smoked,' I says.

Eva ignored me. She was too busy watching Alfie flick through her magazine.

'Who do you think is better-looking, Alfie?' she says. 'Lulu or Cilla?'

Alfie took a puff on the cigarette.

'Tough question,' he says, blowing out a smoke ring.

'It's only that we have this game we play. "Fab Or Flake Off?" Margaret reckons Cilla's Fab, but I reckon she's a Flake Off. I can't stand her music. Lulu's prettier, too, don't you think?'

'I'd have them both,' he says, grinning.

Eva took another puff, her eyes twitching again. She looked down at her magazine. Alfie winked at me.

'I'm going back to my work,' I hissed. 'If the nurses come back and find us talking, we'll be in trouble.'

The way the two of them was speaking to each other was making me feel uncomfortable.

Alfie gave me a funny look, stubbing his cigarette out on the floor. He ignored me and turned to Eva.

'I'd best be off, then. Nice to meet you, Eva. I'll see you around.'

As he left, he tipped his cap at her.

'You never told me you met a fella up the lodge,' Eva says, as soon as he was out of sight.

'There ain't much to tell,' I says, avoiding her eye. 'Anyway, I got this washing to be getting on with.'

I tried to get past her, to go to the store cupboard, but she was blocking my way. She grabbed my arm.

'Do you think Alfie's attractive, then?' she says.

127

I tried to shake her off, but her grip was too tight.

'He's all right, I suppose. For a man.'

Eva pulled me closer to her.

'Only I saw the way he was looking at you, Margaret. I think he likes you.' As she spoke, her voice was getting louder and louder.

'What makes you say that?'

'Isn't it obvious? Didn't you notice him flirting with you just now?'

'Flirting? Don't be stupid, Eva. You know me. I ain't one to get involved with men.'

I pushed past her, picking up the basket of dirty laundry.

'Well, that's a relief,' she says. 'If you want my honest opinion, I think he's an arsehole. A heartbreaker, if ever I saw one. I couldn't bear to see you get hurt.'

What was she saying about Alfie? Why was she being so nasty all of a sudden?

'He's like a lot of fellas,' she says. 'Full of himself. I could tell, the way he spoke to you. He was being patronising. Do you know what I mean by patronising, Margaret?'

I shrugged. I said I wasn't sure.

'It means he's looking down on you. I'd be careful. A man like that could take advantage, do you know what I'm saying?'

What was Eva talking about? Alfie was a nice lad. He'd done me a favour. There was no need for her to be so unkind.

As I was carrying the basket of laundry over to the sink, I noticed something poking out from underneath the sheets – a letter of some sort.

Eva had gone back to reading her magazine.

'When I think about it, Margaret,' she says, 'you're definitely more of a Cilla than a Lulu. And I mean that in the nicest possible way.'

I thought of asking Eva to read the letter for me, but what if it was from Alfie? I didn't want her finding out what we'd done. I had an idea then.

'Eva,' I says. 'You know reading?'

Eva laughed. 'What do you think I'm doing now, Margaret?'

'Is it hard to learn, though?'

I was curious to know this, because I'd always been told I was incapable. There was no school at St Mary's. You had little choice. It was either make baskets, or work in the laundry.

'Depends on the person,' she says, not looking up from her magazine. 'For you, it probably would be.'

'Could you teach me, then?'

'Teach you?' Eva frowned. 'It's a bit late for that, isn't it? You're nearly 30.'

It was the way she said it. It upset me, so I left her alone, putting the letter in my apron pocket for safekeeping. Later that night, I would hide it under my mattress.

If it was important, I'd find out soon enough.

31

1969

After that day, I couldn't stop thinking about Alfie.

It must be love, I thought, for it felt just as Cilla described it in one of her songs, like a yo-yo. I kept hoping Eva would have other chores for me to do that involved going up to Manor House, but, ever since then, she'd insisted on going there by herself, even if it was raining.

Then, one day, I saw him again.

Every Tuesday night, the nurses put a film on for us in the recreation hall. Most of the films they showed was rubbish: cowboys and Indians, which I hated. The odd time, you would get a Laurel and Hardy, which I didn't mind, but mostly it was cowboys. Tonight was different, though. We was going to watch the musical, *Calamity Jane*.

Like the dances, the nurses made the girls sit on one side and the men on the other. Eva wasn't in the mood to go that night, so Janet came with me instead.

I spotted Alfie straight away. He was sat in the back row with Frankie. Like Janet, Frankie had Down's syndrome. He was a cheeky little sod, awful fond of the ladies. He was always doing these funny little dances – wiggling his hips like Mick Jagger – or asking for a peck on the cheek when the nurses wasn't looking. I wanted to be close to Alfie, so I says to Janet, 'Let's go and sit at the back.'

We shuffled our way down the row, past the other girls, until we got to the end. As soon as Alfie saw me, though, he turned his head away, looking annoyed. Had I done something to upset him?

One of the nurses switched off the lights in the hall, making it pitch-dark. The men started making noises. *Woooooo!* The women joined in until Nurse Cunningham, who was working the projector, yelled at us to be quiet or she'd get the belt out. This was followed by lots of shushing. *Shush! Shush!* Then the projector lit and the music started and Doris Day come on the screen, dressed as a cowboy. *Whip-crack-away!* It was wonderful. One of the best films I'd ever seen. When Calamity Jane fell in the mud in her white dress, it made me think of the day I met Alfie, and when she sang about her secret love, I cried, for I knew just how she felt. I looked over to see if Alfie was enjoying it, too, but he had his head down, staring at the floor.

After the film was over, they made us get into two lines, men and women, before ordering us to follow them back to the villas. Nurse Cunningham and Nurse Fitts went from one end of the row to the other, counting. Me and Janet was waiting at the front. Alfie and Frankie was stood in the line beside us. Frankie blew Janet a kiss. Janet laughed, blowing one back.

'He's gorgeous,' she says.

Nurse Fitts and Nurse Cunningham was still counting heads at the other end of the row when Alfie leaned over and whispered in my ear.

'Where were you the other night?'

'What do you mean?' I says, confused.

'I asked you to meet me in the alleyway on Sunday, remember? I was waiting for you for ages. You never came.'

'You waited for me? When?'

'I wrote you a letter. Did you get it?'

The letter. Of course.

'Yes,' I says. 'But I can't read.'

Alfie shook his head. He seemed to understand then.

Frankie was still blowing kisses at Janet. I saw Nurse Cunningham coming down the row towards us, tapping each person on the shoulder.

'Watch it, you two,' I says.

Alfie leaned in then, his shoulder brushing mine. I shivered.

'Meet me at seven o'clock,' he says. 'Sunday night. Down the alleyway behind the recreation hall.'

Before I could answer, the nurses started shouting at us to follow them: men and women, in two separate lines, got marched off in opposite directions. It didn't matter, though. This time, I had understood his message.

At St Mary's, you learned to be cunning. You always had to be one step ahead of the nurses. It was snowing that Sunday, so I borrowed a man's overcoat from one of the cupboards and slipped out of the villa, sneaking my way over the courtyard to the recreation hall. The lights was already off – for they used to close it early on a Sunday, after the evening church service – and everything was quiet. I caught the smell of smoke coming from behind the building.

'Alfie,' I whispered. 'Is that you?'

Alfie stepped out of the alleyway, dropping his cigarette on the ground. It glowed for a second, before sizzling out in the snow. He gave me the signal to follow him, then, once we was halfway down, he grabbed the sleeves of my overcoat, pinning me against the wall.

'Give us a kiss,' he says.

I won't lie – it felt good. I didn't even mind that he tasted of cigarettes. I'd been waiting for this moment forever.

'Your hands are freezing,' he says, taking his gloves off and giving them to me.

Shakily, I put them on.

Alfie laughed. 'Where did you get that coat? It's like a bloody marquee!'

'It was all I could find,' I say. 'I can take it off if you want?'

'Never mind,' he says, grinning. 'It's what's underneath that counts.'

What happened next shocked me. Alfie's cold hand shot up between my bare legs, making me cry out.

'Easy, love,' he whispered, putting his other hand over my mouth. 'Just let it rest there. It'll warm up soon. I promise.'

32

24 AUGUST 2015

Do you ever get the feeling someone's following you? I've had it a few times lately. Wayne would say it's all the TV dramas I watch. He'd say I'm being far-fetched, but some days I'm sure I can sense someone close by. Not a bad person. More like that guardian angel in *It's a Wonderful Life*. I used to enjoy watching the film with Janet every Christmas at St Mary's. Both of us was always in floods of tears at the end.

It's getting dark as I make my way back from the shops. Autumn is on its way. There's a cold breeze on the High Street. I pull my coat tightly around me and take my pink gloves out of my pocket, slipping them on. I wear my gloves all year round, even in summer. Wayne gave them to me a few years ago, as a present for my 70th birthday. They're Marks and Spencer's, I'll always treasure them. As I walk past Sainsbury's, I see David standing behind the counter. I wave and he waves back. I think about popping in. It always looks so cosy with the lights on, but I'm not sure I'm up to talking to anyone right now.

Just then, I see her. A red-haired woman staring at me in the glass. I stop dead in my tracks, my heart beating fast. For a split second I think it's you, Cilla, then I realise it's just my own silly reflection.

I don't want to go home. It's too quiet. I don't want it to be just me and my own thoughts. Putting my headphones on, and pressing play on my CD, I drift off in the other direction, towards the harbour. I've not thought about Alfie for ages – years, in fact – but Cilla's death has brought everything back, the memories.

The sun is setting when I get to Peter Cushion's bench. Cilla is whispering in my ear, telling me how nothing stays the same forever; none of us, she says, knows what the future has in store. I wonder how many sunsets I have left? I'm 75 now, so there can't be that many. Cilla was younger than me when she died. Now, though, it's as if she's here again, sat right beside me, talking to me about the good times and the bad times, just like an old friend.

'We could only try to make the most of each day as it came along,' she says.

We had so little time together, Cilla, but I made the most of every day I had with you.

Rocking back and forth on the bench, I repeat her words, softly to myself, like a lullaby, over and over again, my eyes blurry with grief.

We could only try to make the most of each day as it came along.

We could only try to make the most of each day as it came along.

33

'C'

My car is parked in Keam's Yard, facing the seafront. This is one of my favourite spots to watch the famous Whitstable sunsets, and tonight's pink and orange sky certainly doesn't disappoint (I've taken lots of photos on my phone to upload to Facebook later).

I'm just about to turn the key in the ignition to start the journey back to London, when I see you walk up the ramp and sit down on Peter Cushing's seat. You look absolutely freezing. I want to wind down the window, call you over. I want to invite you to sit in the car with me, to warm yourself. On the radio, Roy Orbison is singing about loneliness, and I watch you rocking back and forth on your seat. I'd love to introduce myself, to talk to you, but I appreciate you've made a new life for yourself. I don't want to overwhelm you, or upset you, by bringing up the past too soon. I'm in such a quandary, really I am. For now, all I can do is watch.

34

1969

After that first night together, me and Alfie would meet up every Sunday in the alleyway. It was the only chance we got to spend time together. Every day of the long working week I looked forward to it. Just the thought of him waiting for me, his cap tipped, his white shirt rolled up at the sleeves, made me smile. It was daydreaming about Alfie that got me through the week, the boredom of it. Whenever I was standing on a cold stone floor, washing dirty knickers in the sink, my hands covered in greasy suds, I would pretend I was in my own kitchen. Our kitchen. I imagined Alfie was my husband, out at work, earning money for the family. I'd say to myself, 'I'd better have this washing done for five o'clock, for my husband will be home soon and there's the dinner to be getting on with.' I'd picture him coming home then. He'd take his shoes off at the door (for in my mind he was always tidy) and kiss me. Sometimes, he would even bring me flowers. This was all in my head, of course, for in real life we had to hide the fact that we was courting. It was our secret. Mine and Alfie's.

At first it was hard keeping it from everyone, especially Eva. She was nosy, so if we was working in the kitchen together and Alfie came in, I had to pretend to ignore him. It used to upset me, but I must be a good liar, for eventually

Eva stopped asking me questions. Just as well, because I was getting fed up with her telling me what I should and shouldn't be doing. Before I met Alfie, I would've put up with it, but because I had him, Eva become less important. Don't get me wrong, she was still my best friend, but I didn't like her sticking her oar in so much. I stopped doing chores for her, too. Like before, if she had wanted me to do her share of the cooking, I would've said yes, but one night, Alfie says to me, 'You know, I've been watching the way Eva speaks to you sometimes. It's not right, Margaret.'

'What do you mean, it ain't right?' I says.

It was a Sunday night, close to springtime, and we was in our usual spot down the alleyway. We'd finished kissing and we was sat on the ground together, like we always did, holding each other's hands, my head resting on Alfie's shoulder, our backs against the wall, our feet leaning on the one opposite.

'Do you want to light my cigarette and I'll tell you?' he says.

He'd started asking me to light his cigarette. It was after we'd seen *Now, Voyager* in the recreation hall. Ever since then, I always kept a box of matches in my pocket, just in case he asked me for a light. I liked to pretend I was Betty Davies in the film. It was romantic.

'Of course, my darling Alfie,' I'd say to him, for that is how we had started talking to each other.

He was kind, Alfie. I'd never had no one care for me like that before. I mean, there was Eva – and Joan, of course – but it wasn't the same. My girlfriends didn't love me the same way Alfie did.

Alfie put the cigarette in his mouth and leaned towards me. I struck a match. He'd taught me to do that. The first time I tried, it kept blowing out. It had taken me a lot of practice, but now I knew to cup my hand around it to protect it from the wind. Alfie put his cigarette in the flame and inhaled.

'If you want the truth, I think Eva's manipulating you,' he says, blowing out the smoke.

'What do you mean?'

'She's getting you to do things for her. Things she can't be bothered doing herself.'

'Like what?'

'Well, the other day, I was in the storeroom, watching you both working, and she got you to mop the bloody floor for her.'

'I don't mind. Eva, she ain't like me, she's—'

'A lazy bitch?'

'Don't say that, Alfie!' I pulled away from him. 'Eva's my mate. My best mate, in fact.'

'And where does that leave me, then?'

'It ain't the same,' I says, crossing my arms. 'I ain't courting Eva.'

'Exactly! So why's she got you running around after her like a bloody blue-arsed fly? Do me a favour, love – next time she asks you to do something, tell her to get lost.'

'Alfie!' I says. 'Don't be horrible. She's a nice girl, Eva. She ain't got used to how things are here, that's all.'

'Rubbish. She's been here six months, at least. She's had more than enough time to get used to things.'

'But she's different. She's clever, for a start.'

'And you're not? Don't put yourself down, Margaret. If you do that, girls like Eva are just going to walk all over you.'

Alfie hacked up a bit of phlegm and spat on the ground. What did he have against Eva all of sudden? Why didn't he want me to be her friend?

'She ain't walking all over me,' I says, annoyed by his talk. 'I have my own mind, thank you very much.'

'Do you? Can't see it myself.'

Alfie said I'd be better off not speaking to Eva. I don't know why he was so against our friendship all of a sudden, but he said I should choose Janet as my best friend instead. Janet was a good girl. Not like Eva. Eva was crafty. A bad influence.

'Do me a favour,' he says. 'Stop acting like a bloody sheep around her.'

I shouted at him then, for I was angry. How dare he speak about Eva like that.

'She's my mate,' I says to him. 'I'll do as I blooming well please!'

'In that case, we're finished,' he hissed, poking me hard in the chest with his finger. 'You and me. Over.'

He threw his cigarette against the wall, stamping it out with his boot. He stood up, pushing me out of the way and making me fall over.

'Don't go, Alfie, please,' I says. 'Please. I'm sorry.'

I was shaking, but he got up and walked off, leaving me sat there on my own.

It was our first-ever row.

35

1969

Later that week, Eva and me was in the kitchen preparing meals for the other patients. Nurse Cunningham had left Eva in charge. I'd not heard from Alfie since our falling-out on Sunday.

'You're quiet, Margaret,' says Eva. 'Are you all right?' I didn't answer her, for I was staring into space, my mind elsewhere. 'Only, if you're not busy, I could really do with some help peeling these potatoes.'

When I didn't respond, Eva came over and put her hand on my shoulder.

I shrugged it off.

'Don't,' I says.

Eva took a step back. 'What's up with you, Margaret? You're not normally like this. Have I done something wrong?' She frowned. 'I've upset you, haven't I? Tell me, Margaret. What was it I said?'

I put down my knife and turned to her.

'Look,' I snapped. 'You ain't done nothing wrong. It's me, OK? Give me them potatoes. I'll help you peel them.'

The kitchen doors swung open with a bang. Alfie came in with Frankie. They was both being really loud, laughing. As soon as I saw Alfie, I felt that frog again, jumping up and down in my stomach. My hands started shaking.

'Shall I fetch us a tea, Frank?' he says.

'Yes please, Alf,' Frankie says, pulling out a crate and sitting down on it.

Alfie came wandering over to the sinks.

'Just filling the kettle, ladies,' he says to us. 'Don't mind me.' He turned on the tap. 'What are you two gossiping about, then? Not me, I hope?'

I couldn't look him in the eye. I put my head down and carried on peeling.

'Leave the kettle there, Alfie,' says Eva, pointing at the stove. 'I don't mind making tea for you both. I'm in charge for the next hour or so.'

'Are you now?' Alfie winked. Placing the lid back on the kettle, he set it on the gas ring. 'That's nice of you to offer, Eva.'

'I aim to please,' says Eva. 'You boys have been working hard today, I'm sure. How do you take it, Alfie?'

'My tea?' Alfie grinned.

'What do you think I meant?' Eva laughed. 'You cheeky bugger.'

'Milk and two sugars,' says Alfie. 'But since it's you making it, maybe skip the sugar. I'm sure it'll be sweet enough as it is.'

'Oh, you charmer,' says Eva.

How come Alfie was being nice to Eva all of a sudden? Ain't she the reason we'd been arguing? Oh, he made my blood boil sometimes.

'Oi,' shouts Frankie. 'Will one of you two lovelies be my girlfriend, then?'

'Shut up, Frankie!' I whispered. 'Silly sod. You'll get us all into trouble.' I pointed my knife at him.

'Easy, Margaret,' says Eva. 'Remember, I'm in charge here. While the nurses are away—'

142

'Margaret,' says Frankie, 'please will you be my girlfriend? Please please please.'

He put his hands together and closed his eyes, like he was praying.

'No, I bloody well can't,' I says. 'Besides, I thought you liked Janet.'

I carried on with my peeling, sneaking a glance at Eva every so often. I watched her pour milk into the two cups, stirring in the sugar with a spoon.

'Take a seat, Alfie,' she says. 'I'll bring these over to you.'

'Grand,' says Alfie. 'Is this what they call silver service then? I always knew we'd end up living the high life, eh, Frank? I could get used to this, couldn't you, mate?'

Alfie sat down on a crate next to him. Frankie nodded, taking an orange from one of the boxes and biting into it like an apple.

'Christ. Frank, give it here,' says Alfie, snatching the orange. 'You don't eat the peel. You need to use your fingers.'

Frankie giggled, the juice dribbling down his chin. He made a right mess. Alfie peeled the orange and handed it back to Frankie. Taking a cigarette from his pocket, he put it in his mouth. He looked up at me and, without thinking, I reached into my pocket for the box of matches, then I remembered. We wasn't speaking.

'Eva, love,' says Alfie, still staring at me, 'have you got a light?'

'Why,' she says, 'I think you might just be in luck, my darling. But only if I can have one of your cigarettes.'

'Sure you can,' says Alfie.

I watched Eva carry the two teas over to where Frankie and Alfie was. She bent over, setting both cups on the floor. Alfie got off his crate.

'Take a seat, Eva. I don't mind standing.'

Eva sat down next to Frankie, who leaned over, puckering his lips at her.

'Give us a kiss,' he says.

Alfie whacked him one over the head.

'Ouch!' shouted Frankie. 'That hurt.'

'Mind your manners, Frank!' Alfie says. 'Eva doesn't want to be molested. Not by you, anyway.'

'Leave him alone, Alfie,' says Eva.

'He needs to learn some manners,' Alfie says. 'You don't speak to women like that.'

'He's all right,' says Eva. 'He's not doing any harm. Now can I have that cigarette, please?'

'You said you'd light mine first,' says Alfie. 'That was the deal.'

Eva put her hand in her apron pocket and took out a box of matches. She struck one. Alfie leaned over. She cupped her hand around his cigarette so he could light it, just like I always did. I was fuming. He then offered her one and she lit it. I watched as she inhaled and blew out a perfect smoke ring.

'Can I have one, please?' says Frankie.

'No you fucking can't!' says Alfie. 'It's bad for you.'

'Eva,' I says, 'when you've done with your cigarette, can you come and give me a hand with the prepping? I can't do everything myself.'

'Do forgive me, gentlemen,' says Eva, standing up. 'My manager is calling me. She's *such* a slave-driver.'

Alfie laughed. 'I'll bet she is.'

I was so angry. I could've punched her in the face.

Eva handed her cigarette back to Alfie.

'Here, have two,' she says.

Alfie put it in his mouth along with the other one. He followed Eva around with his eyes, pretending to smoke both cigarettes at the same time. Frankie was laughing so much at Alfie, I thought he might fall off the crate.

'What's so funny?' I shouted. 'Ain't you two got work to do? Lazy lot.'

There was a thud then, like something had fallen off the roof.

'Shit!' says Alfie. 'What was that?'

Frankie got up off the crate and ran towards the window. 'It's a bird, it's a bird.'

He was jumping up and down on the spot, pointing at the floor.

'Let me see,' says Alfie. 'Is it dead?'

Me and Eva both followed the boys over to where the noise had come from. Sure enough, there was a pigeon lying on the ground. It must've fallen from the rafters. Its wings was stuck together with oil or something, its little eyes gummed shut. It was still alive, though, for its breast was beating like mad.

'Poor thing,' I says. 'It's frightened.'

'I can't bear to look at it,' says Eva, turning her head away. 'I'll be sick.'

Alfie lifted the bird up in both hands, swinging it round fast.

'Boo!' he says, holding it right in Eva's face.

Eva screamed and dropped the mug she was holding, smashing it on the floor. She ran off, shutting herself in the store cupboard. Alfie burst out laughing. He looked down at the bird in his hand, parting its wings with his fingers.

'It's half dead already,' he says. 'Might as well put it out of its misery.'

I couldn't take my eyes off its heart: it was pumping hard and fast, like it might explode at any minute.

What Alfie done next was one of the most horrible things I've ever seen. He grabbed the pigeon by the neck and twisted the head clean off. Blood spurted out onto his fingers, drops of it landing on his boots. Even without a head, the bird carried on flapping, its wings fluttering, like it was trying to get away.

Frankie was hysterical by this point: he was curled up in a ball on the ground, sobbing. Alfie picked up a broom and started bashing the bird with it. He kept on bashing it until it stopped moving.

'C'mon then, Frankie boy,' he says, kicking what was left of the poor bird into a corner. 'We got work to be getting on with.'

I was shocked. I couldn't believe what I'd just seen.

Frankie got up. He was shaking, his eyes red from crying. Alfie pushed him out of the door.

'Thanks for the tea, Eva!' he yelled.

As he left, he turned to me and smiled.

'Make sure Eva gives you a hand with cleaning up this mess.'

Eva had not seen any of what happened. She'd been hiding in the cupboard the whole time.

'Eva,' I says, knocking on the door quietly. 'Are you OK?'

There was no answer, so I pushed the door open. Eva was crouched on the floor with her hands over her head. She was shivering.

'It's my nerves,' she says. 'How can he be so cruel when he knows about my nerves?'

Even though I was angry with Eva, the shock over what had happened with the pigeon made me feel sorry for her. I was confused. Not just by Eva's flirting, but by Alfie. Why was he being so two-faced with Eva, especially after what he'd said to me about her the other night? What was he playing at? It didn't make sense.

'He's a man, ain't he?' I says. 'They're all the same.'

Eva wasn't listening. She was rocking back and forth on the floor, muttering to herself. I decided to leave her and her nerves alone. Grabbing my coat from the hook, I went and stood outside by the back door. I needed to be by myself. I might've said something I regretted otherwise.

36

24 AUGUST 2015

Back at the flat, still wearing my coat, I throw myself into an armchair and stare up at the ceiling.

What if they think I'm mad? What if they don't believe me? Even Wayne, my best friend, thinks I'm starting to lose my marbles.

'People don't come back from the dead, Margaret.' Ain't that what he said to me? 'Cilla's gone.'

I'm frightened, you see. What if they lock me away again? I grab a cushion and hold it tight against my stomach. If only Cilla would show her face, then they'll know I'm not lying. They'll know I'm telling the truth.

The truth is, I ain't even sure I believe myself. Are your letters real, or did I dream them? I reach down beside the armchair and pick up my handbag. Unzipping it, I look inside. The letter and the postcard are still there, so I'm not making it up. What was it Sainsbury's David said when he read them to me? I'm finding it hard to remember. Maybe I made some of your words up in my head. You sent me money, though, and I've spent most of it: a record and a birthday card for Wayne, a new haircut for me. I can't normally afford to do extra stuff like that.

I reach for my CD player and my headphones, which are

tangled up in a heap next to me. I place them in my ears, like tiny white seashells, and press play. Lying back in the armchair, I take a deep breath and close my eyes. Cilla begins to speak. Her voice washes over me like waves, breaking up the silence and the loneliness in the room. She's talking about her first pregnancy, her joy at feeling the baby move for the first time inside her, and her fears that it would be 'imperfect' in some way. My eyes well up at the thought. Are you ashamed of me, Cilla? Am I not what you expected me to be?

My living room curtains are wide open and the lights are off, but the full moon makes the objects around me glow. Cilla is still talking to me. She whispers that her baby was perfect, a miracle. Cradling her baby in her arms, she says she'd never been happier in her whole life. I start to cry, a sense of sadness rising deep from the pit of my stomach, a sadness that quickly switches to frustration.

'Why was you taken from me, Cilla?' I say the words out loud. 'Why so soon?'

Tearing the headphones from my ears, I press eject on the CD player. I rip out the CD and throw it on the floor. Bright moonlight floods the silver disc and for a moment I see your face and my face reflected in it, like a mirror. Frustration turns to anger.

'It ain't fair, Cilla,' I say. 'Why did you have to go away?'

My mind is spinning. Sinking back into the armchair, I close my eyes; try to shut out the different voices in my head. The memories keep on coming, though. They won't let me rest.

37

1969

The next morning, Eva was sat opposite me at breakfast. We hadn't spoken a word to each other since the day before, not one word. I was stirring a spoon around my bowl of porridge. I didn't feel much like eating. Eva asked me to pass her the water jug. I pushed it across the table, not looking at her.

'Thank you,' she says, pouring herself a cup. She took a sip. Her hand was trembling. 'I think you and I need to have a talk, don't you? Only I've noticed things have been different between us recently. You've not been yourself. I thought we were friends, right?'

'I suppose so,' I mumbled, staring at my reflection in the back of the spoon. How ugly was I compared to Eva?

'Are we?' she says. 'Best friends speak to each other, don't they? They tell each other everything.'

'I ain't hiding nothing from you.'

'I didn't say you were. It's me, I've not been—'

'I've had a lot on my mind.'

'Like what?' Eva reached over the table and put her hand on mine. 'Talk to me, Margaret.'

'It's nothing. Let's forget it, Eva. Let's just try and be friends.'

* * *

That afternoon in the laundry room I had some time to myself, for Eva had gone on an errand. I used to do a lot of thinking when I was washing things. Laundry was good for that.

You've been unfair to Eva, I says to myself. *She ain't got a clue about what's been going on with you and Alfie. You giving her the silent treatment, it ain't right. She's your friend. Girls should stick together, be there for one another.*

I decided then I'd make it up to her. It wasn't Eva who was in the wrong, poor thing. It was my fault. I was the one telling lies. I was angry with myself. And to top it all, Alfie had been horrible to me. I went off to the cupboard at one point and had a little cry.

While I was sat in there, I heard footsteps outside. There was a knock on the door. A little voice says quietly, 'Margaret, are you in there?'

'Who is it?' I says.

'It's me.'

'Who?'

'Frankie.'

'Give me a minute, Frankie, love. I won't be long.'

Drying my eyes with the corner of my apron, I checked my reflection, using the bottom of a tin of Ajax as a mirror. I opened the cupboard door to find Frankie standing on his own by one of the baskets, rummaging through a pile of girls' dirty knickers.

'Oi, you,' I says. 'Get your bleeding hands out of there. Lads ain't allowed to touch them!'

Frankie jumped, turning around to face me, his cheeks bright red.

'Oh, p-p-please, I'm sorry,' he says. 'Don't tell no one, p-please!'

He got down on his knees, joining his hands together in prayer.

'What are you doing here anyway?' I says. 'You ain't allowed in the laundry room and you know it.'

'Alfie sent me, miss,' he says, putting his hands on his head, almost as if he was expecting me to give him a clip round the ear.

'Alfie? What does he want?'

'He says, he says . . . He says . . .' Frankie looked like he was concentrating ever so hard.

'Calm down, Frankie, tell me what Alfie said.'

'He says . . . He says . . . He's . . . He's . . . sorry.' Frankie beamed at me.

'Is that all he said?'

'No.' Frankie paused. He slapped himself on the forehead, like he was trying to remember something. 'Alfie says, "Same t-t-t-time next week, then?"'

He grinned at me, glad to have delivered his message at last.

I was as relieved as Frankie, to be honest. So I wasn't in Alfie's bad books anymore.

'Tell Alfie it's OK, Frankie,' I whispered. 'Tell him I forgive him.'

Frankie smiled, clapping his hands. 'Oh! Oh, b-but there's another thing.'

He pointed a finger at me.

'What's that?'

'Will you . . . ? Will you . . . ?'

His face was getting redder and redder. He was fiddling with his pockets, stretching them inside out, until they was hanging out of his trousers, twisted like old socks.

'Will I what, Frankie?'

'Will you . . . ? Will you . . . b-b-be my girlfriend?'

He wiped his forehead and stared up at me, waiting for an answer.

'*Frankie!*' I laughed. 'That's ever so nice of you to ask, but you know it ain't allowed.'

Frankie made a sad face. He looked at me, puckering his lips.

'Just a k-k-kiss, then,' he says, leaning in and offering his cheek. 'Just the one.'

'Oh all right then.'

I checked to see no one was looking, before giving him a quick peck. He let out this little 'whoop', gave his hips a wiggle, then raising his fist in the air, he turned to run off, legging it towards the door.

38

1969

When Eva came back, around three o'clock, I was by the sink, busy rubbing salt into a white petticoat. As soon as I saw her, I put my head down. She was humming a tune. It was one that I recognised, but I couldn't remember the name.

'Everything been all right, then?' she says.

'Yeah,' I says, quietly. 'What you been up to?'

'Me? I've just been up Manor House.'

'You was gone ages.'

'Was I?' Eva yawned. 'Only Nurse Fitts asked me to take some clean washing up to Mrs Dingley's place earlier. She can't half talk, that woman. I couldn't get away. How have things been here?'

I started telling her what had happened with Frankie.

'What was Frankie doing back here again?' Eva looked puzzled.

'He wanted a kiss.'

'A kiss? From you? Little devil.'

Eva took her apron off the hook and put it over her head.

Now that we was speaking, I thought it might be a good time to make it up to her.

'Eva,' I says, 'I'm sorry about the other day. I didn't mean to get angry with you.'

Eva smiled. 'Let's forget about it,' she says, tying her apron in a bow at the back.

'I mean it, though. I was being horrible. It ain't like me.'

'Honestly, it's fine. It was that bloody bird. It set me off.'

Just as she said it, the door banged open and Nurse Cunningham came storming into the room, making us both jump. She was like a nasty jack-in-the-box, that woman, always popping up when you least expected.

'How many times do I have to tell you?' she yelled. 'No slacking during working hours. You've both got jobs to be getting on with, yes?'

We nodded.

'Get on with it, then.'

Nurse Cunningham stormed into the store cupboard where we kept our washing things. She used to check it every week, to see we had enough soap and bleach. I went back to my washing and Eva started sorting through the baskets. All of a sudden there was a loud shriek and Nurse Cunningham came running out with one of Eva's magazines in her hand.

'Whose is this?' she says, flicking through the pages. 'Disgusting,' she says. 'Absolute filth!'

Eva's face was a picture. She started twitching.

Without thinking, I says, 'It's mine, miss. It's my book.'

Nurse Cunningham rolled up the magazine and pointed it at me.

'This is yours, is it?'

'Yes, miss.'

I looked over at Eva, who had a hand over her mouth.

'Forgive me if I'm being ignorant,' hissed Nurse Cunningham, leaning into my ear, 'but what use has a girl like you got for a magazine?'

'I don't know what you mean, miss.'

155

'"I don't know what you mean, miss",' she says, mimicking what I'd just said. 'Well, you can't bloody read for a start!'

She banged the rolled-up magazine on the sink.

'Only I like to look at the pictures, miss.' My voice was shaking.

'Really?' she says. 'That is interesting. So exactly what kind of pictures does a non-reader like you like looking at, then?'

'Just pictures. You know, of things.'

She was frightening me. I wasn't sure what I'd done wrong.

'Things?' she says, snorting. A blue vein throbbed on her forehead. 'And what kind of *things* are we talking about here?'

Before I could answer, she tore open the magazine at the middle pages and threw it on top of the draining board. She grabbed the back of my neck, pushing my head towards it.

'Shall we have a look at some of these *things*, then?' she says, flicking through the pages. She was going so fast that some of them was ripping off in her hand. She stopped at a poster of Cliff Richard and Una Stubbs. 'You know what this is?'

'It's Cliff Richard,' I stammered.

'Pornography,' she says. 'That's what this is.'

'I don't understand, miss.'

She was squeezing my neck with her fingers. It hurt.

'Oh, but you do. Don't try playing the innocent with me, Small. Why do you think they locked you in here all those years ago?'

'I don't know, miss. I was only seven—'

'You're feral, you are. Do you know what that means?'

I shook my head. Nurse Cunningham laughed.

'I didn't think so. Well, let me spell it out for you.'

She carried on turning the pages of the magazine like a maniac, stopping at a picture of Mick Jagger.

'Why, it's the Devil himself,' she says, her cheeks puffing

like they was about to explode. 'Like looking at him, do you? Does it give you a little thrill down there?' She pointed towards the hem of her apron. 'Feral little sluts you are, the lot of you. Isn't that right, Finch?'

Eva went running into the storeroom, slamming the door behind her.

Nurse Cunningham turned to me and whispered.

'Used to be a good friend of the military, that one, but we soon put a stop to her antics.'

'Military?'

'Soldiers.' Nurse Cunningham raised her eyebrows. 'She likes her men in uniform.'

What was she saying? That Eva was up to something during the war? I didn't understand.

'This,' she says, holding up the magazine, 'is being confiscated. We can't have you going down the same road to moral depravation. And as punishment for looking at filth, I'm putting you in the side room.'

Without saying another word, she rolled up the magazine, grabbed my arm and dragged me outside.

39

1969

'You won't see daylight in this place I'm taking you to,' says Nurse Cunningham, pulling me across the courtyard. 'It'll be pitch-black.'

'But I ain't done nothing.'

'Enough!'

She pinched my arm. It didn't half hurt.

We stopped outside Villa 17. It was different from the other villas. There was no windows at the front, only a big wooden door with bars on it. From inside, I could hear screaming and howling. I wasn't sure if it was man, woman or human, even: it sounded like a monster. Nurse Cunningham took a set of keys from her belt and undid the lock. The door creaked open. She pushed me inside.

The first thing that hit me was the smell: a mixture of piss and sweat. The room was dark. Whoever was inside was growling, like a dog.

'Be quiet, you brute,' says Nurse Cunningham. 'I've brought you a friend.'

The growling stopped then. There was a shriek of laughter, followed by clapping noises. Nurse Cunningham lit up a gas lamp, the light making huge shadows on the walls. I hardly dared look, but from what I could see the room was

158

completely empty, apart from a blanket and a chamber pot that had been knocked over, leaving a puddle of piss on the floor. In one corner, a woman was rocking back and forth in her knickers. She was a lot older than me: heavy-looking, with curly black hair. Oh, she was wild. She was grinning and clapping and muttering gibberish, the corners of her mouth bubbling with spit. I recognised her then. It was Dora, the violent one who used to be in our children's ward, the one who used to attack the staff.

'Margaret's come to play with you, Dora,' says Nurse Cunningham. 'I trust you'll make her feel at home.' Dora growled. Nurse Cunningham carried on. 'Margaret here has been a very bad girl. You know what we do with bad girls at St Mary's, don't you, Dora?'

Dora stopped clapping. She turned her head to look at me. She was staring, her eyes yellow and bloodshot. She started howling.

'Please don't leave me with her, miss,' I says. 'I'll never look at another magazine again, I promise. It was a mistake.'

'I think we've got ourselves a bit of a scaredy-cat here, Dora,' says Nurse Cunningham, dangling her big set of keys. 'Needs toughening up. What say I leave you two alone for a bit to get to know each other better?'

Dora let out a loud cry. She jumped off her feet, went straight for Nurse Cunningham. She grabbed her by the leg and was about to sink her teeth into her, when Nurse Cunningham screamed. She dropped the gas lamp onto the floor, where it smashed into tiny pieces. The light flickered and went out. I could hear Dora rolling around in the broken glass, laughing and growling to herself. Her hands and her knees must've been cut to ribbons, but she didn't care. Nurse Cunningham bolted out of the door, slamming it shut behind her.

I heard a yell coming from outside, then a voice saying, 'Quick. Come and look in here, Alice.'

Dora stopped screaming. A panel on the door slid open, letting in some light. She was sat up now, sobbing quietly to herself in the middle of the floor. Through the bars, I saw two pairs of eyes looking in. Nurse Cunningham and Nurse Fitts.

'You can't leave her in there, Violet,' says Nurse Fitts. 'It's too dangerous.'

'Rubbish, Alice. She needs to be taught a lesson. She won't learn otherwise.'

'Stop it at once, Violet,' says Nurse Fitts. 'She'll kill her. Give me the key.'

Dora started growling again.

'That's it, Dora,' says Nurse Cunningham. 'Show us what you're made of.'

Apart from the light from the panel, the room was pitch-black. I could hear Nurse Fitts and Nurse Cunningham still talking outside. Nurse Fitts kept saying, 'No, Violet, it's not right, it's cruel,' but Nurse Cunningham just laughed.

'That's it, Dora, good girl,' she brayed, egging her on.

She was clever, that one. As a nurse, she knew she wasn't allowed to hit me, so she was getting Dora to do her dirty work for her.

'Teach her a lesson,' she says, laughing. 'I'll put extra jam in your pudding tomorrow, Dora.'

At that, Dora lunged straight at me, but I managed to dodge her. Running to the other side of the room, I hid myself in a dark corner. There I curled myself into a ball, short of breath, hardly daring to move. There was a sudden scream, then Dora went quiet, her voice a whimper, like a dog left alone by its owner.

I don't know how long I was in there for; it could've been seconds, but it felt like hours. Eventually the door opened and Nurse Cunningham came running in. She grabbed my arm, pulled me up and ordered me to follow her outside.

40

1969

'Get up, you lazy thing.' Nurse Cunningham shook me awake. 'You're not on holiday, you know.'

She gave me a fright. I must have blacked out, for I woke up screaming, thinking it was Dora, come to finish me off. Then I realised I was in a different room, lying on an old mattress, its thick ticking scratching my neck. I rolled over onto my back, staring into Nurse Cunningham's face.

'C'mon then,' she says. 'Get moving. There's work to be done.'

I sat up, groaning. It was freezing. I was wearing nothing but my knickers and a vest. They must have stripped me the night before, only I had no memory of it. I rubbed the crusts from my eyes.

'I've brought you a few cleaning cloths and a bucket,' says Nurse Cunningham. 'This floor will need a good scrubbing, it's filthy. Once it's dry, I want you to give it a going-over with Blue Steel. I'll be coming back in a few hours to check you've done it properly. No slacking! If it's not up to scratch, you'll be spending another night in here.'

I shuffled off the mattress, crawling onto the floor on my hands and knees.

'Oh, for heaven's sake, girl, get up!' she barked. 'God gave you two legs, not four.'

'Where's Eva?' I says, standing up slowly, the blood rushing to my head. 'I need to see Eva.'

'Never mind about her. Take this!' She shoved a cloth into my hand. 'I'll leave the hatch open to let some light in.'

'Can't I have food first, miss? I'm really hungry.'

'I'll bring you something to eat after you've finished. Not before then.'

She stood there watching me as I got down on my knees. I started scrubbing.

'That's it,' she says. 'Keep going.'

The floor was hard. My knees hurt. I wanted to tell her to shut up, to quit her bloody braying, but I knew it was best to say nothing. I didn't want to spend another night in there. Or worse, be put in the side room again with Dora.

An hour or so later, there was a knock at the door. Nurse Cunningham went to open it. Nurse Fitts was standing there with a tray. She looked worried.

'How's she getting on?' she says.

'She's learning to keep her mouth shut. Not a peep out of her this past hour.'

'Good. I've left one of the high-grade girls in charge of the ward, Violet. Do you want to go and check she's all right for now? I can take care of this one.'

'I can do,' says Nurse Cunningham, sounding annoyed.

'If you wouldn't mind, Violet. Only I don't want to leave the girls alone, unsupervised, for too long.'

Nurse Cunningham leaned over and hissed in Nurse Fitts's ear.

'I know your game, Alice, and I'm warning you. Don't be soft with her. None of your mollycoddling. This is for the patient's own good.'

After she was gone, Nurse Fitts says, 'You can take a break now, Margaret. I've brought you some food.' She put a tray down on top of the mattress. 'Well, go on, then,' she says. 'Tuck in.'

What she brought me wasn't much: a tin plate, with a potato and a bit of Spam on it, along with a small bowl filled with cold custard and a cup of water. There was no cutlery. They didn't allow it, in case you tried to cut yourself, or pick the lock. I ate with my hands, polishing the lot off.

The next evening, they sent me back to the ward. Eva was sat up in bed. She looked worried. It was obvious she'd been waiting for me.

'Are you OK?' she says. 'What did they do to you?'

I told her what had happened. How they'd locked me in a room with Dora, then made me scrub the floor in my vest and knickers.

Eva looked horrified. 'You shouldn't have been blamed for it,' she says, her eye twitching. 'It was my magazine, not yours. I can't believe they did that to you. I feel terrible.'

She tried apologising, but I told her there was no need.

'Eva,' I says, climbing into bed, 'what did Nurse Cunningham mean when she says you was friends with the soldiers?'

Eva sighed. 'This has really upset me,' she says. 'She's a twister, that woman, she twists things. I can't believe the nerve of her. She's so insensitive. Speaking ill of the dead.'

'Are they dead, then? Your friends?'

'They were killed in the war,' says Eva. 'I used to write letters to them both, when they were off fighting. Such beautiful men.'

'Is that why your nerves is bad? Your friends dying?'

Eva shrugged.

'What did happen to your nerves, then? Why are you in here?'

Eva went quiet for a while. She was looking at her hands, pulling at each of her fingers, one by one. Eventually she spoke.

'If I tell you, do you swear not to mention it to anyone else?' I nodded. 'It was my stepdad, Thomas. He got them to put me away.' Eva shook her head. 'I don't really like talking about it.'

I reached across the bed and put my hand on hers.

'Tell me, though.'

Eva swallowed. 'He raped me.'

'What's rape?'

I whispered the word, for I knew it was something wrong. I just didn't know how wrong.

'Don't you know?'

I shook my head.

Eva told me her father had been a pilot. He got sent out to France during the war. He died when his plane got shot down. After his death, her mother went to pieces. She had this 'friend', Thomas.

'He was always coming round ours,' says Eva. 'Even before Dad died. Mum used to say he was company for her while Dad was away, but I knew there was something going on between them. She denied it, of course.'

'What do you mean?'

'Well, Mum would make him tea and they'd sit up late playing cards, smoking, drinking, whatever. They could both drink a hell of a lot. Thomas gave me the creeps. One night, after I'd been out to the pictures with my friend, I came home to find him passed out on the armchair in the front parlour. There was an empty bottle of gin on the table beside him. Mum was nowhere to be seen.'

'Where was she?'

'In bed. I figured Thomas must've carried her upstairs. She was probably incapable of walking. She used to get into a right state, Mum. Anyway, I was trying my best to be quiet, tiptoeing about and that. I didn't want to wake him. Clumsy idiot that I am, though, I kicked over an ashtray that was on the floor. It went flying across the room, nubs and ash everywhere. Thomas sat bolt upright in his chair.

'"What time do you call this?" he says to me. His face was purple and his eyes were bloodshot. I hated him, Margaret. I hated the way he spoke to me. I hated his drunkenness. I hated the fact he was always in our house, getting up to God only knows what with my mother while my poor father was not long in his grave.

'"What's it got to do with you, where I go, or who I'm with?" I said to him. "You aren't my dad, Thomas! What I get up to has got nothing to do with you."

'Straight away I wished I'd kept my mouth shut. He glared at me, got off his chair and staggered over to where I was standing, his eyes locked on me the whole time. He came right up close, so I could smell the liquor on his breath. Oh, Margaret, he was horrible, he really was! He cleared his throat, then he spat in my face. The next thing I knew, he was raising his fist. He punched me hard in the cheek. We started fighting. I grabbed both of his arms, tried to push him away from me, but he was strong. There was a crash, blood and glass all over the place; he'd forced my hand into a lampshade. I shouted for help, but he clamped my mouth shut with his hand.

'"What are you doing?" I screamed at him. I'd never been with a man before, Margaret. It hurt like hell, so I bit him on the lip. He cried out, but still Mum didn't wake. I don't think she heard a thing. It was all over in a flash. He finished his business, pulled up his trousers and ran out of the front door. Two months later, I learned I was pregnant.'

'You had a baby?'

'Not quite,' she says. 'Let me finish. As soon as I realised I was expecting, I told Thomas about it. He was terrified I would say something to Mum. He swore me to secrecy. He blamed me for what had happened, said it was my fault, that I'd *seduced* him.

'"What'll your mother think, Eva?" he said. "Her only daughter, a whore. She'll be ashamed of you. She'll chuck you out of the house, baby and all. You'll be homeless, destitute."

'I believed every word of it. I was frightened. I've never felt so alone in my life, Margaret. I had nobody to turn to. Anyway, he forced me to say it was one of the local lads that got me pregnant, and then he went and grassed me up to the Board of Control. I was hysterical. I tried telling Mum what had really happened, but she didn't believe me. Thomas had managed to convince her I was delusional.'

'What about the baby, then?'

Eva's eyes looked sad. 'I miscarried after a few months,' she says. 'I wasn't even showing any signs. I shouldn't have said anything to anyone. I've been going over it in my head for fifteen-odd years. If I hadn't told Thomas, I wouldn't be here, you see. They would never have locked me away.'

Later that night, when we was lying in our beds, Eva reached her hand across and took mine. We lay like that for a while.

'Margaret,' she whispered to me, 'do you miss your mother?'

I thought about it for a while.

'Not really,' I says. 'You can't miss someone you never knew.'

Eva's eyes widened. 'You never knew your own mother? How come? What happened to her?'

'She died when I was born. Giving birth to me was what killed her.'

'Don't say that. As if you could help being born.'

'I sometimes wish I wasn't born. Don't you think it would've been better?'

'No I don't. For a start, you would never have met me. And how would I have survived here without you?'

'I do think about her, though, sometimes. My mother.'

'Have you got any other family?'

'Only Grandma, but I ain't heard from her since they vanished me. She's probably dead by now. We got each other, though. We don't need no family.'

Eva squeezed my hand. 'I do love you, Margaret,' she says.

41

Another letter comes in the post this morning, in a pink envelope, with the same writing on the front, so I know straight away it's from you, Cilla. I sit down on the stairs and open it. Fifty quid and a lottery ticket. Shakily, I hold the slip of paper in my hand, staring at the numbers.

03, 15, 20, 24, 40, 47

Do these numbers mean anything? A birthday? A phone number? An address? There's no sound in the hallway, apart from the clock ticking. I feel like I'm on *Countdown*, so I panic. I need help. I look for a pattern, but I can't find one. The numbers make no sense to me, so I give up and pick up the letter that came with the ticket instead. Unfolding it, I spread it out on my knee. You've written more than usual. I study the words, tracing the shape of each one with my finger, trying to work out what they mean: a curly smile, drawn sideways in black pen, and some kisses. It's no use, though. Words are gobbledygook to me.

There's a rat-a-tat-tat at the door. I look up. Through the glass, I see Wayne standing outside. It's Wednesday, though, his day

169

off. What's he doing here? In a panic, I put the money and the letter back in the pink envelope. I shove everything in my handbag and hang it over the banister. I undo the latch and open the front door.

'Morning,' says Wayne. 'I wanted to pop in for a quick chat. Mind if I put the kettle on?'

42

'C'

You looked so unhappy the last time I saw you. I thought a lottery ticket might cheer you up, give you something to look forward to. I'm tempted to buy one for myself as well. After all, life is about taking chances, isn't it? You never know, we might both win!

43

1969

On Sunday night, I sneaked out at seven o'clock, my usual time, to meet Alfie. I couldn't wait to make things up with him. This whole fight over Eva had been silly. I just wanted to be with him, to spend time together. When I got to the alleyway, though, there was no sign of him. I sat and waited, but he never showed.

Something must have come up, I thought. *It will be OK. Alfie loves me. When we see each other again, it will be just like old times.*

When I got back to the ward, I couldn't find Eva, neither. I was looking everywhere for her.

'Have you seen Eva?' I says to Janet, who was sat in front of the big television in the day room.

'She went to pick flowers or something,' says Janet. 'It wasn't long after you left. Do you want to watch *Cilla* with me?'

Normally I would've gone to find Eva, but *Cilla* was my favourite programme. I loved it when she done the dance routines. Me and Janet would get off our chairs and copy the moves to her songs: 'Step Inside Love', 'Yo-Yo', 'Dancing In The Street'. We learned them all. Sacha Distel was performing on her show that night – 'Raindrops Keep Falling On My

172

Head'. We knew all the words, so we sung along. After it was over, we had a cup of tea, then Janet went to bed and I stayed up waiting for Eva in the day room. By nine o'clock, Eva still wasn't back, so I went to bed myself. About half an hour later, she came sneaking into the ward.

'Did you get some flowers, then?' I whispered.

'Flowers?' She sounded confused.

'Quiet over there!' one of the nurses shouted. 'Lights out in ten minutes.'

'I'll tell you in the morning,' whispered Eva.

She never did tell me, though.

And I forgot to ask.

I was desperate to see Alfie. He'd not been in the kitchen all week. Annie must have had him doing other jobs for her up the manor. On Tuesday night I went to watch a film again in the recreation hall, hoping I might see him. It was John Wayne, his favourite. I went alone, for even Janet didn't want to come with me. As soon as I said the word 'cowboy', she rolled her eyes. Eva wasn't fussed, neither. She said she was having an early night. It turned out it was a waste of time. Alfie wasn't even there. Frankie was, though. He waved at me from across the aisle. After the film was over, I thought I might get a chance to ask him about Alfie, but the nurses separated us into lines straight away, marching us out. On my way back to the villa, I remembered there was a dance being held in the recreation hall that Saturday. They held them once a month.

Maybe I'll see Alfie then, I thought.

44

1969

Later that week, me and Eva was in the kitchen having our tea break. Frankie came wandering in with a big wooden crate in his arms.

'All right, lovelies?' he says. 'I brought these for you, Eva.'

'Cabbages?' says Eva. 'Just leave them over there, Frankie.'

Frankie grinned, putting the crate down on the floor.

'Do I get a kiss from you, then?'

Eva laughed. 'Go on, then, if you insist.'

She pulled up her sleeve and held out her arm. Frankie got down on one knee and began rubbing his lips on her hand.

'That's enough,' says Eva, pulling away.

Frankie looked disappointed.

'Margaret, maybe you can teach Frankie how to kiss properly,' she says to me.

'No, I bloody well can't!' I says, annoyed with her for suggesting it.

'Can't you teach me, Eva?' he begged. 'Please?'

She shook her head. 'Margaret's a better kisser than me. Try her.'

Frankie pointed at me. 'Is what she says true?'

'Course it ain't, you daft sod,' I says. 'She's winding you up, Frankie.'

'I think you're both gorgeous,' he says. 'I wouldn't mind either of you as my girlfriend.'

He stood up on his tiptoes and closed his eyes, puckering his lips again.

Eva laughed. 'You should be so lucky. Haven't you got work to do?'

Frankie nodded. 'Can I have a cup of cocoa?'

'Oh, go on then,' Eva says. 'Margaret will make you one.'

Eva started humming that tune again. The one I could've sworn I'd heard before. I filled a saucepan with milk, set it on top of the gas ring and started looking on the shelves for the cocoa. There was all sorts of packets and boxes. I couldn't read the labels. I lifted down a small brown tin, wedging the lid off with my knife. I should've smelled it first, but I didn't think. Instead I just mixed it with the milk in the saucepan, then I poured it into a cup. I handed it to Frankie, who tipped it into his mouth. Well, I've never seen anyone go so green in my life. Frankie looked like he was about to vomit. He spat the drink everywhere. All over the floor and all down himself.

'What have you done to him, Margaret?' says Eva, picking up the tin. 'This isn't cocoa. It's gravy browning!'

'Oh my God, I'm ever so sorry, Frankie,' I says.

Poor boy. I felt terrible.

Eva, however, was doubled over with laughter. She found it hysterical.

'Don't worry, Margaret,' she says. 'I'll help you clean it up.'

Someone's in a good mood, I thought.

45

1969

It was the Friday before the dance. Eva was chopping cabbages
for a soup, while I was busy making a trifle. I was laying slices
of Swiss roll in the bottom of a bowl when Eva let out this
little cry. I thought she'd found a bug or something – she
was always overreacting to things – but then I saw her pull
a bit of paper out from between the cabbage leaves. She
read it and burst out laughing. When she saw me looking,
she put her hand over her mouth.

'What's so funny?' I says.

Eva folded the bit of paper in her hand, slipping it into
her apron pocket.

'Oh, nothing, Margaret. I was just thinking about what
happened with Frankie and the gravy.'

'What have you got there?'

'The cabbage?'

'In your pocket.'

'Oh, this?' She patted her pocket. 'It's just a note, a
reminder to myself, that's all.'

'To yourself?'

Eva's eyelid twitched. 'It's a note, Margaret. What's the
big deal?'

'Show me.' I held out my hand.

'It's only a bit of paper.'

'I want to see it.'

'Why? You can't read.'

'I know I can't,' I says. 'I thought you and me didn't have secrets, though.'

'Secrets?' she says, laughing. 'I haven't got any secrets.'

Eva took the piece of paper from her apron and gave it to me, her hands shaking.

'Well?' she says. 'Satisfied?'

I stared at the jumble of words on the page. Apart from a few letters that I thought I recognised, it made no sense to me. I knew something wasn't right, though, for I had the frog feeling in my stomach again. I handed the note back to her.

'What does it say, then?'

'It's just a list of things that I need to do this week. What did you think it was?'

'Forget about it. It don't matter.'

I opened up a tin of fruit cocktail and sloshed it over the Swiss roll. I was confused. I might not have been able to read the words, but I know what kisses look like. Why would Eva be drawing kisses to herself? My first thought was one that I quickly blocked from my mind. Surely Alfie wouldn't be writing letters to Eva? Not my Alfie. I'd seen him flirting with her a bit, but that's just the way men are. Besides, he hardly had a good word to say about her. He said she was lazy, not to be trusted.

46

1969

I woke up on Saturday morning feeling ill. I didn't make it to breakfast. I barely made it to the toilet because I felt so tired and weak. I crawled back into bed. Nurse Fitts came over to see me.

'You don't look well,' she says. She checked my temperature, but it was fine. 'Maybe it's just something you ate.' She brought me a cup of water and put it next to my bed, along with a chamber pot, in case I needed to be sick. 'Don't worry about work today. Get some rest.'

'What about the dance?' I says. 'I was looking forward to it, miss.'

'It's probably not a good idea, Margaret. Not tonight. There's always next time.'

I was so disappointed. I lay there all afternoon, praying I'd be better by Sunday. At least then I might get a chance to see Alfie again.

Later that evening, Eva was getting ready for the dance. She was fidgeting. She must've brushed her hair at least seventy times. She asked if she could borrow my hair clip.

'You're only allowed one,' I says. 'It's the rules.'

'No one will notice. Give it here.'

I handed her my clip and she fastened it on the other side of her head.

'There,' she says, doing a twirl. 'How do I look?'

'All right.'

'All right?' She sounded disappointed.

'You look lovely. As always, Eva.'

Eva bent over and picked something up from the floor next to her bed.

'Before I forget, I wanted to give you something. It's not much, but it might make you feel a bit better.' She handed me a bunch of flowers wrapped in newspaper. 'I picked them myself,' she says. 'There's a letter for you, too.'

She unfolded a bit of yellow paper and read it to me: '"Seventeenth of May, 1969. To my dearest friend Margaret. I will always treasure our special friendship and the love that you've shown to me in all my days here at St Mary's. Yours always, Eva x."'

Nurse Fitts came in.

'I hope I'm not interrupting anything, girls,' she says. 'If you're planning on going to the dance tonight, Eva, you'd best join the others in the queue.'

'Yes, miss,' said Eva, standing up. She looked emotional, like she was about to cry. 'Bye, Margaret.'

'I'll see you later, Eva, love,' I says. 'You have a good time tonight.'

I lay back down on my pillow, clutching the note that she'd given me. Just before she left, she turned around and gave me a wave. Then she was gone.

47

1969

After Eva went, I couldn't sleep. I kept thinking of Alfie, thoughts of him going round in my head like horses on a carousel. Rather than lie awake in bed, I went for a walk to clear my head. The ward was empty; everyone was at the dance. The clock on the mantelpiece struck ten. Still in my nightdress, I stood by one of the big windows in the corridor. From there I could see the recreation hall. Inside, the lights was on and everyone was singing about drinking a drink to Lily the Pink. It was one of Alfie's favourites. He said I reminded him of 'Jennifer Eccles', one of the girls in the song.

'Why's that?' I asked him, so he sang me the words.

Jennifer Eccles was a girl with lots of freckles, he said, who the boys made fun of.

'That ain't nice!' I says, slapping him on the wrist.

Alfie laughed. A few days later, I got my own back on him, when I learned the rest of the words to the song.

I said to him, 'If I'm Jennifer Freckles, or whatever her name is, then you must be Mr Freers with the sticky-out ears.'

It was my turn to laugh. Alfie wasn't happy. He didn't speak to me for the rest of the day.

Laughter was coming from inside the recreation hall. Through the window, I could see everyone dancing, even

180

the nurses. They used to teach us the actions to the songs –
'Twist And Shout', 'Hokey Cokey' – then, in them later years,
'Y.M.C.A' and 'Chirpy Chirpy Cheep Cheep'. I wished I was
with them, having a good time.

As I watched the dancing, I sang along to 'Lily The Pink'.
When it got to the part of the song where Lily the Pink
dies, and her soul goes to Heaven, a huge bolt of lightning
flashed up in the sky followed by a crash of thunder. The
lights went off in the recreation hall, screams coming from
inside. Frightened by the noises, I ran back to bed, pulling
the covers over my head.

I must've fallen asleep, for I woke up in the middle of the
night to the sound of footsteps and Nurse Cunningham's
voice.

'This one might have an idea,' she says.

'What's its name?' A man's voice this time.

'Wake up, dear.' Nurse Cunningham shook me. 'There's
a gentleman here. He'd like a word with you.'

It was pitch-black. The curtains was drawn. Someone
shone a torch in my face and I squinted into the light.

'What's going on?' I says, still half asleep. 'Who's there?'

'There's been a power cut,' says Nurse Cunningham. 'It's
Eva. She's gone missing.'

'What?' I sat up. 'She was at the dance, though.'

I looked at Eva's bed. It was empty.

'Listen,' says Nurse Cunningham, pointing to the man next
to her. 'This is PC Hunt. He's looking for any information
that might help us find Eva. Do you understand?'

I blinked. Through the torchlight, I could just about make
out a man in a helmet with a moustache.

'I don't know where she is, Nurse.'

PC Hunt says, 'Ask it if Miss Finch mentioned anything
yesterday, before she left.'

'Did Eva say anything to you earlier?' says Nurse Cunningham. 'Were you aware that she was planning on running away?'

'Does it recall anything odd about Miss Finch's behaviour yesterday?' says PC Hunt to Nurse Cunningham.

'Was Eva acting strange?' she says to me.

Why was Nurse Cunningham having to explain everything to me? Did the policeman think I was foreign or something? It's what it sounded like, the way he spoke to me.

'She gave me a letter,' I says, pulling the note out from under the covers.

I handed it to Nurse Cunningham. PC Hunt shone his torch on it. He began reading aloud to Nurse Cunningham what Eva had wrote.

'So this is Margaret, yes?' he says, shining his torch in my face again. Nurse Cunningham nodded. 'Can you ask it . . . her . . . when she received this?'

'When did Eva give you the letter?' says Nurse Cunningham.

'Earlier this evening,' I says. 'Before she went to the dance.'

'And she didn't mention anything about her plans to run away?' says Nurse Cunningham. She crossed her arms.

'No,' I says. 'But I can't believe she'd run away without telling me. Me and Eva, we're best of friends. Something must've happened to her. She would've told me otherwise, I'm sure of it. Maybe she got lost or something. She might still be out there, wandering about.'

'Is there any likelihood of that?' says PC Hunt to Nurse Cunningham. 'Has the patient run away before?'

'Not while she's been at St Mary's, Constable,' says Nurse Cunningham. 'She was in another home previously.'

'What was the name of that home?'

'It's not there anymore. It was in Broadstairs. They shut it down. That's why they transferred her here. We keep her old records in the office, though. You can have a look through them if you like, but to be honest, this is a bit out of character. She was prone to being hysterical at times, but not one for taking risks. With the boys, though . . . Well, that's another matter.'

'What do you mean, with the boys?' said PC Hunt.

'Well, when they first took her in, she was what you used to call "a moral imbecile". I'm going back twenty years, you understand.'

'Meaning she was . . . ?'

'I hardly need to spell it out to you, Constable, do I? At least, I'd rather not in front of the patient.' Nurse Cunningham cleared her throat and lowered her voice. 'Let's just say she liked her men friends.'

'Right,' says PC Hunt. 'And was she normal otherwise?'

'Well, I wouldn't go that far,' says Nurse Cunningham. 'She had what you might call psychological issues.'

'I see. And given Miss Finch's interest in men, is there a possibility that this could be linked to your other disappearance tonight?'

'Very possibly,' says Nurse Cunningham.

'And what's his name?' says PC Hunt, taking a pencil and paper out of his jacket pocket.

'O'Connell,' says Nurse Cunningham. 'Alfred O'Connell.'

48

26 AUGUST 2015

Wayne opens the kitchen cupboard and lifts out two mugs:
the Phil Collins one that I got given last week, and my royal
wedding one. Andrew and Fergie. I know they got divorced,
but I ain't got the heart to chuck it away. He pours milk into
the two mugs – semi-skimmed for him and full-fat for me –
and puts three sugars in mine. He pops a sweetener in his.

'I thought you was off to London today,' I say, taking a
slurp of tea. 'For your birthday.'

'I am,' he says. 'Later. I just wanted to call in and check
you were OK.'

I glance at Wayne's face. He looks worried, not like
someone who is meant to be celebrating their birthday.

'There's cake if you want it,' I say. 'Jamaican ginger. If
I'd known you was coming, I would've put a candle in it.'

'I wanted to talk to you about something, Margaret.'

He sounds serious. My stomach tightens.

'You ain't got another job, have you? Don't tell me you're
leaving?'

He shakes his head, then he asks me if I've thought about
seeing a doctor.

'There ain't nothing wrong with me,' I say. 'Apart from a
few aches and pains.'

He tells me I ain't been myself lately. All this business about Cilla.

'Maybe a doctor can help?'

I know where this conversation is going. It's obvious. Wayne thinks I'm losing my mind. If I ain't careful, they're going to lock me away like they did before. I saw a programme about it on television. They made an old lady answer lots of questions. Some of the questions was quite difficult: they confused her. When she got them wrong, they told her she had a disease in her brain and she would need looking after. Exactly what they did to me when I was seven. All those years wasted because they thought I was mad.

'I ain't going to let it happen again!' I shout.

I push the table away and my mug falls over the edge. There's a smashing sound. Phil Collins' face lies in pieces on the kitchen lino. Both me and Wayne jump to our feet.

'Whoa, what's got into you today, Margaret?' he says. 'This isn't like you.' He picks up the bits of broken mug, dropping them in the bin. 'Listen. If you tell me where you got this, I don't mind popping out and buying you a new one.'

'Rock Bottom . . .'

I've barely finished my sentence before I remember Wayne's birthday present. How could I forget? Leaving him to clear away the mess I've made, I hurry upstairs to my bedroom, where I wrap up the record as best I can, to make it look nice. I tie string around the outside and stick a silver bow, left over from Christmas, on the front. On my way back down the stairs, I grab the birthday card from my handbag, which is hanging over the banister.

Wayne is mopping the floor.

'Happy birthday,' I say, handing him the card and present.

'You shouldn't have,' he says, but I can tell he's pleased.

185

We sit down again at the table together.

'What should I open first?'

I point at the present and Wayne undoes the string, tearing it open.

'*Dick Tracy*? Amazing!' He turns the record over, looking at the back and front cover. 'I've been wanting to buy this one on vinyl for ages. Where did you find it?'

'Same place I got my Phil Collins mug,' I say, relieved that I'd got something right.

'Honestly, this is the best present ever. So thoughtful. Thank you so much, Margaret.'

'Don't forget about the card,' I say, pushing the pink envelope across the kitchen table. Wayne picks it up.

'It's already open,' he says, laughing. 'Did you forget to lick it?'

It's then I realise my mistake. Wayne is holding a lottery ticket and a fifty-pound note in his hand. I must have mixed up the envelopes.

'This is too much,' he says, shaking his head. 'I can't accept fifty quid from you.'

He starts reading the letter inside. It's too late. My heart crumbles in my chest. I'm going to have to tell Wayne my secret.

49

1969

'I don't know quite how to put this, Margaret,' Nurse Fitts said, her voice shaking. 'I'm still in shock myself. Something terrible has happened to Eva.'

My heart was pounding.

'What is it, miss?' I says.

'I'd better read you this,' she says.

She sat me down at a table in the ward and made me a cup of tea. Then she read the newspaper story out loud.

Tuesday 20th May, 1969

The Whitstable Courier

"A Dreadful Tragedy"

Body of mental patient found dead
on Whitstable beach

The body of a woman has been discovered washed up on Whitstable beach. Police have identified the body, declared dead upon arrival, as Eva Finch, 42, a patient at St Mary's Hospital in Canterbury. Miss Finch had been missing since Saturday. It is thought that she, and fellow patient Alfred O'Connell, 37, also reported missing, may have made an attempt to run away together during Saturday's power cut, which affected large parts of the South-East. Both patients had attended a dance held at the hospital earlier that evening.

A rowing boat with the name *Mariana*, belonging to Mr F. J. Walsh, of Middle Wall, Whitstable, has also been reported missing. It is alleged that the pair may have stolen it as a means of furthering their escape.

The woman's body was discovered at 6.30 a.m. on Monday by Tankerton resident Dr Michael Goodge, who had been walking his dogs along the seafront before work. He said, "This is a dreadful tragedy for all concerned."

Mrs Violet Cunningham, Chief Ward Supervisor at St Mary's Hospital, said staff and patients at St Mary's were "shocked and saddened" by the news. She said "Eva was a great contributor to hospital life, helping to supervise the hospital's laundry facilities. She will be greatly missed. We are praying that Alfie gets returned to us, safe and well."

The whereabouts of Mr O'Connell are yet to be discovered. Today, Canterbury Police issued a "Missing Person's Statement" asking for anyone with information on Mr O'Connell's disappearance to come forward. Mr O'Connell is described as approximately six feet tall, with red hair, slightly protruding ears and a Northern Irish accent. He was last seen on Saturday evening, wearing hospital patient's clothing: cap, shirt and slacks in charcoal grey, along with heavy black lace-up boots. All Mr O'Connell's clothing is said to be marked with the name of the hospital and his personal identification number: 367.

Nurse Fitts folded up the paper and asked me how I was feeling about the news. I could barely speak. I was in complete shock. It was impossible to take in – Eva's death and Alfie's vanishing. In my head, I came up with some horrible notions about what they was doing together that night, but I did my best to block them out. Eva was dead and there was a good chance Alfie was, too: I didn't want to think wrongly of either of them. Besides, I didn't know the truth of what happened and there was no use guessing. Eva was my best mate. Hadn't she told me that time and time again? What she wrote on that letter was lovely. She wouldn't have written something like that if she didn't mean it.

And Alfie, he loved me. I know he did, for he said so. He said I made him laugh. OK, I might not have been as pretty as Eva, but that didn't bother him. He'd seen me at my worst, crying, having tantrums, getting angry. But he would just laugh it off, you see, for that was his way. I never saw him get down about stuff for long, not really. He was a good man, my Alfie. I loved him with all my heart.

The following Sunday, they held a memorial service for Eva in the recreation hall. Me and a few of the others helped with the catering. We done turkey roll, egg and cress sandwiches cut into triangles, bowls of crisps, cheese and pineapple on sticks, sausage rolls, Battenberg cake, and a strawberry flan served with a big dollop of Dream Topping. You name it, we done it. All the things Eva would've liked. I remember hoping she'd be able to see the table from Heaven, for we'd put everything on paper plates especially, with doilies, napkins and what have you. And we had fresh flowers, not dried ones. It was ever so nice. Eva would've been happy. We done her proud that morning. I even said that to the nurses. We done Eva proud, I says. And they agreed.

A few days before, Nurse Fitts had suggested I might like

to sing something at the service. When she asked me what song I'd like to do, I thought about it for a while, then I said 'Yesterday' by Cilla Black.

'That sounds like a lovely idea, Margaret,' she says, but Nurse Cunningham piped up, saying it wasn't religious enough. She said it had to have something about Jesus or God in the words.

'What's your favourite hymn?' she says.

'"Onward Christian Soldiers",' I says.

'Bit raucous for a funeral.'

'A bit what?'

'Too lively,' says Nurse Cunningham. 'Pick something else.'

So I chose 'All Things Bright And Beautiful', for in my mind Eva was both of them things.

The weather that day was lovely. Gorgeous sunshine. The girls all wore these old green dresses, with white lace collars, that they made you put on for special occasions. They was tight round the neck and they made you sweat. During the memorial, I sat right at the front of the recreation hall, as if I was family. I suppose in a way I was: who else did the poor girl have?

I spotted Frankie sitting in the row across from me, with the rest of the men. He was crying his eyes out. He had such a soft spot for Eva, bless him. When it was my turn to go on stage and sing my song, I was shaking, but afterwards everyone said I sounded good, even Nurse Cunningham, and she wasn't one to dish out praise.

I only wished Alfie and Eva had been there to see it.

50

Silence. I listen to the clock tick-ticking. Wayne puts the note down on the table.

'Was this meant for me?'

I shake my head, my voice trembling. 'No. No. It was a mistake.'

Wayne looks confused. 'So if *you* didn't write this—'

'How could I? I don't even know what it says.'

Wayne picks up the note again and reads the words out loud.

'"*Dear Margaret, just a little something to make you smile and maybe bring you a bit of luck. I know it must be hard for you. I still haven't quite plucked up the courage to introduce myself, but I will soon, I promise. In the meantime, with love, C x.*"'

I try to swallow, but my throat sticks. I never doubted myself once. I never thought my mind was playing tricks on me. Hearing Wayne say it out loud, though, this is the proof I finally need.

'Who is *C*?' says Wayne.

'*C* is for Cilla.'

Wayne puts down the card and sighs.

'We've had this conversation before, Margaret. Cilla's dead. You remember, yes?'

A sort of anger wells up inside me. Anger mixed with

191

sadness and joy and pain. I'm not angry with Wayne, though. I'm angry about the way they treated me back then, the awful things they made me do because of my disability.

The words explode from my mouth.

'Not that Cilla!' I scream. 'I ain't talking about *that* Cilla. I'm talking about the other Cilla. *My* Cilla.'

51

'C'

*I was down in Whitstable again today, looking at properties.
I'm quite the regular here, what you locals might call a DFL, a
Down From Londoner. Anyway, it got me thinking about the
future, and how much of our future you might want to be a
part of. Obviously, I don't want to put any pressure on you at
this stage. I don't want you to think I'm following you down
here – that isn't my intention. I've always loved the town. I
spent many a summer in the bay when I was younger, so I
have a soft spot for the place. I can't seem to keep away. For
me, there's something special about Whitstable; every time I
try to leave, it pulls me back like the tide. Of course, now that
I've found out you're living here, I have even more reason to
stay, and I'm so looking forward to us being together, if that's
what you want. I know we have a lot of catching up to do,
Margaret, but I can't wait to hold you in my arms, to tell you
how much you are loved.*

52

1969

I'd not been feeling well since Eva's death and Alfie's disappearance. It's hard to explain. I didn't want to see anyone. I just wanted to be by myself all the time. I was tired, really tired. And I was eating a lot more than usual. At dinner, I'd beg the nurses for seconds, even if it was Spam, which I hated. I'd put on a bit of weight, too. Either that, or them dresses in the cupboard had shrunk.

One day Nurse Fitts says to me, 'Margaret, I've been speaking to the doctor and we think you should have a break from working for a couple of months. You've had a big shock. You need to rest.'

'But I like my job,' I says, for it was true.

Working kept me busy; it stopped me thinking about things too much. Nurse Fitts was having none of it, though.

They moved me to a different villa then, a more private one. It's only for a few months, they said, until you're back on your feet again. There was three of us in the villa: me, Betty and Dorothy. It was much smaller than the ward, and because there was fewer of us, we had more space. Each of us had our own room, but we shared a bathroom and a lounge, which had a television. I used to watch a lot of telly then: *Coronation Street*, *The Benny Hill Show*, *The Good Old Days*. It helped me relax, take my mind off everything. *Blue Peter* was my favourite; I'll never forget when the elephant peed on the floor and the zookeeper slipped in it. It made me laugh so much.

One night that summer, the nurses let us stay up late to watch the men landing on the Moon. They treated it as a big occasion. Nurse Fitts came over to the villa especially. She brought us a tray filled with cheese and onion sandwiches and a bottle of dandelion and burdock. Dorothy drank most of it. She was a big girl. Betty was the opposite. She was like a little field mouse. She barely spoke.

'Seven hundred feet to go!' says Nurse Fitts. 'Shall we do a countdown?'

Dorothy burped. 'I *beg* your pardon,' she says, shoving another cheese and onion triangle in her mouth. Poor Betty was hid behind a cushion the whole time.

Five hundred feet!

'How did they get up there?' I says.

'In a rocket,' says Nurse Fitts. 'Look, Betty. They're about to land.'

Betty peeped out from her cushion, then went straight back behind it again.

'I can't believe it,' says Nurse Fitts. 'I've actually got goose bumps.'

She held out her arm, so we could see. We watched Neil Armstrong come down the ladder.

This is one giant leap for mankind, says the man on TV.

'They look like Bill and Ben,' I says, for the astronauts was bobbing up and down like puppets on strings.

Nurse Fitts didn't hear me, though. She was too busy staring at the telly with her mouth open.

'Who would have thought they'd be able to send a man to the Moon?' she says. 'It just goes to show you, girls, anything is possible. *Anything.*'

She leaned across to the table and poured herself another glass of dandelion and burdock. I was surprised she didn't spill it everywhere, for she never took her eyes off the television, not once.

'Can we go to the Moon, miss?' says Dorothy, who was standing by the window, pointing up at the sky. Her mouth was stained purple and she had crumbs down the front of her dress.

'Maybe,' says Nurse Fitts. 'Times are changing. Who knows what they'll think of next. It's exciting, isn't it?'

Betty let out a little whimper.

We stayed up past four in the morning. It was the longest I'd never been to bed in my life. Later I lay on my pillow, looking out of my window. I left my curtains open all night, for it was comforting to think Neil might be up there, looking down on us. Waving at us all in his big white spacesuit.

53

1969

The next day I woke up feeling dreadful. I had a headache, and pain at the bottom of my stomach, like cramp. Every time I went to stand up, I felt dizzy. I had to lie down again. The sun was shining through the window, where I'd left the curtains open. It was blazing hot. I put a pillow over my head to block the light. Someone knocked on the door. It was Nurse Fitts.

'Margaret, are you in there?' she says, opening the door. 'Why weren't you at breakfast with the others this morning?'

I sat up with a jump, knocking my pillow onto the floor. Nurse Fitts was standing at the end of the bed.

'What time is it, miss?'

'Ten o'clock,' she says.

I couldn't believe I'd been in bed that long. Normally I was up by seven.

'I ain't been feeling well,' I says.

Nurse Fitts leaned over, put her hand on my forehead. 'You're a bit hot, actually. Have you been sick?'

I nodded. 'It was earlier on.'

'Wait here,' she says, going off to the kitchen.

She came back a few minutes later with a bucket and a cold flannel. She picked my pillow off the floor, plumped it up and put it back on the bed.

'Lie down,' she says, placing the flannel on my head. 'This'll help cool you down. If you need to be sick again, use the bucket. I'll see if I can get Dr Firmin to come over and have a look at you.'

I was woken a few hours later by the noise of a key turning in the front door of the villa. I heard a man's voice.

'Which room is it?' he says.

'Through here,' says Nurse Fitts, knocking once, then opening my bedroom door. She came up to my bed and knelt over me. She felt my forehead again. 'I've brought Dr Firmin over to see you, Margaret. You remember Margaret, don't you, Doctor?'

'I do indeed,' he says. 'I always fit your spectacles, don't I, Margaret? Now, what appears to be the problem?'

I told Dr Firmin all about the vomiting and the dizziness. He got his telescope-thing out of his bag and listened to my heartbeat, then he took my temperature.

'It's probably just a bit of a stomach upset, Margaret,' he says. 'Give it another day and see how you're feeling then. I doubt it's anything serious.'

Something had been worrying me, though: something Eva said to me once. I hadn't had my period for a while, you see. Usually I was as regular as Big Ben, but for the past few months I hadn't seen any blood when I went to the toilet. I tried to remember the last time I'd had one, but it was hard. So much had happened lately. I'd not been feeling my usual self at all.

Recently I'd seen a film on the telly. *A Taste of Honey*. I'd stayed up late in the villa, watching it on my own one night, after the others was gone to bed. It was about a girl who had a child by this lad. She was only young, a good bit younger than me, but it had got me panicked.

What if I was pregnant with Alfie's baby? Just thinking about it made me feel sick. I kept pushing the thought to the back of my mind. I couldn't be pregnant, though. Me and Alfie was always careful. When we met up on a Sunday, or whatever, Alfie always done this thing before we finished.

'Don't worry, Margaret,' he'd say. 'It's safe.'

It must be something else. If I was expecting . . . Well, it didn't bear thinking about. They'd punish me, put me in that room with Dora again, make my life hell. They didn't treat pregnant girls nice in them days, not if you wasn't married.

How would I know if I was pregnant, though? I daren't ask Dr Firmin about it, for he'd make me tell the nurses. I wished Eva was still alive. She would've known what to do. And Alfie. It'd been two months since he disappeared. Where was he when I needed him?

54

1969

'You look like you're putting on weight, Margaret,' says Nurse Fitts.

It was a sunny day in September. We was walking around the hospital grounds together. The nurses had started doing that with me once or twice a week to stop me sitting around in the villa, moping all the time.

'No I ain't,' I says, pulling my overcoat round me and tightening my scarf.

'I'm not saying it's a bad thing,' she says. 'Quite the opposite. It suits you. You look healthy.'

I wasn't sure what to say to that. Over the past month or so, the sickness had stopped, but my stomach was growing. I'd started wearing bigger dresses. I even kept a spare one under my bed, just in case they ran out and only had small ones. The larger sizes helped me hide my bump.

One night when I was lying in bed, I felt the strangest thing, like someone was tickling the inside of my belly with their finger. It wasn't unpleasant, just odd, as if I had tiny bubbles popping inside me.

'Aren't you hot in that coat, Margaret?' says Nurse Fitts. 'It's mild today.'

I shook my head. 'I'm fine, miss,' I says. 'Honestly.'

We carried on walking into the woods. An old woman with curly white hair came along the path towards us, with a big basket of eggs on her arm. She waved.

'Hello there, Alice,' she says. 'I've not seen you in ages. How are you keeping?'

'I'm well, thanks, Annie,' says Nurse Fitts. 'Yourself?'

'Oh, I'm grand. Busy, but grand. You know how it is.'

'Do you know Margaret?'

The woman looked at me, squinting.

'I don't believe we've met, no.'

Nurse Fitts says to me, 'This is Mrs Dingley. She manages some of our services up at the lodge. Margaret's one of our laundry girls.'

'Oh, really?' says Mrs Dingley. 'Well, I must say, you're doing a wonderful job there, Margaret. I even had Lady Maudsley telephone me herself the other day. She wanted to say how impressed she was that the girls of St Mary's had managed to get Lord Maudsley's smut stains out of her antimacassars. Like new, she said.'

She turned to Nurse Fitts and whispered, 'Here, wasn't it terrible about that girl and the O'Connell boy?'

'Yes, it was a shock for us all,' says Nurse Fitts.

Mrs Dingley shook her head. 'A terrible tragedy,' she says. 'Any word on the police finding him?'

'It's been a few months now,' says Nurse Fitts. 'It's not looking hopeful, is it?'

'It's such a shame,' says Mrs Dingley. 'I know he got into trouble working in the cripple mat shop, but I never had any problems with him myself. He was a good lad.'

So this was Annie Dingley. I felt awkward and embarrassed. I'd been in her house that time, drunk her tea and ate all of her biscuits, and she didn't know. Still, it was good to hear her say nice things about Alfie. He always spoke very highly of Mrs Dingley, too.

Mrs Dingley started talking about Eva then.

'I only met the girl once or twice, but I got the impression—'

Nurse Fitts interrupted her. 'Margaret was good friends with Eva,' she says.

'Oh,' says Miss Dingley, laughing. 'Well, look here, ladies, I'd best be getting on. I've got these eggs to deliver to Mrs Stockle in the village. It was lovely to meet you, Margaret. Keep up the good work.'

She patted Nurse Fitts on the arm.

'Good to see you, Alice,' she says.

After Mrs Dingley was gone, Nurse Fitts says to me, 'Margaret, I wanted to have a chat with you, actually.'

'Chat about what?' I says, tugging at one of the buttons on my coat.

'About how you're feeling, after everything that's happened recently.'

'What do you mean?'

'Only I was having a chat with Dr Firmin the other day—'

'What was you saying about me?'

'Nothing bad, don't worry. We just thought it might be a good idea if you started back in the laundry again. What do you think?'

I said to her I would like that.

She told me she would start me off nice and gently, with one or two shifts a week, to get me back in the swing of it.

'I'll have a chat with Nurse Cunningham this afternoon,' she says. 'We'll look at putting you on the rota. Does that sound OK?'

I nodded, relieved it wasn't something else she'd wanted to talk to me about. For now, at least, my secret was safe.

* * *

It was good to be back in the laundry room, even if it was only once a week. I'd missed being there. The work was boring, but it helped me keep my mind off things. And I had a lot on my mind then, believe me. Over the past few weeks, I'd come to a decision. I was going to keep my baby. It was mine and Alfie's. I wasn't going to let them take it off me, no blooming way. Every night I'd lie in bed talking to it. Sometimes it answered me back with a kick. I told it all about its father, what a lovely man he was. How one day he might come back to St Mary's, to fetch us. How we'd all live together, in a proper house. Just like Grandma's. In a proper street with a park, swings and a corner shop: all them things normal people have. We'd be a family. Me, Alfie and Tickle, for that's what I'd started calling the baby. I'd never had a family, not a real one, so I says to Tickle, 'This will be good for us. Me, you and Alfie, together forever.'

I knew in my heart, though, it wasn't going to happen. People like me, people with learning difficulties, they didn't let us have children, you see. Not back then. Some women, they even stopped them from having babies. They used to give them an operation. I know it, for it happened to Marjorie, a woman in one of the other wards. She got caught out seeing this lad, so they took her away for a few days to a place in London.

'Marjorie, love,' they says to her, 'we're taking you on a little holiday.'

They wasn't, though. They was lying to her.

When she came back, you should've seen her face; it was ever so sad, one of the saddest things I've ever seen. She knew, you see. She knew what they'd done to her. This awful thing, to stop her having children. After that day, she barely said a word. She used to be ever so chatty, Marjorie, but after what happened, she stopped talking. It was like she couldn't bear to speak no more. It was like they'd vanished her tongue.

55

1969

It was coming up to Christmas. I was still living in the villa with Dorothy and Betty, but Nurse Fitts had said they was going to move me back into one of the wards in the new year.

'You're looking much better,' she says.

I was dreading it, though. One of the good things about being in the villa was that it was private. I had my own room in there, so I could get dressed and undressed without anyone seeing. Same with the bathroom. There wasn't loads of people queuing up to get in. Don't ask me how I done it, but so far I'd managed to hide my pregnancy from everyone. It got easier now it was winter. People stopped asking me why I was wearing a coat and scarf. If they did, I just told them I was cold.

It snowed heavy that year. Everything outside was lovely and white. I used to like Christmas at St Mary's. We put up decorations, a big tree with lights, and we helped the nurses hang paper chains from the bars on the windows – strips of old newspapers that we'd painted ourselves. The staff relaxed a bit, too, even Nurse Cunningham, especially after she'd had a few sherries. Every year, she was the judge for the Christmas cake competition. Each of the villas took part. I remember me and Dorothy made a lovely cake with rum and lots of currants. I done the icing and we put a baby Jesus made of green marzipan on the top. We didn't win, we came fifth place. They gave us a tartan ribbon and a satsuma each, as a prize.

On Christmas Eve, the Salvation Army used to pay us a visit. I always looked forward to them, for they brought us presents. They was clothes, mostly. Second-hand ones: bedsocks and bed jackets, pullovers, mittens and what have you. Sometimes you even got chocolate or sweets, but not very often. Dr Firmin would dress as Father Christmas and we would all get in a line to see him, waiting our turn. A few of the nurses would help him hand out the presents. They gave out red parcels for the women and black for the men. The children's parcels was pink and blue. You didn't get to choose, you got what you was given. That year, I got two handkerchiefs and a card.

After they done the presents, the Salvation Army would put on a show for us in the recreation hall. I used to love it, for they played all of the old carols: 'Little Donkey', 'Hark The Herald Angels Sing', 'Silent Night'. I knew all the words. Normally it cheered me up, Christmas, but this year was different. The hymns made me feel sad. When they played 'Have Yourself A Merry Little Christmas', I cried, for it made me think of my two best friends I'd lost. Nurse Fitts must've seen I was upset. She came running over.

'Next year will be better, Margaret,' she says, putting her arm around me. 'I promise.'

'No it won't, miss,' I says.

I was shaking inside my coat. I could barely look her in the eye.

Nurse Fitts squeezed my shoulder. 'It's Christmas. Don't be sad.'

'I can't help it.'

'I know it's no consolation, Margaret, but I lost my father earlier this year. It's hard, isn't it? When you lose someone you love?'

I didn't say nothing. I was thinking of Tickle, all safe and warm inside me, without a clue what was going on.

I don't want to bring you into this place, I thought. *Not here, not to St Mary's. You're better off staying where you are.*

What would Nurse Cunningham do if she knew my secret? She'd go mental.

If she tries to harm you, I'll throttle her with my bare hands.

I remembered what they'd done to poor Marjorie. I had to get us out of there, away from that bloody place, before it was too late. The band started playing 'Away In A Manger'. And that's when I had the idea. The idea of how we might escape St Mary's.

56

1969

Every year the Salvation Army brought a couple of vans. They always parked them in the courtyard outside the recreation hall. From where I was standing, I could see them through the window, their roofs covered in snow. I stuffed my Christmas card and the two handkerchiefs in my pocket, then, checking no one was looking, I sneaked out of one of the side doors to the recreation hall. At the end of the corridor was a fire door which led to the courtyard. Someone had left it open, so I got out easy enough. Snow was coming down thick and fast as I trudged across the courtyard with my head down. When I got to the van, the front doors was locked. The back ones wasn't, though: no one had bothered. I crawled in, closing them quietly behind me. There was loads of stuff in the back: cardboard boxes full of books and leaflets, and instruments. I shuffled to the end on all fours and hid myself behind a few of the boxes. Pulling my coat over my head, I lay there for a moment with my eyes closed, listening to the band. They was playing 'The First Noel'. When they finished, everyone clapped and cheered. Not long after, I heard a few voices outside the van.

'That went all right, I thought,' says one of them.

'Them handicapped kids is lovely, though, ain't they?'

says the other. 'Every year they break my heart. They ain't got tuppence. Almost cried a couple of times. I could feel myself welling up like a right nancy.'

'Makes you realise how lucky we are, Fred. I know I like to have a moan about my own kids and the missus now and again, but those poor little mites . . .'

The door opened and both men climbed into the front of the van.

'You might need to get out for me and give that window a wipe from the outside, Bob. I can't see a bloody thing.'

I felt a big draught of cold air as one of the men got out again. There was a scraping noise.

'Is that better, Fred?'

'Yeah, that should do it, mate.'

The man got back in the van, slamming the door shut.

'God, it's cold tonight, innit?' he says. 'Freeze your bleedin' knob off in this weather. We dropping the van off in Whitstable, then?'

'Yeah,' says the other, starting up the engine. 'Got to leave it in the garage, just off Harbour Street. Only the wife needs it for the morning. They're playing an old people's home in Canterbury. I can give you a lift on to Herne Bay in my own car if you like?'

'Perfect, mate. Perfect. I got my hip flask in my pocket. Fancy a drop of whisky?'

'Go on. Just the one. Seeing as it's Christmas.'

'The season to be jolly.'

Both men laughed then, as the van moved out of the courtyard.

Lying hidden in the back, my head jammed up against the spare tyre, I watched everything flash past: the moon between the tops of the trees, the big iron gate, and the long swirly path that led away from St Mary's. Everything was rushing backwards. I was frightened. Apart from the odd trip into town, I'd not left the hospital in over twenty years. And if it wasn't for the baby, I would've stayed. It sounds terrible, but I'd got used to being there. St Mary's was all I knew.

'Shall we stop off at the Nelson for one?' says one of the men.

'Good plan, mate,' says the other. 'Twist my rubber arm. We've got time. It's only eight o'clock. The missus ain't expecting me back till ten.'

'Famous last words, Bob. Remember last year?'

'How could I forget, Fred? Gave me a right earful. Had the silent treatment all the way through Christmas dinner. Women, eh?'

The two men got out of the van, slamming the doors shut behind them. I lay there, thinking to myself. If I stayed in the van they would find me. It was better if I went now, while I still had a chance. I crawled my way back over the boxes and opened the door. Stepping out onto the street, I closed the door behind me. There was noises coming from the pub, men's voices. It sounded busy. The windows was all steamed up. Next door to the pub was a butcher's shop; a row of turkeys was hanging upside down by their feet. I wrapped my coat around my stomach, put my hood up and carried on walking down the road towards the High Street. Everything seemed so big, so huge. I wasn't used to being outside. At St Mary's, they hardly ever let you go anywhere, and definitely never anywhere on your own. The nurses always came with you. Being alone was frightening.

Snow was still falling. A group of carol singers was outside the Duke of Cumberland. The sound was comforting, so I stopped for a moment to listen to 'O Come All Ye Faithful'. I hid myself away, behind a family: a mum, a dad and two children. A normal family. It made me sad to think that I had no family of my own, because Christmas is a time to get together with everyone. What about those of us who don't have families, though? I turned away and carried on walking.

Further down the road, on the other side of the street, was the parish hall. They had a DJ on that night. He was playing 'Gimme Shelter' by the Rolling Stones. Noise and laughter was coming from inside. I crossed the road, climbing up the steps that led to the main entrance. There was a porch at the top. It was a good hiding place from the wind, so I sat down.

What on earth have I done? I thought. *I ain't got no home to go to, no money. Nothing.*

I was beginning to think it would've been better if I'd stayed at St Mary's. I thought of going to the police station and giving myself up. Then one of the front doors swung open and a woman, all dressed in black, came staggering out. She had long black hair with a fringe, and loads of dark make-up round her eyes, lashes like spiders. She stood staring at me for a long time, swaying back and forth, moving her hips round to the music. She hiccuped, giggled, then slid down on the floor next to me. She took a brown paper bag out of her duffel coat pocket; inside was a green bottle. She unscrewed the top and started drinking, laughing to herself, nodding her head along to the music. She nudged me in the side with her elbow.

'You've got a good heart, hen,' she says. 'I can tell. A pure soul. Not many of us left these days. Would you like a wee swallae?'

I couldn't work out her accent. It was a bit like Alfie's, but different. She passed me the bottle.

'No thank you,' I says. 'I don't drink.'

She looked at me for a moment in shock. Then she says, 'Good for you, hen. Good for you. I'm Lorna, by the way.'

The woman held out her hand for me to shake. She had on black fingerless gloves: even her nails was painted black.

'My friends call me "Lorna Doone", but I'm never doon.' She laughed. 'What's your name?'

This Lorna, she wasn't half speaking funny.

'Margaret,' I says.

'Maggie? Och, really? I had an Auntie Maggie once. Great legs. Superb dancer. Taught me the Gay Gordons when I was knee-high. She's dead now, God rest her soul.'

Lorna took another slug from the bottle.

'Here, what do ye think o' the DJ, then?' she says. 'Ah think he's fan-bloody-tastic!'

'I've not been in,' I says.

'You mean, you've been sat out here by yourself all night? A wee lassie like you? It's freezing, for Christ's sake! You'll catch your death.'

She leaned over and whispered in my ear. Her breath was awful, even worse than Nurse Cunningham's.

'Listen, Maggie,' she says. 'I'm absolutely blootered, so forgive me if I'm acting dafty. I don't mean it.'

I nodded. She was staring at me, her head rocking from side to side.

'You look scared, hen. Are you sure you're OK? Here, have a wee sip o' this. It'll calm you down.'

Lorna handed me the bottle. She was being kind. I could hardly say no. I put my mouth around it and swallowed. It felt like my throat was on fire. I choked.

'What is it?'

'Gin. You mean to tell me you never tried gin?'

I shook my head.

'Och, you haven't lived, hen.'

I handed her back the bottle. She took another sip.

212

'Here,' she says, putting her hand on my leg. 'What ye doin' for Christmas?'

'I ain't that bothered about it, really.'

'No plans, then?'

I didn't answer. My insides was still burning from the gin. Lorna took another swig.

'Are you on your own tonight, hen?' She burped. I nodded. 'Aye? Sure, why don't you come over to my house? I'm on my own, too. We can get plastered. You and me. Woman to woman.'

'Yes,' I says, not quite sure what she was talking about.

'I'm just doon the road. Regent Street. Sounds posh, but it isn't. Do ye wannae head over there now?'

I nodded. What else could I do? I had nowhere to go. I didn't have any other choice.

Lorna screwed the cap on the bottle, putting it back in her duffel coat pocket. She stood up, swaying, then she held out her hand for me. I grabbed it. She pulled me up.

'Take my arm, hen,' she says.

I did as I was told. She smelled of perfume, damp clothes and cigarettes.

We walked down the steps of the parish hall together. Lorna was all over the place. On the way to her house she sang 'Big Spender', hitching up her skirt and doing high kicks. It was just as well the streets was empty, because I was trying my best to hide in case anyone saw me. This Lorna wasn't half drawing attention to herself.

57

1969

'Shite, I dropped my keys,' says Lorna. 'Where did they go?'

We was standing outside Lorna's front door.

'Ah, here they are. No need to panic, hen,' she says, bending over to pick them up. 'You'll have to excuse the mess, Maggie. I'm not the tidiest of lassies.'

Why is she talking about dogs? I thought to myself.

The hallway was dark. There was a big pile of yellow newspapers by the front door. On the way in, one of the papers got caught on Lorna's foot. She kicked it out of the way.

'You see this room on the left,' she says. 'That's ma bedroom.'

She leaned in, flicking on the light.

Lorna's room was a mess. In all of my time living at St Mary's, I'd never seen anything like it. The bed was unmade and there was loads of dirty cups and plates on the floor. It smelled of fried fish. And cat's piss. Everywhere you looked there was paintings. On the wall, on the floor, on the bed. On one shelf was lots of jam jars filled with brushes and dirty water.

'Before you say it, Maggie,' says Lorna, taking off her coat and throwing it on the bed, 'I know what you're thinking. They look like fannies.'

'Fannies?' I says.

'My paintings. I'm putting together an exhibition of my work doon at the community centre. "Natives", it's called.'

'"Natives"?'

'Oysters,' says Lorna. 'These are all paintings of oysters. I do other stuff, too, of course. Street scenes, portraits, you know. You have to. Oysters don't pay the bills.' She pointed at the bed. 'You can put your coat doon there if you want,' she says. 'Then I'll take you through next door and we can have another wee swallae.'

'I'd rather keep my coat on, if you don't mind, Lorna.'

'Suit yourself, hen. I won't be offended. I know it's cold.'

Lorna switched the bedroom light off. I followed her down the hallway, into the next room.

'This is the parlour,' she says, almost tripping over a little black cat as she went in.

It meowed. Lorna swore at it, kicking it out of the way.

The parlour was even messier than the bedroom. There was loads of books and ornaments everywhere. Plants that looked like they needed watering, and a small Christmas tree with a few baubles and a bit of tinsel, but no lights.

'You take a seat, Maggie. I'll put the fire on and then I'll fetch us a few toddies.'

I nodded. Despite the mess, it felt quite nice to be inside with someone taking care of me.

Lorna lit the fire, then went into the scullery. She came back a few minutes later with two mugs, setting them both down on the table.

'Get that doon your gob, Maggie,' she says. 'Good for warming the cockles.'

She chinked her mug against mine.

'Cheers,' she says. 'Nice to meet you, hen.'

I took a sip and nearly died. It was even worse than the

gin. My eyes watered. The black cat rubbed against my ankle, meowing.

'Ignore that one,' says Lorna. 'Furry wee shite. Always wanting food.'

'What's she called?' I says, stroking the little thing on the head, for she was very cute.

I'd always wanted a pet of my own. You wasn't allowed them at St Mary's.

'It's a he,' says Lorna, picking a box of matches off the table. She struck one, lit a candle. 'Mungojerrie. There's another one, Rumpleteazer, but I don't know where she is.'

'Funny names,' I says.

'T. S. Eliot,' says Lorna.

'What?'

'He was a poet,' she says, as if I should know what she was on about. 'Died a few years ago. Wrote a book about cats.'

She took a gulp of her hot toddy, smacking her lips.

'So what were ye doing out on your own tonight?'

I pretended I was too busy looking at the cat to hear her. Lorna laughed.

'Och, you cannae understand me, Maggie, can you? I'm sorry, hen, it's the way I talk. You'll soon get used to it.' She was staring at my hands. 'Ah take it you're not married, then?'

'No,' I says.

'I don't blame you,' she says, jabbing me in the arm with her finger. 'Men are a bunch of fucking bastards, excuse my English. You see my ex, Kenny? He left me last year. For a *man*.'

I nodded. What was she on about?

'Kenny's an artist, too, mind,' she says, tearing the plastic off a packet of cigarettes. 'We're a right queer lot. Eccentric, you might say. You smoke, Maggie?'

I said I didn't.

'Never mind,' she says. 'Not much of a talker, are you, hen? It don't bother me. It's nice to have company on Christmas Eve.'

Lorna ripped the gold foil out of the top of the packet, scrunching it in a ball and throwing it in the ashtray.

'I tell you what, Maggie,' she says, leaning over the candle to light her cigarette. 'Have you ever had your fortune told?'

She blew out a cloud of smoke.

'My fortune?' I says. 'I ain't got any money, if that's what you mean.'

'Let me see your palm. Give it here.'

I looked at her, confused.

'Your hand, hen,' she says. 'The right one.'

I put my hand on the table.

'Other way up,' she says. 'Your *palm*, sweetheart. That's it.'

Lorna took my hand, her cigarette still hanging from her mouth. She spread my fingers out, squinting at my hand.

'Och, hen, you've not had it easy now, have you? Your head and heart line are joined together. You don't see that very often.'

'What do you mean?' I says, trying to work out what she was looking at. What could she see that I couldn't? It just looked like lines and crosses to me.

'Oh, look,' she says. 'See the mark beneath your wee finger? That's a bairn.'

'I ain't never been burned,' I says, trying to move my hand away from the candle flame.

'No, you big dafty.' She laughed. '*Bairn*, not burn. It means baby. You're going to have a baby, Maggie.'

All of a sudden, I felt frightened. How could she tell all that just from looking at my hand? It didn't make sense. Was she a witch or something?

'Oh dear,' she says, the ash on her cigarette growing longer and longer. 'That's sad.'

'What is?' I says, panicked. 'What can you see?'

Lorna took another drag of her cigarette, a bit of ash dropping off the end onto the table.

'You'll never marry,' she says. 'Does that bother you, hen?'

I said it didn't.

Lorna put her cigarette out in the ashtray.

'Someone from your past is coming back, though,' she says.

'Really?' I says.

My heart was beating faster. I knew Alfie wouldn't have left us both like that. He was alive, then. Ain't that what Lorna was telling me?

'Alfie?' I says.

She peered very closely at my hand.

'Och, I cannae see,' she says. 'Too many lines and crosses. I'm not as good as I used to be. You're all right, though. You've got a long life ahead of you. I can tell you're a fighter, hen. These lines go quite deep.'

I began to feel strange. Dizzy.

Lorna downed the rest of her toddy.

'Do you want another drink?'

'No, thank you,' I says, for if I looked up to the ceiling, it felt almost as if the room was spinning, like a cartwheel going round and round and round.

'Bit of a lightweight are ye, hen?' says Lorna. 'That's OK. I'm Scottish. It's in ma genes.'

She went off to the kitchen again. Mungojerrie jumped up on my knee and starting purring. He was doing this funny thing with his paws. Pat pat pat. His claws was digging into me.

Lorna came back in with another drink.

'Oi, you, piss off!' she shouted.

I jumped up straight away. The cat went flying out of the room and I went to run after him. Lorna laughed.

'Not you, Maggie, you daft sod! I meant the cat. Sit back down, hen.'

I did as I was told. Lorna had started rocking back and forth again. When she went to take a seat, she missed the chair, nearly fell on the floor. For the first time, I noticed how red her eyes was. She lit a cigarette and took another drink, spilling some of it on the table.

'You and me, we're having real communication problems tonight, aren't we, hen? I need to teach you some Scottish.'

She drank the rest of her toddy, then let out this awful cry. I watched as she fell forward, banging her head on the table.

'Lorna, love? Are you OK?'

I reached over to take her hand. It felt floppy, like a dead person.

'I'm sorry, Maggie,' she says, sitting up, mumbling into her hands. 'I've had too much to drink. I don't mean to get you doon.'

'That's OK,' I says, not really sure what to do, or whether to call a doctor, for Lorna's eyes was red and sleepy-looking.

'I should probably go to bed,' she says. 'Do you want to stay over, Maggie?'

'Can I?'

Lorna stood up, swaying. She pointed at the couch.

'It's yours if you want it, hen.'

I nodded. 'Thank you, Lorna.'

'I'll get you a blanket,' she says, staggering out to the hallway.

There was a lot of crashing and banging, then some swearing. Everything went quiet. I stood there in the living room for ages, waiting. Lorna never came back. After a while I thought she might have hurt herself or something, so I went to have a look. From the end of the hallway, I could see that her bedroom light was still on, the door wide open. I crept down and looked inside. Lorna was fast asleep on her bed, with Mungojerrie curled at the bottom by her feet, purring. There was a big pile of towels lying on top of an armchair. I crept into the room and grabbed a couple. The smell in there was dreadful. I had to hold my nose, it was making me feel sick.

I sneaked back down the hallway into the living room and made myself a bed on Lorna's couch, putting all the cushions down one end, as pillows, and covering myself with the towels. They didn't look too clean, so I kept my clothes on. The fire was still burning, so I was warm enough. It was only when I lay down that I realised how tired I was. My feet was throbbing from all the walking I done earlier, but at least the spinning in my head had stopped.

'Happy Christmas, Tickle,' I says, my head sinking into the pile of cushions. 'You and me is going to be OK. I promise.'

I wrapped my arms around my stomach, rocking us both to sleep.

58

1969

I woke up to a hissing sound. This awful smell hit me. Lorna was standing by the door with a tiny bottle in her hand, spraying it everywhere. I sat up on the couch, rubbing my eyes. Choking, I picked my glasses up off the floor and put them on.

'Christ, it really stinks in here,' she says. 'I know it's freezing outside, hen, but I'm gonna have to open this window. Sorry. I hope you don't mind?'

There was a gust of cold air.

'Don't bother me,' I says, shivering. 'What's that smell, Lorna?'

'Pagan,' she says. 'My favourite perfume. Helps hide the smoke. I swear by it.' She sniffed at me, screwing up her nose. 'Do you want a wee squirt?' I shook my head. Lorna was looking at me funny. 'Forgive me, hen,' she says. 'It sounds awful, but I cannae remember your name.'

'Margaret,' I says, getting up off the couch. I yawned, stretching my arms.

'Och, Maggie, that's it. Silly me. Well, I don't know about you, Maggie, but I feel absolutely terrible this morning. Shall I fix us both some hair of the dog?'

I looked at her, saying nothing. Was she going to start talking about Lassie again?

Lorna set the bottle of perfume on top of the fireplace and went into the scullery. Mungojerrie followed her in. I watched her opening the fridge. She looked inside, frowning.

'I've got some tomato juice in here. I could make us a Bloody Mary?'

She lifted out a carton, sniffed it. Mungojerrie began rubbing on her ankles, meowing.

'Piss off, you wee shite,' she says, kicking him out of the way. She started coughing really badly then. 'Don't mind me,' she says, bending her head over the sink like she was going to be sick. She hacked something up in her throat and spat. 'Better out than in, I suppose.'

Lorna wiped her mouth with the sleeve of her dressing gown, patting her chest. She went on tiptoe, reached up and got a couple of glasses down from one of the top cupboards. She put them on the sideboard, filling them up with tomato juice, then she poured in something else from a bottle. It looked a bit like water.

'Too cold for ice,' she says, bringing the two drinks into the living room and handing me one. She went over and sat at the table, lit a cigarette.

'Anyway, Happy Christmas.' She raised her glass. 'Cheers, hen. It was nice to meet you.'

'And you, Lorna,' I says, taking a sip. 'Happy Christmas.'

I'd never had tomato juice before. I wasn't sure about the taste, to be honest, but I carried on drinking it anyway. I didn't want to upset Lorna.

'Nice, aren't they?' she says, smiling. 'Good for sorting your head out. One for the road, as they say.'

I nodded, taking another gulp.

'So . . . er . . . M-Martha,' she says. 'Are you seeing your family today? I cannae remember what you said your plans were last night.'

'I ain't got no family,' I says.

'I see.' I noticed she'd drunk half her Bloody Mary already. 'So, where do you live?'

'Canterbury.'

'Oh, that's all right, then. Not too far for you to get home. Only I did'nae want to leave you stranded last night. A bonny wee lass like yourself out on her own.'

'What are you doing today, Lorna?'

'Me? Ah . . . I've got some painting to be getting on with. I might take a walk doon the beach. Collect some shells.'

'You ain't got no family, then?'

Lorna frowned. 'No, no. Not doon here. In Scotland, yes. Also, I've . . . I've . . . arranged to meet a friend for lunch later. She's on her own, too, and . . . uh . . . Yeah . . . So . . .' Lorna looked up at the clock on the mantelpiece. 'Shite, will you look at the time? It's nearly ten! I'm meant to be in the pub in a few hours. Look, it was lovely meeting you, hen. We had a good night, from what I can remember.'

She laughed. A little laugh, like she was embarrassed by something.

'I'll just stay here then, shall I, Lorna?'

'I beg your pardon?' She picked up her glass.

'On the sofa. I can wait here for you if you like. Until you come back.'

'What do you mean? Wait for me?' Lorna downed the rest of her Bloody Mary.

'While you're having lunch. I can look after the cat if you like.'

'Do nae worry about him. He can look after himself.' She stood up, putting her empty glass down on the table. 'God, will you look at the state of this room. I'm going to have to get the brush out.'

'I can do that for you, Lorna. I'm good at cleaning.'

'Yes, well . . . Look here, hen, I've got to go and get ready. Are you OK to see yourself out?'

'But you said last night—'

'Listen . . . Mar—'

'Margaret. My name's Margaret.'

'Yes, of course. Well, Margaret, to be totally honest with you, I do nae have a clue what I said to you last night. I was blootered.'

'Blootered?'

'Drunk. Pissed as a fart. Off my head. I don't mean to be rude, hen, but I'm sober as a bloody judge now and I need to get on with my day. On. My. Own. Do you get me?'

I nodded. 'Yes, Lorna. Thank you for letting me stay. It was very kind of you.'

'That's no problem, hen. Now, have you got everything? All of your belongings, yes?'

'Yes, Lorna. Only—'

'Great, well, in that case, let me just show you the door.'

I got up off the sofa and stood there in the middle of the floor. I didn't want to leave. I had nowhere to go. Lorna pointed towards the living room door.

'The way out's just doon the end of the hallway, yes? Mind the step.'

'OK,' I says, staying where I was. 'Thank you, Lorna.'

'You're not moving very fast, hen. Do you need me to help you?' Lorna grabbed me by both arms. 'Look!' She pushed me into the hallway. 'It's just doon here.' She barged ahead of me and opened the front door. 'Off you go then, hen.' She waited until I was by the entrance, then she shoved me outside. 'Have a good Christmas. You take care now.'

I turned back round to say goodbye, but she slammed the door in my face. I stood there for a minute, not going anywhere; then slowly, I made my way to the end of the path and opened the gate, heading down the road on my own.

59

1969

I was lost. I got right down to the end of the street where Lorna lived and I didn't know where to turn. I looked around to see if anyone was about, anyone who could help me, but the roads was empty. I'd never known such quiet, not like this. I was used to noise, people screaming, nurses telling you to shut up all the time. I walked past houses, rows and rows of them, all squashed together in a line, like the beds at St Mary's. I never thought I'd say it, but I almost wished I was back there, warm under the blankets. My head hurt and my hands was freezing. I could barely move my face. My glasses had steamed up. It was hard to see where I was going. There was lights on in most of the houses. They looked cosy, with Christmas trees in the windows. My feet was aching, so I sat down on a wall in somebody's front garden, the snow soaking into my backside. I pulled my coat round me, shivering.

'It's all right,' I says to Tickle. 'I'm going to look after you.'

My teeth was starting to chatter. I turned to look at the house behind me.

Through the window, a group of children was running around in front of a lovely big fireplace, which had candles and Christmas cards on it. There was two girls, a boy and a baby. I couldn't help staring at them, they looked so happy. Even from outside, you could hear music and laughter. The girls was dancing round the room, holding each other's hands, twirling about in their skirts. The little boy came up to the window, a toy aeroplane in his hand, pretending he was about to crash it into the glass. He stopped doing it when he saw me, then he stuck his tongue out and ran back to the others. The mother came into the living room. She had on a posh dress and oven gloves. I heard her shouting at them to keep the noise down. I got off the wall and started moving on down the road.

I don't how I done it, but I managed to find my way back to the High Street. My stomach was rumbling. I'd not eaten since the day before, and I'd no money to buy food, neither. I cursed myself for not thinking to bring money, but where would I have got it from? I would've had to steal it from one of the nurses' handbags and that ain't right. I don't agree with stealing things. Besides, it was Christmas. All the shops was shut. What use was money to me?

I carried on walking until I came to the parish hall, where I'd met Lorna the night before. I climbed up the steps and sat inside the porch for a bit to get myself warm. I was there a long time. It felt like hours. A few cars went past, but that was it. I didn't see any people, not a soul. They was all in their houses having Christmas dinner, I supposed. I wished I was back at St Mary's having turkey with everyone. They did good food at Christmas, not the usual rubbish. I wondered if anyone had noticed I was missing yet, and then I started panicking. What if they sent the police out to find me? Would I go to prison? Or would they put me back in St Mary's? And poor Tickle . . . What would happen to my baby? I felt sick at the thought. I knew I had to carry on.

I got back on my feet and wandered further down the High Street. The wind was icy that day. It felt like I had tiny bits of glass stuck to my cheeks. I kept on touching my face, then looking at my finger to check I wasn't bleeding. I'd never been so cold in my life.

I came to another lot of houses, just behind the High Street. The lights was on in one of them, so I went up to the front door and knocked. I didn't know what else to do. I was so cold and my mouth was dry with thirst.

A child answered the door. A boy. He had on a paper hat. His smile vanished when he saw me.

'You're not Auntie Doreen,' he says, frowning.

'I know I ain't,' I says. 'But can you help me, please?'

I could barely speak, my mouth was frozen.

'Who is it, Paul?' says a voice from inside.

'Come here, Daddy,' says the boy. He put his thumb in his mouth.

A man came to the door. He was tall with long hair and a beard; he looked a bit like Jesus.

'Please . . . sir,' I says. 'Can you help me?'

The man took one look at me.

'Sorry, mate,' he says. 'I don't want to know you.'

He slammed the door in my face.

I turned and walked away, for what else could I do? Stand there banging on the door until they let me in?

Margaret, I says to myself, *you've got to keep trying. Keep going until you find someone kind enough to give you a glass of water. Maybe a bit of food, if you're lucky.*

I felt even smaller and more vanished than ever. St Mary's might've been horrible, but it wasn't like you was invisible. At least the people there talked to you. People in the outside world, though, they couldn't care less. They didn't give a damn about people like me. The only time they spoke to you was if they was being rude, or calling you names. I hate those words they used to call us. It hurts. When somebody shouts those things at me, it makes me feel like I am nothing.

I carried on walking until I came to a path that led to the beach. The sky was grey and cloudy still, but the snow had stopped. I crunched over the pebbles towards the sea and sat down on one of the wooden fences. The wind was even icier down there. I looked at my fingers; they was beginning to turn blue. I put my hands inside my armpits, to try and keep them warm.

Whitstable beach.

This is where they found Eva's body, I thought. *Drowned.* My eyes filled with tears. I closed them and said a little prayer to God, asking him to keep me and the baby safe. When I looked up, like a miracle, I saw a boat in front of me. It was tied to a post, further up the shore. I jumped off the fence and wandered over. There was nobody about, so I lifted the tarpaulin and climbed inside. I lay down, pulling it over my head. It was cold and uncomfortable in the boat, but I was so very tired and at least I was sheltered from the wind. Curling myself into a ball, I closed my eyes, wondering how on earth I was going to survive.

'What've you got there, you little rascal?'

I heard a woman's voice over the barking. I ain't scared of dogs, not normally, but this one was going mental. A big nose, wet and black, appeared under the tarpaulin, followed by a tongue and a set of sharp teeth. The dog went on barking. I heard crunching on the stones.

'Stop it, Snowy,' says the woman. 'Here, let me put you back on your lead.'

The nose and mouth disappeared.

'There's a good boy,' says the woman. The dog whimpered.

I spoke up. 'Excuse me, miss,' I says from under the tarpaulin. 'Can you help me, please?'

As if by magic, the tarpaulin vanished. Above me I saw only sky and a woman's face, leaning over. She had a woolly hat on, with hair poking out at the sides.

'Good heavens,' she says. 'What on earth are you doing in there?'

60

1969

Her name was Sandra. She was a nice lady. She took me back to her house. It was along the seafront. It was pretty. Blue and white, with a tiny balcony that looked out over the bay. Once we was inside, she put the kettle on, then she went upstairs. She came back down with a blanket, wrapping it around my shoulders to keep me warm.

'Would you like me to run you a bath?' she says.

I thought about this for a moment. My teeth was no longer chattering, but my fingers and feet was still numb with cold.

'Would it be warm, though?' I says. 'The bath.'

'Warm?' Sandra laughed. 'Of course it'll be warm. I do have heating, you know.'

I was about to blurt out about the baths at St Mary's, how cold they was, but I stopped myself.

'Ignore me, Sandra. I'm being silly.'

She smiled. 'It's Sandie,' she says. 'Let's get you in the bath, then, shall we?'

Sandie's bathroom was beautiful. Everything – the sink, the tiles, the floor – was bright white, and it was so quiet and peaceful. There was no shouting or screaming, like at St Mary's. I lay there for ages, up to my neck in foam, listening

231

to the tap dripping, swirling the warm water around with my hands, breathing in the smell of lavender and soap. I stroked my swollen belly, rubbing it lovingly with bubbles. I thought of Tickle, snug as a bug inside me and, just for that moment, I felt safe in my own little world. Just for that moment, I allowed myself to forget about the trouble I was in.

After my bath, I patted myself dry with one of Sandie's fluffy white towels and changed into the clean clothes she had left hanging for me behind the door: a pair of thermal tights and a floaty nightgown covered in little flowers. It felt so nice to be out of the scratchy dress they made me wear at the hospital. It's hard to describe, but the bath had made me feel like a new person almost, softer, and more relaxed.

When I came downstairs, Sandie was cooking in the kitchen. The smell made my tummy grumble with hunger. I offered to help with the preparations, but she told me to relax.

'Take a seat,' she says, pulling a chair out from under the table.

She gave me a cup of tea. I held it in my hands, enjoying the warmth. Like everything in Sandie's house, the cup felt cosy and comforting.

While she stirred a saucepan of gravy, she told me she was on her own for Christmas. Her husband had died recently.

'I don't have many family left,' she says. 'I didn't really feel like celebrating. This year I thought it would just be Snowy and me, so I didn't even bother getting a turkey. We're having roast chicken, though, with all the trimmings. How does that sound?'

I nodded, my mouth watering. I was starving. Snowy came over and put his head on my lap. I started stroking him. He was a lovely big dog. A Dalmatian. Sandie adopted him after her husband died.

'He's company for me,' she says, putting a massive plate in front of me, a plate filled with chicken and roast potatoes and parsnips and carrots and sprouts. I ate it quickly and when she offered me seconds, I said yes, gobbling them down just as fast. Then we had Christmas pudding with brandy butter, coffee and After Eight mints. I felt ever so lucky.

After dinner, Sandie asked me if I wanted to go to the living room and watch some television. I was stuffed, I could hardly move, but I got up and followed her in. The room was cosy, with a rocking chair and a log fire and two dog ornaments either side of it. On one of the walls was a big painting of a fisherman in a boat. We sat down on the sofa together, with Snowy curled up on the floor by our feet.

'It's a shame the Queen's not doing her speech this year,' says Sandie. 'I always look forward to that. Christmas isn't Christmas without the Queen.'

Sandie looked sad. She poured herself another glass of sherry.

'Why ain't she doing a speech, then?' I says, for we always used to watch it at St Mary's.

'I don't know,' says Sandie. 'She gave a written address instead. It's what inspired me to have you over for dinner.'

'What did it say?'

'They read it out on the wireless this morning, just before I took the dog out. She talked about the lonely, the sick and the elderly. She said she hoped that they would all receive warmth and companionship over Christmas. Well, as soon as I saw you lying in that boat on your own, I remembered that. It struck a chord with me, and I just knew I had to help you.'

Sandie looked at me, smiling. We sat there for a bit, just staring at the TV, then she said, 'I do miss him, you know, my Bill. Especially this time of year. He was a kind man. Always so kind.'

I started crying. I don't know if it was the thought of Sandie losing her kind husband, or the fact that I was on my own, or that Alfie was still missing. Everything seemed to come to a head just then.

'Sandie,' I says, 'I don't mean to be rude. You've been ever so nice, but I need to go home. I need to go back to St Mary's. I've made a mistake. I'm lost. I've got no money. I don't know what to do. Can you help me?'

Sandie put her hand on my shoulder.

'Margaret,' she says, 'whatever you've done, I won't judge you. I promise.'

There was something about Sandie. I trusted her. She was kind. The kindest person I'd ever met. She gave me a handkerchief, left me to dry my eyes while she went and made us both another cup of tea.

When she came back, I told her everything.

'Are you sure you want me to phone them, Margaret?' Sandie says. 'Only I don't mind if you want to stay the night.'

'I need to go back,' I says. 'I'm in enough trouble as it is.'

Sandie nodded. She picked up the phone, dialling the number.

'Hello. Is that St Mary's Hospital?' she says, twisting the phone cord with her finger. 'I've got one of your patients staying with me in my home . . . Margaret, yes, that's the one. I found her on the beach about midday. She was lost. I've taken her in and given her some food, she was freezing, poor thing. She seems fine, yes. A little shaken, but that's understandable given the circumstances . . . Mrs Evans. Sandie Evans . . . That's right, Island Wall, Whitstable . . . In a van, I think . . . I know, wasn't it? Yes, that's great. I'll be here. See you then. Thank you. Bye.'

She hung up the phone.

'They're sending someone over at eight to take you home,' she says. She picked up a magazine what was on the floor and sat back down next to me on the sofa. 'Are you sure you're all right?'

'I ain't got much choice, have I?' I says. 'What do you think will happen to me?'

Sandie sighed. 'I don't know. It's hard to say. Listen, love, I hope everything works out for you. I mean that. The baby, too, of course.'

I shrugged. 'What time is it?'

'It's just gone five. You've got a few hours yet.' Sandie pointed at her magazine. '*Cinderella* is on,' she says. 'Shall we watch that? It's been an emotional day. We both need cheering up.'

Sandie got up and switched the channel over. It was the part where the Wicked Stepmother makes Cinderella do all the chores. I didn't say anything to Sandie, but it made me think of Nurse Cunningham – of what she might do when she found out I was pregnant.

I'll know soon enough, I thought. *They'll be coming to get me in a few hours.*

I picked up one of Sandie's cushions from the sofa and held it in my arms, like it was a baby.

61

1969

'How long has it been, Margaret?' says Dr Firmin, after he was done examining me.

'Since May,' I says.

I was lying on his couch, shaking. I pulled my dress back down.

He was writing things in a little book.

'And you never told anyone?' he says.

'No, Doctor. I was too frightened.'

Dr Firmin put his pen down and looked at me.

'You do know how serious this is, Margaret?'

'Yes, Doctor.'

'A woman like you can't possibly have children. You know that, yes? You're fully aware of the implications?' He used such big words. It was hard to follow. I nodded anyway. 'It's far too late for a termination.'

'What's that?'

'An abortion.'

'I don't understand.'

'What I mean is, if we'd known about this earlier, we could've given you an operation. To stop the baby being born.'

'What do you mean, stop?'

'Never mind,' he says. 'It's too late for that now. There's no point even discussing it. I'm going to have a word with Nurse Cunningham. See if she can help us sort out this mess.'

Of course, I'd told Nurse Cunningham everything as soon as I got back to the hospital. I had to. I was ever so nervous about what she might do to me: all the way back in the car, I'd been retching. The driver kept asking if I was OK, if I needed him to stop, so I could be sick. In a funny way, it was a relief to tell them – to get it all out of my system. As soon as I had said the words *I'm pregnant*, I relaxed. Even though Nurse Cunningham was furious with me (in all of my days at St Mary's, I don't think I'd ever seen her so angry, which is saying something), I thought, *that's it. She can say what she likes. I've told her now. Whatever happens, happens. There ain't nothing I can do to stop it.*

I remember sitting in her office, just staring at my feet, while she called me a whore and a slut, and a lot of other words what ain't nice. Not once did she lay a finger on me, though. Not once. She wouldn't have dared, you see. This was because of the baby. She might've been able to shout at me, call me horrible words and what have you, but she couldn't hurt me. *Sticks and stones*, I thought to myself. *Sticks and stones.*

Dr Firmin called Nurse Cunningham back into his office. They was both talking about me as if I wasn't there.

'We can't possibly put her back in the ward, Dr Firmin,' says Nurse Cunningham. 'I don't want any of the other patients getting an inkling of this.'

'Don't you think it might be good for them to find out about it?' he says. 'As a deterrent to this sort of behaviour?'

'Use her as an example, you mean?' says Nurse Cunningham. 'Maybe, Doctor, but later. Much later. Right now, I don't want anyone seeing her in this state. Besides, there are one or two women in the ward who've lost children. I think this will only upset them. There's one in particular who could react quite violently.'

'I see,' says Dr Firmin. 'In that case, what do you propose doing?'

Nurse Cunningham sighed. 'We can put her in a separate villa for now. The baby must be due quite soon, though. She can't possibly have it here. There's a place I know of for women in her predicament. In fact, we've taken in patients from there before. I'm going to call them first thing tomorrow morning and see if they'll have her.'

'What's happening?' I says. 'Where are you putting me? I ain't going to no prison.'

'Prison?' Nurse Cunningham snapped. 'Prison? Why, prison is far too good for a whore like you!'

'Steady on now, Nurse Cunningham,' says Dr Firmin. 'She's expecting a baby. We can't go upsetting her too much.'

'Oh, but she makes me mad, Doctor,' says Nurse Cunningham. 'I always knew something would happen to this one. It's in her blood. And according to her records, her mother was the same. Couldn't keep her legs closed.'

'Oi!' I says. 'Don't you be horrible about my mother. It ain't right! She's dead. You don't speak ill . . .'

Nurse Cunningham smiled. She looked evil.

'I could tell you a few stories about your mother,' she says.

'That's enough now, Nurse!' says Dr Firmin. 'Stop taunting the patient. It's hardly helping matters.'

'God, I've had enough of this place,' says Nurse Cunningham, pulling me off the chair. 'C'mon, you. Let's get you somewhere private.' She dragged me towards the door. 'Just one more year, I keep telling myself,' she says. 'One more year until I can get out of this hellhole. A bloody life sentence, that's what it's been. A bloody life sentence.'

I looked back at Dr Firmin. He nodded at me then, as if to say goodbye.

I spent the night in one of the side rooms. The next morning there was a knock on the door. It was Nurse Fitts. She was carrying a tray.

'I've brought you eggs and bacon,' she says. 'You need to keep your strength up. Don't mention anything to Nurse Cunningham about it, though.'

I sat up in bed, taking the plate from her.

Nurse Fitts sat down on the bed next to me.

'I wish you'd told me sooner, you know,' she says. 'It's all starting to make sense now. That big coat you had on over summer. You should've said something.'

'I thought you'd be angry with me,' I says, tucking into my breakfast.

'Well, I can't say I'm over the moon, Margaret, but these things happen. We could've got you help much sooner.'

'I don't want them to take my baby from me, miss,' I says.

She put her arms around me.

'Things will get better,' she says. 'You might not think so now, but they will.'

'Where am I going, then? I heard Nurse Cunningham say they was going to put me somewhere.'

'There are special places for pregnant women who aren't married.'

'What sort of places?'

'I don't know all the details. I only spoke to Nurse Cunningham very briefly this morning, but you're being sent off to a home for a while. Until you have the baby.'

'A home?' I says. 'What sort of home?'

'It's a place called Lady Oak Lodge.'

Lady Oak Lodge. It sounded ever so grand.

'Is it posh?' I says.

'I wouldn't go that far,' she says.

Nurse Fitts took my empty plate off me, putting it back on the tray.

'It's a home for unmarried mothers in Ramsgate,' she says.

A shiver ran down my spine then. You see, it was the first time I'd ever really thought of myself as a mother.

62

1970

From Ramsgate station, we got a bus to Lady Oak Lodge. You couldn't see it from the road, for it had trees and bushes all around it. You had to go down a lane to get there. Me and Nurse Fitts got a bit lost to begin with. We had to stop an old lady and ask for directions. The lady gave me this awful look and pointed at a large sign with a picture of the baby Jesus and Mary on it.

'Of course, it's not somewhere I'm familiar with myself,' she says.

'Some people can't help themselves, can they?' says Nurse Fitts, after the lady was gone. 'I only asked her for directions. I didn't want her blooming opinions.'

'What do you mean?'

'Never mind, Margaret,' says Nurse Fitts. 'She's not worth worrying about.'

Lady Oak Lodge was nowhere near as big as St Mary's. It looked more like a house. There was a courtyard out the front, with a few cars parked in it. You went in through a porch; all covered with ivy, it was. You had to ring a bell first.

I wasn't expecting a nun to answer the door. This was

241

Sister Hilda. She was a tall lady, even taller than Nurse Fitts. She had glasses round her neck on a chain.

We followed her into a long, dark hallway. It was very clean. The walls and floors was polished wood. Right at the end of the hallway stood a grandfather clock and, next to it, a big staircase, with a red carpet what went all the way up to the top.

Sister Hilda took us into her office, a tall room with high windows. She sat down behind a desk. There was two chairs in front of it. The chairs was from the church. They had that bit at the back what you put the hymn books in.

'Sit,' she says.

There was a big vase of flowers on the desk.

'I like your flowers,' I says.

'Lilies,' she says, frowning at me. 'A symbol of purity.'

She turned to Nurse Fitts then.

'Have you got the necessary documents?'

'Yes, of course, Sister,' says Nurse Fitts, taking an envelope out of her bag and handing it over.

Sister Hilda tore the envelope open. She pulled out the papers, spreading them out on her desk like playing cards. She put her glasses on and started reading.

'So this is Miss Small?' she says, not looking up.

The way she said Miss, it reminded me of the noises snakes make. Missss.

'That's me,' I says.

'I wasn't talking to you,' she snapped. 'I was talking to Nurse Fitts.'

Nurse Fitts says, 'Yes, Sister, that's right. Margaret Small.'

'Well,' says Sister Hilda. 'This is interesting, very interesting indeed. I'm not sure we've had a case quite like this before. Is this a usual occurrence at St Mary's?'

Nurse Fitts was fiddling with the strap on her handbag. Her face was red.

'No, Sister,' she says. 'Of course not. It's never happened before. At least, not to the extent that we've been unable to arrange for the patient to have an . . .'

Nurse Fitts started spelling a word out then, letter by letter. I didn't recognise it at the time, but it began with an A.

A is for Alfie, I remember thinking to myself.

'I see,' says Sister Hilda, coughing. 'And one presumes that, on reflection, you'll be putting measures in place to ensure that nothing like this ever happens again?'

'Oh, yes, Sister,' says Nurse Fitts. 'Naturally. Both sexes are kept entirely separate. We are very strict about that. We—'

'Clearly not strict enough,' says Sister Hilda, looking up from her desk. She took her glasses off. 'Nurse Fitts,' she says, 'I think you need to have a good, hard look at these so-called strict policies of yours. The Devil is a slippery beast. One knows from experience that he will find his way into even the smallest of cracks.'

Who was she calling a devil? I thought. Not me, I hoped.

Nurse Fitts bowed her head. 'Yes, Sister. We're doing all we can. Like I said, this has never happened before and I've been working at St Mary's for over twenty years.'

'Well, make sure it doesn't happen again,' says Sister Hilda. 'As you would expect, the adoptive parents who use our facility have certain standards of quality. It's one reason why we keep the mothers with us for six weeks after the birth.'

'I'm not following you,' says Nurse Fitts. 'What do you mean by "quality"?'

'Put it this way, dear,' says Sister Hilda, stroking the leaves of the lily plant with her fingers. 'One can ignore a mother's immoral tendencies. These are not things that a child tends to inherit. However, certain genetic defects, handicaps . . .'

243

'I see,' says Nurse Fitts.

Sister Hilda cleared her throat. 'It's the baby's welfare that concerns me,' she says. 'To put it rather bluntly, Nurse Fitts, no one wants to adopt a handicapped child. Indeed, there's a fair chance that Miss . . .' She stopped, as if she had forgotten my name.

'Small,' I says. 'Margaret Small.'

Sister Hilda glared at me, then continued. 'There is, of course, a good chance that Miss Small's baby will turn out to be perfectly normal, in which case, finding parents shouldn't be a problem. We have a very long waiting list for normal, healthy children. If, on the other hand, the baby should develop the same defects as the mother, then we'll need to look at putting it into an orphanage – or indeed, depending on the severity of the handicap, an institution like St Mary's.'

Sister Hilda was talking too fast for me to take it all in. I wanted to ask Nurse Fitts what she was going on about, but I felt like I wasn't allowed to speak. Every time I tried to say something, she gave me a look, or told me to be quiet.

Eventually Nurse Fitts stood up to leave.

'Goodbye, Margaret,' she says, patting me on the shoulder. 'Good luck with everything. I'll see you in a few months' time.'

Sister Hilda told me to stay where I was. They left me on my own. I sat on the chair, staring at the white lilies, wondering what I was doing here and what on earth they was going to do to me next.

Sister Hilda told me to pick up my case and follow her. We walked down a long hallway, then started climbing all the way up the big staircase with the red carpet. It took me a while to get to the top. Sister Hilda kept having to stop and wait for me to catch up. She had a big set of keys in her hand. She kept swinging them back and forth.

My room was on the top floor, right at the end of a long corridor. There was no windows in the corridor, just lamps on the walls, all the way down. Only a few of them was working.

Sister Hilda turned the key in the lock. She pushed the door open. The room was tiny, with two beds and a tall, dark wardrobe. The beds had metal bars at the end and there was crosses above both of them. If you was lying on your pillow at night and you looked up, you would see Jesus hanging there, wearing his crown of thorns. There was a small window with grubby red curtains. On one of the walls, between the two beds, was a framed picture: words, sewn in different colours of the rainbow. They looked quite pretty. I asked Sister Hilda if she would read it aloud to me.

'"O God thou knowest my foolishness; and my sins are not hid from thee." I suggest you spend this time alone in prayer,' she says.

She left me alone then, closing the door behind her.

63

1970

I'd only been in the room an hour or so before there was a knock on the door. I went to answer it. It was Sister Hilda.

'This is Joyce,' she says, pointing to the black woman stood behind her with a suitcase. 'She's going to be sharing a room with you.'

Joyce looked at me and smiled.

'Hello,' she says. She had on a yellow dress with a matching hat and navy stockings.

'Hello,' I says. 'My name's Margaret.'

Sister Hilda says, 'Leave your suitcase on the bed, Joyce. You can unpack it later. Now, if you'd both like to come with me, I'll give you a short tour of the home and let you know exactly what is expected of you. You will find that we run a very tight ship here at Lady Oak Lodge.'

We followed her back down the corridor. When we got to the top of the steps what we'd come up earlier, she told us to stop.

'This is the main staircase,' she says. 'You'll need to clean it every morning. And when I say clean, that means getting down on your hands and knees and scrubbing it hard with soap, a cloth and a boiling hot bucket of water. Once a week, on Sunday, you will polish it top to bottom with Blue Steel. Understood?'

I nodded. Joyce looked at me, rolling her eyes. Sister Hilda rubbed her finger along the banister.

'This will need polishing daily.'

Joyce let out this big booming laugh.

'You are joking, Sister?' she says. 'Look at the size of me. How on earth is a woman like me meant to get up and down these stairs on my hands and knees?'

Sister Hilda was furious. 'I fail to see what you find so amusing, Miss Campbell. Unless it so happens that you are possessed and what I am in fact hearing is the Devil's laughter?'

Joyce's mouth fell wide open with shock.

'Stair cleaning must be completed by nine a.m., before the arrival of any visitors,' says Sister Hilda. 'You are both forbidden to access the main stairs after that time, but you may use the servants' stairwell at the back of the building. Is everything clear so far?'

'Yes, Sister,' I says. 'I used to do the cleaning at St Mary's, too, you know. I was very good at it.'

'That's nice, dear,' says Sister Hilda.

Joyce nudged me. 'You like cleaning?' she says. 'Oh my days. Are you mad?' She shook her head, let out another big laugh.

Sister Hilda told her to be quiet.

Sister Hilda took us into the recreation room. There was two women sat in the middle of a long table, watching *Top of the Pops* and chatting. The singer Mary Hopkin was on.

'I frigging love this song,' says one of the women. She was a skinny blonde with bobbed hair.

She stood up and took two cigarettes out of a packet – started wafting them about, like she was conducting a choir. She was laughing to herself, waving her arms like a windmill, going 'La la la la, la-la, la la la la, la-la'.

247

She sat down, giving one of the cigarettes to the other lady.

'God, I'm knackered,' she says. She put her feet up on the table. 'Those were the days, right, Martha?'

'They weren't half, Paul,' says the other one, putting the cigarette in her mouth. 'Look at us now. Ruined, we are.'

Apart from her bump, this one was skinny, too. She had dark curly hair and freckles. Both women was laughing. They lit up their cigarettes and started singing along to the music again. They was being ever so rowdy. Sister Hilda marched up to the television and switched it off. Pauline muttered something under her breath. Martha stuck her two fingers up at Sister Hilda behind her back. I was shocked. I'd not seen women behaving like that before. Like men, almost.

'Ladies,' says Sister Hilda, 'I'd like you to meet Joyce and Margaret. They're staying with us for a few months.'

Martha looked at Pauline. She pulled a face, pushing her bottom lip out with her tongue. Pauline burst out laughing. I felt a churning in my stomach and my cheeks was hot. I looked at Joyce. She was staring down at her feet, like she was embarrassed.

After Sister Hilda had left the room, Joyce and me both pulled a chair out from the end of the table and sat down.

'Hello,' I says. 'I'm Margaret. This nice lady next to me here is Joyce.'

Joyce didn't say nothing. She looked uncomfortable. The two women was sniggering.

'I see,' says Martha. She looked at Pauline. They both burst out laughing.

Pauline says, 'I'm ever so sorry about my friend. She don't get out much.'

She poked Martha in the ribs. Martha squealed.

Joyce banged her hand on the table.

'Here!' she says. 'What's so funny, then? Are you laughing at the colour of my skin?'

The women went quiet.

Martha says, 'What are you talking about, darlin'? Of course not! I love coloured people. My last two boyfriends were coloured.'

'What is so funny, then?' says Joyce. 'Why are you laughing? Tell me.'

'Private joke,' says Pauline, taking a puff of her cigarette. 'You won't get it.'

Martha leaned over the table. She flicked her cigarette in the ashtray.

'It's Joy they call you, innit?' she says. 'Listen, Joy, we ain't racists. Are we, Paul?'

Pauline shook her head. She blew out a big cloud of smoke, coughing.

'Far from it,' says Martha. 'I mean, if you ask me, coloured people make the best music. In fact, I was saying that to you just the other day, weren't I, Paul? I said to you, didn't I? I said coloured people make the best music.'

'I thought you said lovers,' Pauline says, grinning.

'Oi!' says Martha. 'Give it a rest, you! Well, that and all. Goes without saying. Once you've had black . . .'

Martha smiled. She ran her tongue around her lips, slowly.

'Ain't that right, Joy?' she says, winking. 'I bet you've got a few stories to tell.'

The two women laughed again. Joyce crossed her arms, putting them on her belly.

'It's Joyce,' she says. 'And he was white, actually.'

The room went quiet.

'So what's it like in this place, then?' I says.

249

Pauline and Martha looked at each other. Martha opened her eyes wide.

'You really want to know?' she says.

'Bloody awful,' says Pauline. 'The nuns make you get down on your knees and say prayers first thing every morning. "Repent! Repent!" they say. Then you got to scrub floors. If that weren't bad enough, twice a day, on a Sunday, we've got to line up in a big crocodile and they parade us all down through the village to church.'

'They treat us like bloody lepers,' says Martha. 'I said to Paul, they might as well give us bells to ring. "The home for naughty girls", they call us. They make us sit at the back of the church. We're not allowed in the pews up front. Like bloody lepers.'

'Why do they do that?' I says.

'Why?' Martha says. She took one look at me and burst out laughing.

'Sorry, I don't mean to be rude to you, love. I was just thinking about something Pauline said earlier, weren't I, Paul?'

'How the hell am I supposed to know what you're thinking, Mart?' says Pauline.

I saw her smirk at something. She covered her mouth with her hand.

Martha says, 'It's because they don't . . . They don't . . .'

She couldn't get the words out. She was laughing too much.

Joyce dragged her chair out and stood up.

'I don't know about you, Margaret,' she says, 'but I'm tired and I've got my unpacking to do. I'm going to bed. Are you coming?'

'Yes, Joyce,' I says. I got up and pushed my chair back. 'It was nice to meet you, Martha. And you, Pauline.'

They was both still sniggering.

On the way up the staircase, Joyce grabbed me by the arm.

'What a pair of bitches they are,' she whispered.

'Who?' I says.

'Who do you think? Those two idiot girls we just met.'

'Martha and Pauline, you mean?'

We was near the top of the stairs. Joyce was a few steps behind me. She was out of breath, huffing and puffing.

'Never trust a skinny woman,' she says. 'That's what my father always told me. Those two are trouble, you mark my words.'

64

1970

Joyce was right about Martha and Pauline. They was bullies. The whole time I was at Lady Oak Lodge, they tormented me. They used to play tricks. They made fun of me constantly.

'Margaret,' Martha would say, when we was on stairs together, cleaning. 'Can you do me a favour and go and ask Pauline for a long weight?'

'What's a long weight?' I'd say.

'Ask Pauline, she'll tell you.'

So off I'd run to find Pauline.

'Pauline,' I'd say, 'Martha sent me to ask you for a long weight.'

Pauline would snigger. 'In that case, why don't you *wait* here for a bit longer then, Margaret?' she'd say.

Then she'd leave me standing there on my own. When they saw me later, they'd both burst out laughing. Another time, they sent me to Sister Hilda to fetch someone called Annette Cloth.

'Who's Annette Cloth?' I says.

'Ask Sister Hilda,' says Pauline. 'She knows her.'

'A net cloth, dear?' says Sister Hilda. 'I think someone is pulling your leg.'

* * *

'Don't let it upset you, Margaret,' says Joyce. 'Those two aren't worth it. You are much better than them.'

We was in our room one night. It was February time, so me and Joyce had been living together for over a month. We was both due to give birth any day now.

Joyce was lying on top of the bed, reading her Bible. I'd been crying for the past half an hour. Earlier, in church, I'd overheard Martha saying to Pauline that I wasn't right in the head. I'd seen her do that face again – where she pushed her bottom lip out with her tongue.

'I bet her baby's not going to be right in the head either,' she'd said.

Joyce says to me, 'It is women like Martha and Pauline who are the ones with the problem, Margaret – not you. Remember, it is always better to be kind than to be smart. Not that either of those two are smart. They are silly girls. They give women like us a bad name.'

'How come you ended up in here, Joyce?'

Joyce put down her Bible and stared out of the window.

'I fell in love,' she says.

'Who was you in love with?'

'The wrong man, clearly.' Joyce sighed. 'He was a pilot in the RAF. I met him in the local park, on my way home from church. It was a hot summer's night, hot for this country, you know? I was wearing a gold dress, swishing the hem back and forth, singing to myself. He was out walking his dog. He stopped me on the path. He said I was the most beautiful woman he had ever laid eyes on. When I told him my name, he said, "Joyce, you are a goddess."' Joyce laughed. 'No man had ever called me a goddess before. He asked me if I wanted to go for cake in the cafe next to the lido. So of course, I said yes. After that day, we met up every Wednesday afternoon. We used to go back to my place. It wasn't until a few months later, when I told him I was pregnant with his baby, that I learned about his wife.'

'He was married?'

Joyce nodded. 'I was very upset when I found out, but with God's help I managed to turn my anger into forgiveness. I have not seen the man or spoken to him since.'

She picked up her Bible again.

'I miss my country,' she says.

'Where are you from?' I says.

'Barbados,' says Joyce. 'I want to go back there one day. It's cold here. And grey. Your buildings are too close together. I find it hard to breathe sometimes.'

I liked Joyce. She was a nice lady. She made me feel welcome. I told her all about Alfie that night, about our relationship, and his vanishing. How I hoped that one day I might find him again.

'You never know, Margaret,' says Joyce. 'The Lord works in mysterious ways.'

Just then, I remembered what Lorna had said.

Someone from your past is coming back.

I opened my mouth to tell Joyce about it, but it was getting late and I was exhausted. I used to get so, so tired in them days.

Joyce went back to reading her Bible. Yawning, I put my head down on the pillow and fell fast asleep.

65

1970

The day my waters broke, I was on the main staircase at Lady Oak Lodge. It was just after breakfast and prayers. Joyce and me was on our hands and knees, sweeping up and down the stair carpet.

Joyce says, 'Cleaning this old building is like purgatory. Always filthy. Look at this dust!'

Martha was busy polishing the banister. She had a cigarette hanging from her mouth.

'Oh, stop moaning, Joy,' she says. 'Cleaning's good for you! Keeps you strong. Pauline swears by it. She said it definitely helped her labour. She said to me, "By the end of it, Martha, my muscles were so supple, the baby just popped out. Like a cork."'

'What rubbish you talk, woman,' says Joyce. 'I don't believe a word of it. It can't be good for any girl, working when she is heavily pregnant.'

Those two was always at each other's throats.

'Look at my feet,' says Joyce. 'They are like balloons.'

Martha says, 'Well, to be fair to our Paul, she was pretty slim to begin with. It's not as if she was carrying a load of extra weight.'

She looked at Joyce.

'Like a sparrow,' says Joyce, tutting. She put her brush down and leaned against the banister. 'It's not natural for a woman to eat so little. A baby needs feeding. I used to see Pauline at mealtimes. She goes pick, pick, pick, like a little bird. Then she lights up a cigarette. "Help me, Lord Jesus," I say to myself. "Will you please rescue me from all of these terrible mothers?"'

Martha flicked ash onto the stairs.

'Do you mind?' Joyce says. 'We have spent the past half hour sweeping this staircase, and now you're making it dirty again.'

'Oh, give it a rest, you lazy cow,' Martha snapped. 'What do you mean, you've spent the past half hour cleaning? I've been watching you the whole time, for Christ's sake. You've been sat on your fat arse all morning.'

Just then I noticed a popping sound. Something warm was trickling down my leg. I had a strange clenching feeling in my stomach, like someone was wringing out a wet cloth.

'Joyce!' I screamed. 'Joyce! Something's the matter with me. Something ain't right!'

Joyce hadn't heard me, for they was both still arguing.

Martha says, 'Admit it, Joyce. You've done sweet Fanny Adams today. Poor Margaret here's been doing most of the work for you.'

'How dare you!' says Joyce, picking up her brush and banging it on a stair. 'Why, I have never met such an arrogant woman in my whole life.'

'You mean to say you never looked in a mirror before?' says Martha. 'Mind you, if I looked like you, I don't think I would either, love.'

'You're a very wicked girl,' says Joyce. 'No wonder you ended up in the state you're in.'

Martha let out this laugh. 'Pot calling the kettle black!'

she shrieked. 'Who are you to be lecturing me about morals? Like I said, you need to take a good look in the mirror. Bloody cheek!'

I stared down at my legs. I had water coming out of me – tiny drops of it on the stairs. I was frightened. My stomach hurt. Oh, the pain of it!

'Joyce!' I yelled. 'Joyce!'

Joyce knew what had happened straight away.

'Good heavens,' she says. 'Martha! Martha, go get help. Quick now! Margaret is going into labour!'

'Fuck!' says Martha, stamping out her cigarette on the floor.

She threw down her duster and ran downstairs to the end of the hallway. She was banging loudly on Sister Hilda's door with her fists.

'What on earth is the matter, dear?' says Sister Hilda, poking her head around the door.

She looked up at where I was sat, and frowned. Joyce had her arm round me. She was telling me to take deep breaths.

'I'll call for an ambulance,' says Sister Hilda. 'But for heaven's sake, get her off the visitors' staircase. Immediately.'

'Where are we meant to put her, though?' says Martha.

'I'll tell the ambulancemen to park at the back. You can carry her out via the service stairs.'

'You are joking, aren't you, Sister?' Martha says. 'Can't we just bring her out the main entrance?'

'Don't be so ridiculous,' says Sister Hilda. 'We can't go parading fallen women via the visitors' entrance. What kind of impression does that give of the Lodge? Now do as I say. Take her down the service stairs. Quick.'

The service stairs, or the servants' passage, as it was some-times called, was through a small door at the top of the main staircase. Joyce and Martha helped me up off the step. They walked me back up towards the top landing. I was doubled over, holding my stomach, breathing slowly, just like Joyce had told me to do.

'This is bloody ridiculous,' says Martha. 'Why can't the ambulancemen just pick her up from the front entrance?'

Joyce didn't answer. She wasn't speaking to her.

When we got to the top, Joyce opened the door what led to the service stairs. I was in a lot of pain now.

'I don't know how we're going to manage this,' says Martha. 'There's no carpets on them stairs for a start. Look how slippery that floor is!'

They took an arm each, supporting me. Joyce let out this big groan. The passageway was too narrow for all of us.

'I'll go backwards down the stairs, then, shall I?' said Martha. 'I mean, it's not as if I might slip and fall or anything.'

Joyce scowled. 'I'm saying nothing,' she says.

'That makes a change,' says Martha.

Both came with me down the staircase. It was very dark. Martha was right, though. It was dangerous. What if one of them fell over? All three of us would've gone tumbling down the stairs, with Joyce landing on top.

It took us about five minutes to get to the bottom. Joyce had my hand. I put my other hand on Martha's shoulder for support. Martha was cursing all of the way down. Sister Hilda was there to meet us at the other side.

The ambulancemen was already waiting to take me to hospital.

66

'You had a baby? I can't believe I didn't know about this.'

We're still in the kitchen. Outside the sky has turned grey and the tree branches are starting to look bare. The cup of tea, what I've been cradling for the past hour, has gone stone cold. The clock is ticking. Wayne whispers, as if someone might be listening in, but there is only the two of us.

'A baby girl.' I push my mug away in frustration, the hurt balling up in my stomach. 'I named her Cilla.'

Wayne rubs his eyes. 'I get it now. All this grieving was to do with baby Cilla, not Cilla Black. Her death must have triggered something in you. Memories.'

'It was a long time ago. I tried to block it out. What happened, you know?'

Wayne nods, as if he understands, but I can tell he's waiting for me to continue with my story. It's a story I've gone over in my head so many times. For the days after I gave birth to Cilla really was the best and worst of times. If I'd had the chance to do things differently, I would've done, but what choice did a woman like me have back then? It wasn't like I could refuse to hand you over. It wasn't like I had any support. There was nowhere safe for me to run away to. Like I said, I had no choice.

Wayne looks at me across the table. He's waiting for me to speak.

'So you'll want to know what happened to the baby, then?'

My glasses are dirty. I take them off and give them a rub with the sleeve of my cardigan, putting them back on again.

'Give me a minute. I'm getting to that part.'

67

1970

Cilla Eva Small was born on 17 February 1970. She was a gorgeous little thing with red hair and sticky-out ears, just like Alfie would've looked if he was a girl. I was only in the hospital for a week, then they moved me back to Lady Oak Lodge.

In them days, it was normal for the mother to stay with the baby for a couple of months after the birth, to feed it and that. One of the midwives at Lady Oak Lodge said I wasn't allowed to look after Cilla, though.

'She ain't capable,' she says. Joyce, who'd had her baby a few days after mine, argued with them.

'What do you mean, she's not capable?' she says. 'Of course she's capable. She's the child's mother, for goodness' sake. She should be allowed to feed her own baby.'

Joyce told them if I had any problems, that she would help me.

So, in the end, the midwife says, 'All right, then, we'll let her feed it.'

It was kind of Joyce to do that. She helped me, you see. It was all I needed, really: a bit of support.

Joyce had a little boy. Ernst, she called him. He was beautiful. Heavy, though: eight pounds and twelve ounces.

I remember Martha saying to me one day, 'He must take after his mother, then.'

After we had the babies, they moved me and Joyce out of our room into the main maternity ward. There was about ten of us in there. We had beds next to each other. Joyce showed me how to breastfeed so it didn't hurt. It was difficult at first, but Joyce was patient with me, supporting me through it all. We done that for the first few weeks, then the midwife says, 'You need to stop breastfeeding now.'

They taught us how to squeeze our milk into a bottle then, using a pump. Once you learned how to do that, you wasn't allowed to breastfeed no more. You used the bottle instead. Joyce told me they only done it so you didn't get too fond of the baby.

Even so, them days and weeks after the birth was the happiest of my life. Cilla was mine, you see. I was allowed to be with her. My baby.

They kept all the little ones in the nursery. It was downstairs, right below the ward. There was a big glass window outside, so you could see in. Each morning I'd wake up excited. I'd get Joyce and we'd rush to put our gowns on. Then we'd run down to see Ernst and Cilla. The babies was in a row of tiny cots. All of the mothers used to sit around with their babies and chat while they was feeding or cuddling them. Me and Joyce spent a lot of time in there.

They had a couple of beds in the nursery, too. Two of the mothers used to sleep in them at night, to keep an eye on things. Martha stayed in one of them beds for a while. Pauline was in the other. If your baby woke up in the middle of the night and needed feeding, they would come up to the ward and let you know.

Pauline and Martha both had little boys. They ended up keeping them. Pauline's fella came up the Lodge one day to see her. He told her he'd made a terrible mistake. He said he loved her; that he wanted to do the right thing by her. They was going to get married, I think.

Martha, she took her baby home with her, for her parents decided it was all right. We'll help you look after it, they said. She called him Paul. After her best mate Pauline, she said. And Paul McCartney: her future husband.

Me and Joyce ended up staying at Lady Oak Lodge longer than most women. They kept me in because of my disabilities.

They says, 'We need you to stay and look after the baby for a while.'

I found out later that they only done that to make sure Cilla was normal before they put her up for adoption. Ain't that terrible? At the time I didn't mind. I was over the moon, actually. It meant I got to spend more time with my baby. It was more than most of them got.

Joyce had a terrible time of it, though. She couldn't find anyone to adopt little Ernst. It was partly because he was mixed-race, you see. Also, most of the parents what came there wanted to adopt girls. They thought boys was trouble. I remember Joyce sitting up in bed one night. She had tears in her eyes.

She says to me, 'I don't know what I'm going to do, Margaret. Nobody wants my boy. My parents won't accept him. What happens if I can't find a home for Ernst? I don't want him ending up an orphan.'

I hardly knew what to say.

In the end, I never did find out what happened to Joyce and baby Ernst, for I left Lady Oak Lodge before them. A social worker came to see me one afternoon.

She says, 'Margaret, the doctor has had a proper look at the baby and he thinks she's perfectly healthy, so we can put her up for adoption now.'

I always knew that day would come. In a way, I'd been preparing myself for it all along. At least, I thought I had. The day they made me give Cilla away was awful, though – much worse than I could ever have imagined.

It was April, not long after my birthday. I was told I needed to take Cilla on a train to London. There was a family who wanted to adopt her. One of the Sisters came with me. I cried the whole way there. It was the worst day of my life. We got off the train, near where the adoption agency was based. London was so big. It was frightening. At the station, there was loads of people, pushing and shoving. I remember holding on tightly to Cilla, in case someone knocked her out of my arms.

When I got to the agency, it was just this office with a row of chairs, so I sat down. Sister sat next to me. She got a ball of wool out of her bag and started knitting a scarf. We waited ages. Cilla was as good as gold, though. She slept the whole time. Not a peep out of her. Then this woman came out in a skirt and jacket. Prim and proper, she was.

'Name?' she says.

I tried to speak, but no words came. I couldn't bring myself to look at her face, neither, so I just stared down at her shoes. They was grey. Grey high heels. I squirmed in my seat, for I realised now she'd come to take my baby. I realised now was the last time I'd get to hold Cilla.

Sister put her knitting down on her lap. She nudged me in the side with her bony elbow.

'Aren't you going to answer the lady?' she says, tutting.

I swallowed, gave her my name. The woman in the grey high heels wrote it down in a book.

'What's the baby's name?' she says.

'Cilla Eva . . . Small.'

264

As I said the words, I looked down at the tiny hand gripping my finger. Cilla was asleep. She didn't even know what was happening. I wished I was as calm as her, but how could I be when it felt like I was being made to let go of all the love in the world?

'Follow me,' says the woman.

I stayed where I was, rocking Cilla back and forth in the chair. I kept my head down, listened to her high heels clip-clopping away, hoping if I ignored her, she would vanish. When I looked up, she was standing behind a counter.

'Bring her here,' she says.

I stood up, walked slowly towards her, my baby in my arms. Every bone in my body wanted to turn away, to turn back.

At the counter, the woman took Cilla off me. I watched as she carried her into another room. She left me standing there for a few minutes, and when she came back, she was empty-handed.

'You can go now,' she says.

That was it. The last time I saw my baby. It was just like handing a bag of clothes over in the laundry room.

68

'C'

When I first saw you, I wasn't sure we'd have a lot in common. I worried we wouldn't have much to talk about, that we'd struggle for conversation, but I'm over that now. It was just me being silly.

I'm really looking forward to meeting you, Margaret. I was nervous at first, but only because I was being cautious. I know it's going to be emotional for us both, but I think you and I are going to cope just fine.

69

28 September 2015

The woman from the adoption agency is called Carol. Wayne helped me get in touch with her. He spent a lot of time looking things up on the computer. It took a few weeks for them to get back to me; at one point, I wanted to give up. I'd had enough, but the thought of seeing Cilla again kept me going.

The adoption agency is in a place called Liverpool Street in London. Wayne has driven me here. It felt like the longest car journey ever, even though it only took a few hours.

London is busy today, like Whitstable in the summer, only a hundred times worse. There's no way I'd be able to find my way around on my own, so I'm glad Wayne is with me. He's arranged for us to meet Carol in one of the cafes in the train station. When we get there, she's already waiting for us. She's a nice lady and I like her voice. It's kind and caring. She reminds me a bit of Cilla, the friendly way she speaks to people. Wayne goes to the counter to order a round of teas, leaving me and Carol on our own.

'I've got a few documents to share with you,' says Carol.

She takes a big brown envelope from her handbag and puts it on the table.

'I can't read,' I say quickly. 'You're going to have to read them for me.'

Carol smiles and takes a few pieces of paper from the envelope. They look old: yellow and creased at the corners. I feel like I'm about to be sick.

'Some of the language they use in these official records is very old-fashioned,' she says. 'I hope it doesn't upset you.'

'It's fine,' I say, folding my arms against my chest. 'Won't be anything I ain't heard before.'

'Right, then.' Carol puts on her reading glasses. 'Let's see what reason they've given for the adoption. "Mother does not have the mental capacity to raise a child."' She raises her eyebrows. 'Don't say I didn't warn you.'

Mother does not have the mental capacity.

The words sting. I would have been as capable as any mother of bringing up her own child. I might've needed a bit of support with it, but I would've been a good mother. Nowadays it wouldn't happen. I saw a programme on TV the other day. A couple with Down's syndrome. They was allowed to keep their baby. They was given support to help them with being parents.

Wayne arrives with the teas, setting them down on the table.

'Who adopted Cilla, then?' I ask.

'I'm afraid I can't give you too many details about the parents, Margaret. For confidentiality reasons.'

I ask her what confidentiality means.

'It means private,' she explains. 'I can you tell you, however, that Claire went to a good home.'

'Claire?' I say, almost spitting my tea everywhere. 'Who's Claire?'

'Claire is what your daughter's adoptive parents renamed her—'

'What's wrong with Cilla,' I burst out. 'Why did they change it?'

I look at Wayne, shaking my head in disbelief.

'It's perfectly normal for adoptive parents to rename the baby,' she says. 'Like I said, though, Cilla went to a good home. She will have had a nice upbringing.'

Just at that moment, the tears come, and they won't stop. I'm sobbing so loudly that people in the cafe are starting to stare. I throw my arms around Wayne, pulling him close. My snot is dripping onto his shoulder, but I don't care. I want to make my hands into fists and scream.

She was my daughter. I never wanted to give her away. She was taken from me.

All because it was the wrong bloody time. Nowadays, I could've kept her. We would've had a life together.

'Have some tea,' Wayne says, pushing the mug towards me.

I sip it slowly, trying to calm myself down.

'Do you want to know the names?' Carol says. 'Of the parents?'

I nod slowly, feel the sugary tea sticking in my throat.

'Thomas and Jean Rowan,' she says. 'They lived in Wimbledon.'

'Wimbledon?' I say. 'Where they play tennis?'

'That's it,' says Carol. 'Lovely area. Lots of open space and very leafy.'

'Are they still alive?' I say. 'The parents, I mean?'

Carol sighs and puts the letters back in the envelope.

'I don't have those details, I'm afraid, but I can give you the names of a few websites where you might be able to find out some more information.'

Wayne gets his phone out of his pocket.

'Go on, then, Carol,' he says, tapping his keyboard. 'I'm all ears.'

70

1970

A week or so after they'd taken Cilla away, Sister Hilda called me into her office.

'You can't stay here anymore,' she says. 'We're sending you back to St Mary's.'

I wasn't looking forward to going back to the hospital. It sounds wrong, but I enjoyed a lot of my time in the Lodge. Not just because of Cilla: there was fewer people there, you see, so I got more support. I learned quite a lot when I was there. It's why I always say smaller places are better for people like me.

It was a hot, sunny day when Nurse Fitts come to pick me up. I'd not done much apart from mope around – that's if I had time. You was always cleaning there. Even after you gave birth, the nuns got you straight back doing stairs again. A lot of the women there used to complain about it, but they wouldn't listen. You wasn't just cleaning, you see, you was repenting for your sins. It wouldn't happen nowadays. I was born in the wrong time.

I felt bad leaving Joyce behind.

I says to her, 'Will you be all right, though?'

She was sat on a big rocking chair in the nursery, holding baby Ernst in her arms. She was feeding him a bottle, singing a lullaby.

'Hush-a-bye-baby on the tree top.'

She looked at me.

'Don't you worry about me, Margaret,' she whispered. 'I have my faith. Jesus will look after us both, I'm sure.'

I gave her a hug and said my goodbyes.

You would think I'd be used to goodbyes by now, but I wasn't. Even though I'd said them loads of times, they still hurt.

'I just want to warn you,' says Nurse Fitts. 'Nurse Cunningham isn't very happy.'

We was in Nurse Fitts's new car. She was driving. I was sat next to her, in the passenger seat. I'd not been in a car for years. Lovely car, it was. Bright orange. A Beetle, I think. Nurse Fitts said she got it second-hand.

'I've been saving up for two years,' she says.

'What's up with Nurse Cunningham, then?' I says. 'Why ain't she happy?'

'You know what she's like,' says Nurse Fitts. 'She's old-fashioned. She's in her sixties now. Doesn't like change.' Nurse Fitts turned on the radio. Dana's 'All Kinds Of Everything' came blaring out of the speakers. 'You know that she's retiring soon?'

'Who is? Dana?'

'No,' says Nurse Fitts, smiling. 'Nurse Cunningham.'

'What's retiring? Is that like when they put new wheels on your car?'

Nurse Fitts laughed. 'Now that you mention it, Margaret, it is sort of like that. Only they'll be replacing Nurse Cunningham. With a newer model.'

'Eh?' I says. I was confused.

'Retirement is what happens to somebody when they get too old to work.'

271

'You mean Nurse Cunningham is leaving?' I says. I couldn't believe it.

'Yes,' says Nurse Fitts. 'In September. She told me the other day she's been working at St Mary's for forty-five years. Can you believe that?'

'I can well believe it, miss,' I says. 'For I've been here for over twenty.'

'God, have you really?' says Nurse Fitts.

She put a cigarette in her mouth and lit it.

'Actually, you're right,' she says. 'Because you arrived not long after me. I started in 1946.'

'1946?' I says. 'What age is you, then, miss?'

'I'll be 43 in July,' says Nurse Fitts. 'I was 19 when I started. Blimey. So that means Nurse Cunningham's been working there since before I was born.'

It was raining. Nurse Fitts switched the wipers on.

'Honestly, Margaret,' she says. 'What have I been doing with myself all of this time? I have no husband, no kids.' She sighed. 'Do you ever feel like you've wasted your entire life?'

I didn't answer her. I was in a world of my own then, listening to the radio, thinking of Cilla.

Nurse Fitts wound down the window, flicking her cigarette butt out onto the road. She wound it shut again. I sat staring at the windscreen wipers as they went swishing from one side to the other, getting rid of all the rain.

71

1970

Nurse Fitts was right. Nurse Cunningham wasn't happy. She wasn't happy at all. She must've been waiting for us both to come back, for as soon as Nurse Fitts had parked her car in the hospital courtyard and turned off the engine, Nurse Cunningham came running out of the main entrance. She was waving her hands at us.

'Alice! Alice!' she was shouting. 'I'd like a word with you.'

She banged on the car window with her fist. Nurse Fitts wound it open.

'About time, Alice! I thought you said you'd be back before lunchtime. It's almost two o'clock.'

'Relax, Violet,' says Nurse Fitts. 'If you must know, we stopped off for a bite to eat on the way back.'

Nurse Cunningham's face looked like it was about to pop.

'A bite to eat?' she says. 'A bite to eat? What on earth have you been doing with the patient for the past few hours? She's not on a Pontin's holiday, for crying out loud. This is a very serious matter, Alice. Very serious indeed.'

Nurse Fitts sighed. 'Really, Violet,' she says. 'The way you're reacting right now isn't helping the situation. If you'll just—'

Nurse Cunningham screamed at her. 'How dare you speak to me like that!'

273

Nurse Fitts wound the window back up.

'Ignore her. Just get out of the car and go inside. I'll get your suitcase out of the boot for you.'

I opened the door and stepped onto the gravel. Nurse Cunningham came running round to my side of the car. She grabbed me by the arm, twisting it, so it hurt.

'Wait here, Small,' she says. 'You're coming with me.'

Nurse Fitts was getting out of the car. She shouted over the roof.

'What are you doing, Violet? For God's sake, leave her alone. She's had a hard enough time as it is.'

'Oh, has she now?' says Nurse Cunningham, squeezing my arm tighter. She shoved her face right up close to mine. 'Hard, was it?' she says. 'I'll show you hard.'

'Let go,' I says. 'You're hurting me.'

'Alice,' she says, 'I'm taking her to see Dr Firmin. Leave her suitcase outside Villa 17. That's where I will be taking her afterwards.'

'Really, Violet,' says Nurse Fitts, 'I don't think it's necessary to put her in a punishment room. I think she's learned her lesson now.'

Nurse Cunningham ignored her. She yanked me by the arm, pulling me across the courtyard and into the main reception.

72

Wayne has signed up to a website where you can find people's family trees. He's got his laptop on the kitchen table and is squinting at the screen, typing fast with his fingers.

'I'm going to search for Thomas Rowan first,' he says. 'Men tend to keep their surnames, so we'll have a better chance of finding the right one.'

'The right one?' I say, lifting two mugs down from the kitchen cupboard.

'There'll be more than one Thomas Rowan, Margaret, possibly hundreds of them. We've got to narrow it down.'

'Hundreds of Thomas Rowans?' I flick the switch on the kettle. 'How are we going to find the right Thomas, then?'

'By looking at the dates, where he lived and when.'

It sounds ever so complicated to me. I feel panicked. How will we ever find this Thomas? What if we choose the wrong one?

Wayne types the name into his computer. He don't even look at the keys, he just taps and taps and taps. He's so quick. I wish I could type, but they never let me learn.

The kettle whistles, steam pouring from the spout.

'Pass me a pen and paper, Margaret,' says Wayne, still tapping. 'I think I might have found our Thomas.'

73

1970

'Everything appears to be in perfect working order,' says Dr Firmin, after he was done examining me. 'It's been a while since you had the baby. I can't see any reason why you shouldn't go back to work straight away.'

'Does that mean I can start on laundry again?' I says.

The doctor raised his eyebrows and looked over at Nurse Cunningham.

'I don't see why not?' he says.

But Nurse Cunningham shook her head. 'I'd like to wait a few weeks before we put her back on laundry, Doctor,' she says. 'We've done a good job of keeping this whole sordid business quiet. I think the patient needs time to reflect in private over her experience. I don't want the other patients finding out what happened. As far as they're concerned, Margaret has been ill for the past few months, which, I think you'll agree with me, isn't too far from the truth, Doctor?'

Dr Firmin nodded.

'I think that's a perfectly sensible idea, Nurse Cunningham. It will give the patient here plenty of time to get used to being back in the hospital. I'm sure the place she has just come from was very different from here.'

'Exactly,' says Nurse Cunningham. 'A very different set of

rules, I should imagine. A few weeks of solitude will allow her to settle in again.'

Nurse Cunningham said goodbye to Dr Firmin. Taking me by the hand, she marched me out of his office, through a big set of doors and across the courtyard to Villa 17.

I was only in Villa 17 for two weeks, but it felt like much longer. The room they put me in had no furniture, not even a bed. There was a blanket on the floor for me to sleep on, but that was it. Apart from when Nurse Fitts came in to bring me food and water, I had nobody to talk to, not a single soul.

I missed sharing a room with Joyce. I missed her big laugh and the sound of her voice when she sang baby Ernst to sleep. Compared to St Mary's, Lady Oak Lodge was like Heaven. The nuns there might have been strict, but they was nothing compared to Nurse Cunningham.

Moving me from a place where I was with other women to a punishment room, just after I'd lost my baby, wasn't right. I'd never felt so alone, so unloved by anyone. Every night, I cried myself to sleep.

One time, I had a dream that they let me keep Cilla. The nurses put a cradle at the end of my bed in the ward, so I could sleep next to her. They said they had made a terrible mistake, that I was capable of being a mother after all.

'She's your baby,' they told me. 'You need to care for her.'

At night, I read her stories – for in my dream I was able to read – and in the mornings I fed her, then I'd put her in a pram, push her around the hospital grounds, just like I used to do with Joan in the old days. For the first time in ages, I was happy. When I woke up the next morning, though, I was alone again, on a hard floor, with only a blanket for warmth. And this feeling that wouldn't go away. This feeling that part of me was missing.

Nurse Cunningham retired in September that year. They held a party for her in the recreation hall. We put up balloons and streamers. There was food laid out for everyone: crisps, biscuits, sausage rolls and so on. Nurse Fitts read a speech she'd written down on a piece of paper. Her hands was shaking as she spoke:

'"I've worked with you for the past twenty years, Violet, and during that time I've got to know you very well. I can't say I agree with your nursing methods, many of which are very old-fashioned – cruel, even – but I wish you the best of luck with your retirement. You will certainly be remembered by all the staff and patients here at St Mary's."'

There was an awkward silence, then everyone started clapping. Nurse Fitts asked Nurse Cunningham to go up on the stage, where a few of us, me included, was waiting in line to present her with gifts. Janet went first. She gave her a gold carriage clock. Everyone clapped and cheered. Bernadette was next. She handed her a photograph album which we'd all helped put together. It had all sorts of things in it, memories and that: the pantomimes we'd done, sports days and Christmas. There was a lovely black and white photograph of Joan and me with Mr Chance when he'd opened the recreation hall that time. I would've liked to keep it for myself, but it was her present. Finally it was my turn to go up. I gave her a big bouquet of flowers. White roses. Nurse Cunningham's favourite.

Nurse Cunningham gave a speech, too. She was quite emotional, her voice was wobbling. Then we all sang 'For She's A Jolly Good Fellow' while some of the younger girls put on a gymnastics display.

She wasn't one of my favourite nurses at St Mary's – she had a mean streak that made her cruel and nasty – but I was still sad to see her go. There are people in your life who you might not like that much, but they're still part of it, if you know what I mean.

They're still a part of your life.

74

29 SEPTEMBER 2015

'Do you want me to make the call for you?'

Wayne is holding his mobile phone. He's had to repeat this question three times. The clock in the sitting room next door chimes the hour.

'I ain't sure,' I says, twisting the sleeve of my cardigan. 'I mean, what if he hangs up? What if he don't want to know?'

'Cilla will want to know,' Wayne says. 'Think about what Cilla wants.'

'What would Cilla want?' I say, repeating your name out loud.

I try to picture what you look like now. I only ever saw you as a tiny baby, but you must be in your forties. The thought of it makes me catch my breath. It sounds stupid, but – up until now – I'd only ever thought of you as a child, my little girl. All the years I've missed, it terrifies me. I won't ever get them back.

Will you call me Mummy when we meet? Even though I wasn't there for you. For your first steps, your first word, the first time you fell over. I wasn't the one putting a plaster on your knee, or tucking you up in bed, like the mothers do on television. You won't remember me kissing you goodnight or telling you everything was going to be OK. I lied to you when I said that, didn't I? Still, I'd like to think you'd want to call me Mummy, even though I've been a stranger to you all these years. I never thought I'd have to say this to my own daughter, my own flesh and blood. Who gets to choose who lives a normal life and who don't? Why is life so unfair?

I wipe my nose with the sleeve of my cardigan.

'Put your phone down, Wayne,' I say. 'Really, what's the use of any of this? I need to forget about Cilla, forget about the past. There's no point dragging things up now. I ain't calling nobody.'

Wayne puts his mobile back in his pocket.

'If you're sure,' he says quietly. 'Maybe you should sleep on it tonight, though. If it really is Cilla trying to contact you, she'll have her reasons. She obviously cares a great deal about you.'

I nod. And then the sobbing comes, loud and uncontrollable – like it might never stop. Wayne passes me a pack of tissues. I take one, wiping the tears from my cheeks and blowing my nose.

'OK, I'll do it,' I say, finally, the words coming out breathless and panicked. 'Cilla would want me to.'

'There's no rush, Margaret. In your own time.'

'I ain't got a lot of time left, though,' I say, looking Wayne in the eye. 'Not at my age.'

Wayne pauses. He smiles. 'You'd better get a move on, then. I'm happy to make the call if you'd prefer.'

I nod. I'm trying to convince myself that it's the right thing to do, but my stomach is in knots. What if this Thomas don't want to speak to me? What if he thinks I'm a bad mother for giving her away all those years ago?

'Was I a bad mother?' I say to Wayne.

'A bad mother?' Wayne shakes his head. 'Margaret, what are you talking about? You had no choice. Stop blaming yourself.'

I look at him, tears forming again at the corners of my eyes.

'It's the system's fault,' he says. 'We're all controlled by the system. Fifty years ago, it was illegal to be gay. If I'd been alive then, I wouldn't have been able to be myself.'

'What do you mean, not be yourself? Who would you be, then?'

'Lots of men who were gay just got married, to a woman. Being gay was a criminal offence. What other choice did they have? It's the same with you. When you were young, they decided people with learning disabilities should be put away in long-stay hospitals. They saw disability as an illness. They used to think the same about homosexuality, too. Things are different now, though, for both of us. Times have changed, thank God. Don't judge yourself the way others judged you in the past.'

Wayne speaks softly and quietly, a whisper almost.

'Your disability is no longer a barrier, Margaret. Don't ever let it limit you. Don't ever let it stop you from doing what you want.'

I look outside into the garden. The sun is setting behind the fence, the only sounds the swishing of cars on the road and the ticking of the kitchen clock. I feel a tickle in my stomach, something I've not felt in a long time. I'm thinking of my reunion with Cilla, of the two of us seeing each other again for the first time since I held her in my arms as a little baby. She is older now, much older, but she is smiling, and we are holding each other close.

'Call him, then,' I say. 'I've wasted too much time already.'

Wayne dials the number he got from the Internet. He puts his phone on speaker so I can hear the conversation. My heart beats fast as we both listen to it ring. A lady answers.

'Hello,' says Wayne. 'I'm looking to speak to a Mr Thomas Rowan.'

'Who is this?' says the lady at the other end of the line. 'You're not phoning about double glazing again, are you? As I said to the last caller, we're too old for new windows.'

'This isn't a sales call,' says Wayne. 'I'm phoning on behalf of a client of mine. She's trying to get back in touch with an old friend of hers, Cilla.'

'Cilla?' says the woman. 'I'm afraid you have the wrong number. There's no one called Cilla living here.'

'Sorry, not Cilla,' Wayne says, quickly correcting himself. 'I mean, Claire.'

There is silence at the other end of the phone. I can hear the sound of my own breathing. After what seems like forever, the woman finally speaks.

'Who did you say you were again?'

'A friend of a friend of Claire's,' he says.

The woman pauses.

'Look, I don't know how you know my daughter, but I may as well tell you. She died. A long, long time ago. Claire had a heart condition. She was only a child at the time. Is this an old school friend?'

Wayne's face turns white as a sheet. I snatch the phone off him, press the red button to end the call. This is too much to take in right now.

'Oh, Margaret, I'm so sorry,' says Wayne. 'I should've taken the call myself. I feel terrible.'

I can't speak because my head is spinning. I want to scream, but the words don't come.

Cilla is dead, I think. *My Cilla. Dead. A long, long time ago. Why did nobody tell me?*

75

29 September 2015

After what happened, I told Wayne I needed a walk to the beach to clear my head. He came with me. We hardly said a word to each other the whole way; Wayne knew I wasn't in the mood for talking. Besides, what could he have said to make me feel better?

I can smell the sea here, salty and sharp. There's a puddle around my feet from when it rained earlier. The purple laces on my trainers have come loose and one of the toes of my socks is soaking wet. I've been meaning to get myself a new pair of trainers for a while now, but I keep putting it off. I've had other things on my mind. It's high tide, so the waves are coming in and out, washing the shingle back and forth. They remind me of the old penny pushers in the arcades in Margate. I used to like to have a go on them. Some days, I won and the pockets of my dress would be heavy with coins. Some days, I lost. I'd head home with a heavy heart, empty-handed.

Today, my heart feels heavy.

I can't tell you how much I was looking forward to seeing you again, Cilla. All the hopes and dreams I'd built up in my head. It hurts too much to remember how happy I was about finding you. My dear daughter, who I held in my arms as a baby, who they only allowed me to love for a very short time.

76

'C'

I'm standing in front of your house. It looks different from the other Victorian properties on Cromwell Road, more modern. It must be 1960s, or thereabouts. Plain-fronted. Red-brick with dark wood-framed windows and doors. There's a small window box filled with red geraniums. Did you plant the flowers yourself, I wonder?

I sit down on the low wall outside and take the parcel I've prepared for you from its plastic Waitrose carrier bag. I've packaged the record in brown cardboard to keep it safe.

I can't help thinking about the different paths our lives have taken. What would have happened if they had allowed you to live a 'normal' life, instead of locking you up in an institution, as if you were a danger or a threat? I can't think of anyone less threatening than you, Margaret.

I hope you like my present.

77

6 OCTOBER 2015

Wayne waves a small parcel at me.

'This was on the landing when I came in. Looks like another present from your mystery sender. There's no stamp on it, though. Any idea who it could be?'

'What do you mean, no stamp?' My voice is groggy.

It's only been a week since I heard the news about my Cilla, and I ain't left the house. I'm still in my nightie, even though it's past ten o'clock, curled up on the sofa watching television. Normally I'm up by seven, but this week I ain't felt like doing much. I've barely had the energy to drag myself out of bed. Really, though, what's the point?

Wayne hands me the parcel.

'It means whoever is sending you these letters has been to your house. He or she posted this through your letterbox. In person.'

I put it down on the sofa next to me without saying a word. Now that I know it ain't Cilla, I ain't interested. Picking up the remote control, I turn the TV up. *Celebrity Antiques Roadshow* is on. Two girls – I say girls, but they must be in their forties at least – are talking to a man in a straw hat about *Black Beauty*. Celebrity this, celebrity that:

what a load of old codswallop. I could've been a celebrity. It's impossible, though, if you can't read the scripts.

Wayne moves the parcel out of the way and sits down beside me.

'Bananarama,' he says, looking at the two girls on the TV. 'I used to love them, back in the day. They were cool. I bet they never imagined they'd end up bargain hunting in Buckinghamshire.'

He laughs, looking at me to see my reaction, but I'm just staring at the screen, lost in my own thoughts.

If it ain't Cilla sending me these letters, then who is it? I don't know anyone else. No friends, or family. Maybe Sainsbury's David was right. Maybe I have a secret admirer. Whoever it is, I wish they'd shown their face sooner. It would've saved me a lot of bother.

'It would've saved me a lot of bother,' I mumble, grabbing a cushion and holding it tight against my stomach.

'Is the TV annoying you?' says Wayne, taking the remote control. 'I can switch it off for you if you want.'

'Leave it on,' I say, rocking back and forth, holding my cushion. I sound rude, but I don't mean to be. Like I say, my mind is elsewhere.

Wayne takes the parcel and taps it on the arm of the sofa.

'How are you feeling today? Don't you want to open this, then? It might be something nice.'

'You open it!' I snap. 'What good will it do me?'

When I was a girl, I used to love opening presents, not that you got many at St Mary's – a pair of socks, or a handkerchief, if you was lucky. Now, though, I'd rather have nothing. If you have nothing, you don't know what you're missing out on. You have nothing to lose, either. Like before I had Cilla, I didn't know what it felt like to be a mother.

Better to never be a mother, than to have a child and for it to be taken away from you.

Wayne speaks softly this time. 'It might help us get to the bottom of this mystery sender, that's all.'

I tut loudly, then sigh. Taking a deep breath, I try to shake off my bad mood.

'I suppose so.'

Wayne opens the parcel. It's a record. A 7-inch single. It's in a plain black paper sleeve with a hole in the middle.

'This doesn't make sense,' Wayne says, reading the label.

I put the cushion down and peer at the record in Wayne's hand. It looks familiar. A dark green label with white swirls. I've seen it somewhere before, but I can't place it.

'What don't make sense?' I say.

'It's a copy of "Alfie" by Cilla Black.'

'"Alfie"?' I say, my stomach flipping over itself.

'Wait. There's something else inside.'

Wayne pulls an envelope from the sleeve and carefully tears it open. Inside there's a fifty-pound note and a letter. He reads it aloud:

'"*I saw this the other day and thought you might appreciate it! Love C xxx*"'

A shiver runs up my spine as I remember something. The other week, when I was in Rock Bottom Records, Sid, the owner, played 'Alfie' for me. If anyone knows who sent this, Sid will.

'Give me the record,' I say. 'I'm going to sort out this bloody thing once and for all.'

I burst out of the house dressed in my nightie and trainers, slamming the door shut behind me. The sound echoes down the street. I don't turn around. I keep on going, walking as fast as I can, my breath heaving in and out like a steam engine.

I can hear Wayne behind me. He's calling out, 'Wait! Margaret! Where are you going?'

But I ain't stopping for no one.

My hip is already throbbing, but I'm on a mission. I head straight for the High Street. A car beeps its horn as I run across the road without looking. The driver, a bald man in a tracksuit, winds down his window.

'Watch where you're going, you stupid bitch!' he yells at me.

I ignore him and carry on walking.

The streets in Whitstable are empty this morning. There's no one around. The sightseers ain't arrived yet. The town is full of them these days. It never used to be. Just as well. If anyone gets in my way, I'm likely to knock them over. One of my purple shoelaces has come undone, but I don't have time to stop and tie it. I pass Hubbard's bakery. Usually I'll pop in for an iced finger, but not today. Outside George's Mini Market, one of the staff is just setting up, hanging up inflatable dinghies and rubber rings outside the shop. I rush past without saying so much as a hello. I'm heading towards Harbour Street.

The sky has got darker and it's starting to rain. I feel a tap on my shoulder. It's Wayne. He's out of breath, walking fast to keep up with me. I may be 75, but when I've got a bee in my bonnet, no one can stop me.

'Margaret,' he says. 'Will you tell me what's going on?'

'I need to talk to Sid,' I say, my breath full of puff. 'Sid will know who sent me the record.'

78

6 OCTOBER 2015

I barge into the shop to find Sid is in his usual spot behind
the counter with his headphones on. He's cleaning an LP,
spraying it with fluid, wiping it round with a blue cloth.
Outside the rain has got worse. My socks feel wet inside
my trainers, but I'm glad to be here. It's warm and dry and
I can get an answer to my question.

'I need to talk to you, Sid,' I say. 'It's urgent. Can you
hear me?'

Sid puts down the record he is cleaning and takes off his
headphones.

'Loud and clear, Margaret. What's the matter?'

'It's about Cilla,' I say. 'Cilla Black.'

Sid looks at me, his eyes sad.

'I know what happened to Cilla,' he says quietly. 'You told
me before – 72 is too young to die.'

He thinks I'm here to talk to him about Cilla's death. Sid
was one of the first people I told when I heard about her
stroke on the radio. We talk about her a lot. He knows how
much she means to me.

'It ain't about her dying,' I say. 'I want to know who sent
me this.'

I hand him the 7-inch single. The cover is wet from the

rain and is starting to curl at the edges. Sid looks at it, puzzled.

'I played you this the other day, didn't I?'

I nod. 'Someone bought it for me as a present. They put it through my letterbox. Only they didn't say who it was from.'

'How strange,' he says. 'I sold the only copy I had last week. A lady, if I remember rightly.'

A lady? So *C* is a woman.

'What did she look like?' I say.

Sid rubs his eyes. 'Let me think. She was attractive. About fifty, or so. Well spoken. Red hair.'

'What day was it?' says Wayne. 'Can you remember?'

'Let me have a look.' Sid opens a green book on the counter and starts flicking through it. 'I keep a record of all transactions in here, you see. What day was it? Maybe Monday or Tuesday last week?'

My heart starts beating fast.

'Here it is,' says Sid, pointing halfway down a page in his book. '"Alfie", Cilla Black, 7-inch single. Five quid. It was last Monday, in fact.'

'Did you recognise her?' I say, leaning over to try and make sense of the words Sid is reading. 'Was she local?'

'I haven't seen around her before, but then we get customers from all over the world coming to the shop. That's about all I can tell you, sorry.'

My heart sinks as Sid hands the record back to me.

'So that's it, then?' I say, disappointed. 'Unless she shows her face, like she said she would in her letter, we ain't ever going to get to the bottom of this one.'

79

1980

Things started changing in the 1970s and 1980s. A lot of people left St Mary's. Not just staff, but patients, too. What happened was, they began saying to us, 'You know if you want to, you can go and live on your own now.' Bernadette was one of the first to go. She was old by that point. In her sixties. They moved her out of the hospital to a flat in Blean, sharing with this other lady, Maureen.

One afternoon, it was around the early 1980s, I was making a pot of tea for the staff. I used to do that for them sometimes when they came on duty. I'd put the teapot on a tray with cups and saucers. Then I'd arrange the biscuits on a plate with a doily and what have you. I enjoyed doing that. They let us have the radio on in the kitchen, so I could listen to all my favourite songs while I was making the tea: 'Summer Nights', 'Take A Chance On Me' and 'Do Ya Think I'm Sexy?' Me and Janet used to have a dance routine to the Rod Stewart one. I shouldn't say it really, for it was a bit rude, but Janet used to get the jam rings and put them on her top parts, like they was boobs, then she done this pouting thing with her lips. *Na na na naaaa na.* It was ever so funny. We was always doing stupid things like that. Life got boring otherwise.

So this one day, Nurse Fitts come in the kitchen and says to me, 'Margaret, the social worker's here to see you.'

I panicked at first. I thought to myself, *what do they want?*

Then I remembered that Nurse Fitts had asked me to put one of my best dresses on that morning. At the time, I'd thought nothing of it. But obviously this was the reason why.

'We'll both be in the day room,' she says. 'Do you want to bring the teas through when you're ready?'

'How does she take it, then?' I says.

I might've sounded grumpy, but I don't like people springing surprises on me like that. It unnerved me a bit.

'It's not a lady, it's a man,' says Nurse Fitts. 'And he'll have milk and one sugar, please.'

I made the teas and put the biscuits on a plate: bourbons, rich teas and pink wafers. I put everything on a tray and carried it in. The tea was spilling over the edges a bit, for I was shaking. I kept thinking, *why is the social worker here to see me? Are they going to vanish me again?*

The social worker was a bald man with a red beard. He had on a green suit. When he saw me come over with the teas, he stood up, wiping his hands on his trouser legs.

'This must be Margaret,' he says, smiling.

Nurse Fitts nodded. 'This is Mr Goody. From the council,' she says.

The tray rattled when I put it down on the table.

Mr Goody says, 'Wait, wait! Let me get you a chair.' He grabbed me a spare one from behind. 'Take a seat,' he says, shaking my hand.

I sat down, then went to pick up the teapot.

'Oh, don't bother pouring,' he says. 'I can manage that myself.'

'Shall I be mother?' says Nurse Fitts.

She took the pot off the tray and poured the tea for us.

I says, 'There's some biscuits, too, sir, if you'd like one.'

'Don't mind if I do,' he says, reaching across the table and grabbing a bourbon off the plate. He took a bite. A few brown crumbs landed on his tie. He brushed them off.

'Margaret!' he says. 'Isn't this marvellous? You've done a great job. We could do with someone like you working in our offices.'

'Where are your offices, then, sir?'

'London,' he says.

'Oh,' I says. 'I don't mean to be rude, Mr Goody, but I don't like it up there in London. It's too busy. Ain't my sort of thing.'

He laughed. 'I know what you mean. Don't worry, though. I'm not going to propose that you move to London. Nothing of the sort.'

He took another biscuit off the plate. A pink wafer this time.

He says, 'How would you feel about moving out of St Mary's, Margaret?'

I choked on my tea then. Nurse Fitts had to give me a hankie, for it was all dribbling down my chin.

'Move out?' I says. 'But where would I go? Are they throwing me out, miss?'

Nurse Fitts smiled. 'No one's throwing you out, Margaret. We wouldn't do that to you. Only we think it would be better for you if you lived outside. In the community.'

I felt sick to the stomach.

'I . . . I don't like it out there, miss,' I says. 'The people, they're cruel. They call me names and that. I've heard them.'

Mr Goody took another biscuit. He says, 'I can understand your concerns, Margaret, but we're thinking it would be for your own good. You're clearly very capable.'

'Capable?' I says.

'Put it this way. If you can get up early every morning and fetch coal to light a fire, not to mention cooking and cleaning, and doing the laundry, then you're not really what we would call "mental", are you?'

'But I can't read nor write,' I says. 'I'm slow like that.'

He laughed. 'There are lots of people that can't read or write. It doesn't mean they need to be locked up in hospitals. Shall I let you into a little secret? I'm a bit dyslexic myself.'

'Are you really, sir?'

'Yes. You should see my spelling. It's atrocious.'

I crumpled up the hanky, wiping my nose with it.

'What if I like it here, though? I got my friend, Janet.'

'There's no reason why Janet can't move in with you. We wouldn't want you to live on your own. You'd be in a group home.'

'A group home?'

Mr Goody then explained to me what a group home was. He said it meant I'd be living with a few others. It wouldn't be straight away, he said, for there was a waiting list.

'If you're happy with that arrangement,' he says, 'I see no reason why you should go on living here at St Mary's.'

I looked at Nurse Fitts. She was smiling.

'It's a good thing, Margaret,' she says. 'There's no need to look so worried. There will still be people helping you out. Trust me, it's all going to be OK.'

80

19 OCTOBER 2015

One morning, a few weeks later, I get back home from Sainsbury's with Wayne to find another envelope lying on the floor. Again, there's no stamp. Whoever has been writing to me has been to my house again. A shiver runs through me, like a ghost.

'Take this into the living room with you,' says Wayne, picking up the envelope and handing it to me. 'I'll unpack the shopping and make us a quick cup of tea.'

I take my coat off, hang it up on the banister and sit down in an armchair. Kicking off my trainers, I switch on the TV and sit with the letter on my lap, watching Jeremy Kyle. A young man with loads of tattoos is arguing with his girlfriend.

Wayne comes in carrying two teas. He sets them both down on the table.

'I don't know what's up with teenagers these days,' he says, looking at the television. 'They have no compassion. You should see some of the idiots on this programme.'

'Here,' I say, giving him the letter. 'Can you read what it says? Not that it matters much.'

Wayne opens the envelope and starts to read. I watch the expression on his face.

'Well, I never, Margaret,' he says. 'I think this might just give you the answers you've been looking for.'

81

19th October 2015

Dear Margaret,

Please forgive me if this letter comes as a shock, but I didn't even know you existed until recently. My name is Christine and I'm your half-sister. It was me who sent you the money and presents in the post: the £50 notes, the lottery ticket, the record. Maybe it wasn't the right way to go about things, but I wanted to treat you, to make up for lost time. I would have made myself known to you much sooner, but I've spent ages mulling over things in my head. I'm sorry it has taken me so long. I suppose I was waiting for the right time, which is now.

To cut a long story short, Mum – our mum – had a stroke last summer. She's fine, don't worry, but not long after, she just came out with it one day. She started telling me all about the daughter she had to give up when she was a young girl, how her parents threw her out of the house not long after she was born and told her, as far as they were concerned, she was dead. She said how sad it made her feel, how if she'd had the chance to live her life all over again, she would've wanted you to have been part of it. Things were different then, though, Margaret, as I'm sure you know.

Anyway, Mum kept going on and on about something in the loft, so I went up there, and after a bit of searching I found a shoebox. It was exactly where Mum had said it would be, on the top floor of my old doll's house, the one I had when I was a little girl. I opened the box up and inside was a photo of mum holding a baby. I knew it wasn't me because I was born in the 1950s. This photo was clearly older. I found a small jewellery box, too, with a lock of red hair inside and the copy of a birth certificate: Margaret Mabel Small, April 7th, 1940.

Both Mum and I would really love it if you got in touch. My address and phone number are on the back of the envelope. I hope, with all my heart, that you reply. As I said, Mum is very frail right now. She would dearly love to see you.

Love and kind wishes,

Your sister,

Christine x

82

19 OCTOBER 2015

Wayne looks at me, folding up the letter. He wipes his forehead with the sleeve of his jacket.

'What are you going to do then, Margaret? Are you going to phone this Christine?'

It's hard to describe my feelings. It's all too much. I can hardly take it in. I feel excited, but, at the same time, I'm shocked. Grandma lied to me: all these years, I've thought my mother was dead. I never thought to question what she told me. I feel overwhelmed.

'I can't phone her,' I say, making up an excuse. 'I ain't got any credit on my mobile.'

'That's easily solved,' says Wayne. 'You can use mine.'

Wayne pulls his phone from his jacket pocket.

'I . . . I can't do it,' I say. 'I . . . I don't know what to say.'

Wayne frowns. 'She's your sister, Margaret. Of course you can talk to her.'

I start crying, not only because I am sad: I'm happy, too. I have a mother and a sister I never knew existed. All my life I've had no family and now two of them come along at once. It's hard to take in. Wayne hands me a tissue and I blow my nose, sobbing and smiling at the same time.

The man with the tattoos on the TV is shouting, 'She's

lying to me, Jeremy! There's no way that baby's mine. I know it. She's been having it off with Keith behind my back. My bloody best mate!'

Wayne picks up the remote control to turn it down.

'Your mother will have had her reasons, you know,' he says. 'She'll have wanted to keep you.'

'I know,' I say, giving a small smile. 'It ain't her fault.'

'You've forgiven her already, then, have you?'

I nod.

'She's my mother, ain't she?' I say.

We sit there for a while, in silence, just staring at the TV, watching Jeremy Kyle with the sound off. I think of my Cilla; of what I would've done if it was her trying to contact me.

Then I ask Wayne to dial the number and give me the phone.

83

26 OCTOBER 2015

A week later, Wayne picks me up in his car to do the drive up to London. The sky is dark and it's raining.

'You've got the address?' says Wayne.

I say yes, but I'd better double-check. I'm always forgetting things. I rummage around my handbag. I find the letter where I left it, folded carefully inside my purse. My mother's address. I hand it over to Wayne.

'Flat C, Bolton Court,' says Wayne. He types it into the satnav. 'Let's hope Irish Gerry knows the way. I haven't got a bloody clue.'

We drive for miles and miles. The traffic is terrible, and we keep having to stop. After a few hours' driving, we have lunch at one of them motorway cafe places. Wayne needs the toilet, so he gives me the money and asks me to do the ordering.

'Tea, strong, with full-fat milk, please,' I say to the lady behind the counter. 'None of that skimmed stuff. And a Diet Coke for my friend, please.'

I order lasagne and chips for me, and a baked potato with coleslaw for Wayne. He's always on a diet, that boy. I tell him he don't need to lose weight. Men shouldn't, though, should they? He's skinny enough as it is.

'Are you nervous?' he says. 'About meeting your mother?'

I stab a chip with my fork, dipping it in ketchup.

'I'm more excited than nervous,' I say. For really, I can't wait to see her.

When we get back into the car, Wayne puts on a Madonna CD, even though he knows I don't like her. I keep telling him she needs to put more clothes on.

'You don't see me dancing about in my bra and knickers,' I says. 'A woman of her age. She should put it away. It ain't right.'

Wayne laughs, turning up the music even louder.

'C'mon Margaret,' he says, waving his hands about, 'strike a pose.'

I put my seat belt on and fold my arms.

'No thank *you*,' I say.

Some people have got a cheek.

It's still lashing it down when we get to Colliers Wood. Wayne parks the car outside Christine's address. He switches off the CD and takes out his electric cigarette.

'You told me you'd given them things up,' I says. 'They're bad for your health, you know.'

'It's better than smoking,' he says. 'Besides, I need something for my nerves.'

'*Your* nerves?'

'I'm feeling nervous for you, Margaret. I'll give them up again next week, I promise.'

'I've heard that one before,' I say, tutting. 'Don't worry about me, by the way, I'm fine.'

We sit in the car for a few minutes, not talking, just listening to the sound of the rain on the roof.

Wayne says, 'Do you know what this reminds me of? Today, I mean. It's like that TV show with Cilla Black.'

'What – *Blind Date*?'

'No! The other one, where they reunited the families.'

'*Surprise, Surprise*,' I say, grinning. 'I used to love that.'

As he opens the car door, he starts humming the theme tune.

'Right, you,' he says. 'Let's go face the music.'

There are three doorbells outside the house. I ring the one for Flat C. Through the coloured glass on the front door, I see a blurry shape moving down the hallway. A lady answers. At first, I think it's my mother, but this lady is a good bit younger than me. She's pretty. In her fifties, I would say.

'It's lovely to finally meet you, Margaret,' she says. 'I'm Christine.'

She goes to give me a hug.

I don't say nothing at first. I'm feeling quite shy, which ain't like me.

'Aren't you going to say hello, then?' says Wayne, smiling at me.

'Hello,' I say quietly, brushing my hair over my face.

'I'm Wayne, Margaret's support worker,' he says, shaking her hand.

'Come in,' says Christine. 'Both of you. It's pouring down. You'll catch your death out there.'

We move into the hallway. It's very plain, cream walls. It smells clean, like air freshener and new carpets.

'Are you OK with stairs,' says Christine. 'There's a lift, if you'd rather . . .'

'Actually, Margaret's hip's not so good,' says Wayne. 'Let's take the lift.'

The three of us squeeze in. It feels a bit awkward.

'How was your journey?' says Christine.

She's looking at me, but I'm at a loss for words. I don't know where to begin.

304

'You're very quiet today, Margaret,' says Wayne.

He turns to Christine and smiles.

'I tell you what, Margaret,' says Christine. 'I'm so jealous of you living in Whitstable.' She presses a button on the lift. 'I've been looking at houses down there for a while now. There's a little seafood restaurant on the High Street. Wheelers. Mum loves it. We've been there a few times—'

The lift stops and the doors opens. All I manage to catch is the word 'Mum'.

I'm about to meet my mother.

84

26 October 2015

'If you two don't mind waiting outside for a minute, I'm just going to pop in and let Mum know you're here,' says Christine. 'She was asleep earlier. I'll need to wake her.'

We wait in the hallway, not speaking. It feels like ages. There's a spider plant by the doorway. Its leaves are brown and it looks like it hasn't been watered in ages. A wheelchair is folded up against the wall. Christine comes back.

'Sorry about that,' she says. 'It's just Mum gets awfully tired. You can come through now.'

Me and Wayne take our shoes off, then go into the flat. It's plain inside; everything is cream, like the downstairs hallway.

'Mum's in her bedroom, just at the end of this corridor. Follow me,' says Christine.

The door is ajar. Christine goes in while we wait outside.

'We've got visitors, Mum,' I hear her say. 'Someone very special has travelled all the way up from Whitstable to see you.'

She signals at us to come in.

The room is dark. The curtains, which are white with pink roses on them, are half drawn. It feels hot and it smells a bit; not bad, just like old people's breaths, old people who have been sleeping for a while. It is then that I notice her. My mother. She's sat up in bed, in the middle of the room, staring into space. She is much smaller and much older than I imagined. When she sees me, she lets out a small cry. What she says next, though, I can't make out. The words. Is she saying my name?

'You remember Margaret, Mum?' says Christine.

A moment's silence, then I hear my mother's voice for the very first time.

'Mar . . . ?'

'That's me,' I say, smiling. I give her a little wave.

Christine pulls up a chair for me next to the bed.

'Here,' she says, 'you sit next to her.' She turns to Mum then. 'This is Margaret, your daughter. Do you remember now?'

Mum screws her face up into a ball, tight, like she's concentrating ever so hard, trying to remember something important.

'Mar . . . ?' she says, louder this time. 'Mar . . . !'

Her eyes twinkle as she realises who I am. Her mouth opens into a smile.

'Mar-ga-ret,' she says slowly, her face beaming.

She lets out a little cry and then the tears come.

'Yes, Mum,' I say. 'It's me. Margaret.'

I take her hand, lean forward, wrap my arms around her tiny shoulders. Her cheeks feel baby soft against mine. Her heart beats madly in her chest. I have so much love inside me, I want to squeeze her, but she's brittle, like a little bird. We sit holding each other for a while. I never want to let her go. Never.

'How about I make us some tea?' says Christine, dabbing a hanky under her eyes. 'You're not in a hurry to go, are you?'

'Go?' I says. 'We only just got here! Besides, we've a lot to catch up on.'

'I'm in no rush to get home, Margaret,' says Wayne. 'You take as long as you like.'

I leave Mum to rest, and the three of us make our way down to the kitchen. Christine fills the kettle and puts it on the gas ring to boil.

'It's so lovely to have you both here,' she says, opening a cupboard and taking down a box of teabags. 'Mum and I have been waiting a long time for this moment. I would've introduced myself earlier, I'm so sorry, but I was torn, you see. I didn't want to overwhelm you, Margaret. The gifts were meant to be a small gesture, a . . . token of my affection. I never wanted to worry you, or—'

'It don't matter,' I say, interrupting her. 'You was only trying to protect me, Christine. Don't worry. I understand. And the gifts was lovely, thank you. They was ever so thoughtful. All of them.'

Christine smiles. 'Hobnob?' she says, putting a packet of biscuits down on the table. We both reach for one. Christine runs her hand through her hair, biting her lip. 'I've been thinking, I probably should've gone about this completely differently.'

'How did you find me?' I say, crunching into my biscuit.

'Well, I already knew your name, of course, and your age, and roughly where you lived, so I just looked you up on the Internet. It was as simple as that, really.'

'I ain't on the Internet, though,' I say. 'I don't do Facebook or nothing.'

'Your contact details are on there. Most people's are. Remember the old days when we had phone books?'

'Phone books was never any use to me,' I say. 'I could never read the stupid things.'

Christine laughs. 'They were cumbersome. You didn't miss much. Anyway, so once I found your details, I didn't do anything for quite some time. If I'm being honest, I wasn't sure if you'd want me contacting you, Margaret. And then one day I was down in Whitstable – as you know, I've been looking for houses – and I popped into Hubbard's, the bakery, to pick up one of their crusty loaves—'

'The ladies there do lovely iced fingers,' I say.

'I know they do,' says Christine, smiling. 'Because you were in front of me in the queue.'

'Buying iced fingers?'

'Yes!' laughs Christine. 'And, of course, I didn't know it was you at that point until after you left the shop and one of the women behind the counter turned to the other, a younger girl – she must've been new – and said, "That's Margaret, she's one of our regulars. She comes in most days." And, of course, I knew then it was you. It was obvious. Plus, you look *so* much like Mum.'

'Everyone knows everyone in Whitstable,' I say. 'You can't keep anything private.'

'Not always a bad thing,' says Christine. 'It was the local grapevine that led us to each other.'

'When was that, then?'

Christine pauses. 'Just over a year ago. By that point, I was coming down to Whitstable quite regularly and I'd often see you around – wandering about town, in Sainsbury's, one time in the record shop. Mum's illness made me realise how little time she has left, and that gave me the push I needed to finally get in touch with you. I'm so glad I did, though. For your sake and Mum's. She's so frail now, bless her.'

'Are you the main carer?' says Wayne.

'I do most of the caring, yes,' she says. 'We get a little bit of help from a young girl from social services, but it's only for a few hours a week. Between you and me, I'm looking into residential care for Mum at the moment. It's better for her, really. And for me.'

'Maybe I can help you?' I say. 'With the caring, I mean.'

'That's a lovely idea, Margaret,' says Christine. 'Let's investigate together. You can help me have a look at some care homes down in Whitstable. Mum's from there, obviously, so it would be nice for her to return to her roots. Plus, as I mentioned to you earlier, I've been looking to buy a property there for myself, too, so I can be close to Mum. And you, of course, Margaret. If you'd like that?'

The kettle whistles. Christine lifts it to pour the tea.

'How do you take it, Margaret?' she says, setting the empty mugs out on the worktop.

'Milk,' I says. 'Full-fat. With three sugars, please.'

'Oh,' says Christine. 'I think we only have semi-skimmed. Sorry about that.'

Wayne gives me one of those looks, as if to say, *Don't make a fuss, Margaret.*

'It don't matter, Christine,' I say, for really, I am beaming inside. I can't help but smile.

'Semi-skimmed is fine.'

85

That afternoon, sat at Mum's kitchen table, over tea and biscuits, I learn about my mother's past – what happened to her in the years after she left me. All my life, I'd grown up believing she died giving birth, but Grandma had lied. Mum was alive, she never wanted to give me up. She was only 16, though, and working at the mill when she got pregnant by a soldier. Grandpa was furious when he found out.

'You're no daughter of ours, Gladys,' he told her. 'You've broken your mother's heart. And mine.'

I was only a few months old at the time, so they kept me. But they threw Mum out of the house. She had nowhere to go, no money, nothing but a bag of old clothes and a Bible.

'As far as we're concerned,' they said, 'you're dead. Our only daughter. We're ashamed of you. We never want to see you again.'

Mum ran away to London, took work where she could find it – in bars, cafes, you name it. She did what she could to survive. One day she was working in a cafe in Piccadilly when a customer asked if he could take her for a drink after her shift. This was Jim, who later became her husband. They got married and moved to Australia not long after.

'So you was living in Australia?' I say.

311

'For a while, yes,' says Christine, nodding. 'I was born in Perth in the late fifties. Mum was never a fan of the heat, though, and she missed living in England, so we moved back to London in the seventies, when I was still a teenager.'

'What happened to Grandma and Grandpa?' I ask her.

I knew Grandma, of course, but I have no memories of Grandpa.

Christine shrugs. She takes a sip of tea.

'He died quite young, I think, not long after Mum left. It could've been a heart attack, but who knows? I believe Grandma died in the sixties, but I don't know the exact details. Mum never had any further contact with her. She was a heavy smoker, though, which might have had something to do with it. Then, sadly, my dad passed away a few years ago, of cancer. Ever since then, Mum's health has got worse. Dad really was the love of her life. She never got over losing him.'

'Just like Cilla and Bobby,' I say.

'I take it you mean Cilla Black?' says Christine, smiling.

'That's right. The singer. Her husband, Bobby, died of cancer, too. He was the love of her life. I've been listening to her autobiography on my CD player.'

Christine puts her hand on mine.

'Yes, I suppose so, Margaret,' she says. 'Mum and Jim were just like Cilla and Bobby.'

Christine's hand feels warm on mine. I like her. She's family. I've never had family before, apart from Grandma, who I can barely remember now, so this is new for me. I open my mouth to tell her about my Cilla, how I thought it was her sending me the letters and the money, but something stops me.

There's no rush, I think to myself, my hand safe under hers. We've got all the time in the world to get to know each other now. All the time in the world.

86

31st October 2015

Dear Margaret (and Wayne),

Thank you so much for your kind invitation to join
you at the GAY FAWKES PARTY at Wayne's house
in Whitstable on Saturday 7th November. Mum and I
would love to come. We're very excited! I've booked a
room at the Hotel Continental, so we can stay over.

Looking forward to seeing you both.

All our love,

Mum and Christine

xxx

87

Wayne takes a tray of cocktail sausages out of the oven and puts them on the kitchen table.

'You can never have enough cocktail sausages at a party,' he says. 'They're always the first to go.'

'Won't they go cold?' I say, for no one I know likes a cold sausage.

Wayne closes the oven door.

'Don't panic, Margaret. We'll give them a quick blast in the microwave when everyone gets here.'

He wipes his hands on his apron and lifts a carrier bag off the floor.

'I might as well give this to you now. It's a present from me.'

'A present?' I say. 'You shouldn't have. You've done enough for me already. Besides, it ain't even my birthday.'

Wayne tells me to close my eyes and puts something in my hands.

'You can open them now,' he says.

The parcel Wayne has given me is wrapped in blue paper with lots of tiny rainbows on it. I tear it open. Inside is a box with what looks like a picture of a phone on it.

'What's this?' I say. 'A mobile?'

Wayne laughs. 'Not quite. It's a voice recorder.'

'A voice recorder?'

'Like a digital tape recorder? I thought we could use it to start recording your story.'

'We're making my audiobook?'

I can hardly speak. I hold the voice recorder in my hands, turning it over, staring at it in disbelief.

'I got you a card, too,' says Wayne, handing me an envelope.

I open it. On the front of the card is a photo of me taken by the Big Wheel in Margate, the day after I had my hair done. My eyes fill with tears.

'Thank you, Wayne,' I say. 'This is the best present I've ever had.'

'There's something else,' he says. 'Let me show you.'

Wayne opens the card and takes out a leaflet.

'They're running a free evening class at one of the colleges. It's a literacy course for adults with learning difficulties. I've signed you up for it.' He grins. 'I thought it might be a good way for you to meet people, too. New friends.'

A familiar song is coming from the kitchen radio. My favourite show is on: *Sounds of the 60s* with Brian Matthew. We look at each other and smile as Cilla's voice blares from the speaker, only this time, she ain't speaking to me, she's singing a song about a red rubber ball. The music is upbeat and catchy, and I can't help but sing along. She's saying the worst is over now, that everything is going to be all right. I believe her, for as she sings, I'm clutching my present from Wayne to my chest and looking out of the window. The sun is just as she describes it. It's shining – like a red rubber ball.

Charisma is the first to arrive. Wayne greets her at the front door. He's wearing a tall, pointed hat, a long black curly wig and a rainbow-coloured robe.

315

Charisma don't look impressed.

'Why are you dressed like that?' she says, taking off her anorak and hanging it on a hook. 'You never said it was fancy dress.'

Wayne twirls around, laughing.

'I'm *Gay* Fawkes. Isn't it obvious? Ta-dah!'

Charisma stares at him. 'Obvious?' she says. 'Not to me, it ain't. I thought you was that Joseph fella with his multi-coloured dream coat.'

She trundles into the kitchen, where I'm busy putting the last of the sandwiches Wayne and I made earlier onto plates: Dairylea and ham, corned beef and, my favourite, Coronation Street chicken.

Charisma throws an Iceland carrier bag down on the kitchen table.

'I brought you some bits and pieces. There's a six-pack of Cheesy Wotsits in there, and some sparklers.'

'Thank you, Charisma,' says Wayne. 'Would you like a drink?'

'I'll have a cider.' She blows out her cheeks and holds her stomach, like she's in pain. 'Not fizzy, though. Better make it still.' Pulling out a chair, she sits down. 'I've had terrible wind this week. Can't have anything too gassy.'

'I only have Strongbow, I'm afraid,' says Wayne, opening the fridge. 'If you leave it a while, it'll go flat, though.'

'That'll do,' she says.

Wayne hands her a can and she cracks it open. It fizzes everywhere, spraying her Meat Loaf T-shirt – and half the sandwiches – with cider. We're in for a good night, I think.

The doorbell rings. Wayne throws Charisma a cloth and goes to answer it. I grab a handful of paper towels to dry the table with. The kitchen is already a tip and the party ain't even started yet.

'Surprise, surprise!' says Wayne.

I turn around to see Sainsbury's David standing in the kitchen. He grins shyly, holding out a bunch of flowers.

'I . . . um . . . I can't stay for the fireworks, Margaret,' he says. 'I just wanted to pop in and give you these. To congratulate you on finding out who your mystery sender is. Wayne was telling me all about it in the shop the other day.'

He leans over to give me a peck on the cheek, but I move my head to the wrong side and we miss each other. We end up just sort of hugging.

He takes a step back and gives me the flowers. I press my nose into them. They smell lovely. So does David. I ask him what aftershave he's wearing.

'David Beckham,' he says, glancing at the clock on the wall. 'It was a present from my girlfriend.'

'You have a girlfriend?'

I don't mean to sound rude, but I always thought Sainsbury's David might be gay. Let's face it, most of the other men in my life are. Apart from Michael Bolton, of course.

David nods. 'We've been together three years. I met her in sixth form college. We're getting engaged.'

Charisma, who has finished patting down her T-shirt, takes a sandwich and shoves it in her mouth.

'I'm not meant to have bread,' she says. 'Makes me fart.'

Wayne laughs. 'It's just as well David brought his aftershave, then. We might need to give the kitchen a spritz with the old *Eau de Beckham* later.'

'Oh, I . . . I . . . can't hang around long, unfortunately,' says David. 'I've got to pick my nan up from bowls.'

'That's a shame,' says Wayne. 'Stay for one drink?'

The doorbell rings again.

'I'll let you answer it this time, Margaret,' Wayne says.

I take off my apron and hang it over the back of the

chair. On my way, I quickly check my hair in the hallway mirror. I had it cut again at Razzle Dazzle last week. It's even redder now. Cilla would be proud. I smile at my reflection, before opening the door to find Christine, and Mum in her wheelchair, waiting outside.

'You look beautiful, Margaret,' says Christine. 'Check out that hair! I can really see Mum in you!'

'Can you?'

I can't help beaming. I look down at Mum and she's beaming, too. I clear away some of the shoes that have been left in the hallway to make room for Mum's wheelchair. Christine apologises for being late.

'The traffic coming out of London was terrible,' she says. 'We got stuck in a tailback. Anyway, the important thing is we're here now.'

Wayne comes bouncing over in his rainbow-coloured glad rags. He kisses both Mum and Christine on the cheek. Christine hands him a few bottles of champagne.

'Veuve Clicquot!' says Wayne, looking at the label. 'Have I told you you're my favourite person, Christine? Do you want me to pop one open now?'

'I think that's a fabulous idea,' she says. 'By the way, Mum and I have got some very special news.'

'Special news?'

'I've put an offer in on a house in Whitstable,' she says. 'It's not a done deal, but it looks promising. A beautiful property, five bedrooms, right on the seafront. Anyone fancy Christmas dinner round ours next year?'

'Me!' I shout, a little too loudly.

I ain't even had a drink yet and already I'm feeling emotional. I want to have a little cry. I'm so happy.

Wayne grabs six champagne glasses from the cupboard and puts them on the table.

'Not for me,' says Charisma. 'Any more bubbles and I'll be spending the night on the toilet.'

'Good point,' says Wayne. 'We'll have enough popping and banging later with the fireworks. We don't need any more loud noises from you.'

We all laugh, even Charisma. Everyone holds out their glasses as Wayne pours the champagne. Mum's hands are a bit shaky, so I hold the glass steady for her.

'Only a drop for Mum,' says Christine.

'Gladys's face is telling me otherwise,' says Wayne. He leans over, whispers in Mum's ear, 'You have as much champagne as you like, Gladys. You're only young once.'

She looks up at me, a huge grin on her face.

Wayne turns to us all then.

'A toast,' he says. 'To new beginnings. Margaret, Christine and Gladys.'

'Margaret, Christine and Gladys,' we all chorus, chinking our glasses together.

Later on that evening, the five of us move into the garden to watch the fireworks. I can't help thinking back to when I was a child, the night they vanished me, all those years ago. It's cold outside, but at least we have each other. I get Mum a blanket and tuck her in. I stand behind her, resting my hands on her shoulders. The stars are shining bright, the night air smells of smoke. Together we watch the Catherine wheels, the Roman candles, the bright lights, flashing up in the sky.

The End

Acknowledgements

The Vanishing of Margaret Small has been over fourteen years in the making, so it feels strange, and a little surreal, to be writing acknowledgements after all this time.

Thank you to everyone at Soho Agency: to my agent, Rowan Lawton. I've said it before, Rowan, but you really have made a huge difference to my life. I'm so grateful for every opportunity you have created through your infectious enthusiasm, tenacity and fighting spirit. You are a true warrior. Thank you for all that you've done, and continue to do, to help bring stories like this one to the world.

Thank you also to Jane Snelgrove and all at Embla and Bonnier UK. I am so delighted to have you as an editor, Jane. It really has been a dream experience, and you have handled 'Margaret' so carefully and sensitively.

Thank you to all at Faber Academy, in particular my tutors, Esther Freud and Tim Lott, and 'The Fabettes' who gave such thoughtful and generous feedback on early draft extracts of the book: Rebecca Thornton, Jill Johnson, Paul Gould, Kate Taylor, Jackie Thomas, Richard Cooper, Bernadette Crowley, Jo Downer, Jude Fisher and Mike Morgan. Also, to Steve 'S.J.' Watson, who I met when I was reading some poems at Polari at the Royal Festival Hall back in November 2011, and who first gave me the idea of applying for the Faber Academy Writing a Novel course. Thanks also to Paul Burston, who runs Polari, for the incredible platform you have created for emerging LGBTQ+ writers. And John McCullough, an outstanding poet and teacher, who encouraged me to find my voice and keep writing back in my OU days.

Thank you too to other authors who have read all (or parts of) the book-in-progress over the years, and given feedback: Anstey Harris, Imogen Clark (who I first met online on an OU Creative Writing diploma back in 2009!), Alex Brown, Matson Taylor, and fellow CB Creative Edit and Pitch Your Novel course buddy Julietta Henderson.

Thank you to my former colleagues at Mencap, especially Ciara Lawrence, who is an amazing spokesperson and media influencer for people with a learning disability. Check out Ciara's Pink Sparkle Podcast!

Thank you to my teaching colleagues. Also to my students, past and present, who continue to inspire me, who – for many years – have been asking, 'Sir, when is your book coming out?' I hope my long and bumpy road to publication has been a lesson in resilience for you all. As a teacher, I've always tried to practise what I preach. 'If at first you don't succeed . . .'

The Vanishing of Margaret Small is also a love song to Whitstable, the little seaside town in Kent where I lived as an impoverished student in the early to mid-nineties. I moved back here in 2021, after 20 years in London – a move in part inspired by the writing of this book. Many of the Whitstable locations Margaret visits are real – Tea and Times, Rock Bottom Records, Hubbard's (to name but a few) – but the characters who inhabit them are entirely fictional. I do hope local readers will forgive me for taking some artistic licence here and there. In 2015, for example, Sainsbury's on Whitstable High Street was just in the process of taking over from Budgens. The shop doesn't have a meat counter either, but I added one just because I wanted to give Margaret a few more people to talk to!

A huge thank you to my parents for always supporting my love of reading and writing. It's taken me a long time to get published, I know, but – as my school reports will tell you – I've always been a slow starter. I got there in the end! Mum, you are always my first reader and I promise to show you Book Two soon. Thanks also to my sister, Jane, for putting up with all of the substandard Roger Hargreaves/Enid Blyton-esque storybooks I wrote for her when we were growing up (remember 'Bessie Beachball'?).

Special thanks to Dan, my partner and travel companion, for supporting me on my (often totally impractical) journey to publication and for taking me all over the world. Also to Prudence the cat, my owner and writing buddy, for always giving me the purrfect reason to come home.

Finally, many thanks to the book bloggers and influencers on social media who have been reading and sharing their love of Margaret Small, both here in the UK and further afield. Your support is hugely appreciated, so if you enjoyed the book, please leave an Amazon review. Readers who wish to get in touch can find me on Twitter @neilalexander_ and Instagram @neilalexanderwriter.

A Note from the Author

When I started writing *The Vanishing of Margaret Small* in 2009, I was working as Celebrity Manager for UK learning disability charity Mencap. It was during this time that I met the most extraordinary woman, Mabel Cooper, whose voice inspired me to pick up my pen and write this story, a story which, after nearly fifteen years of edits, rewrites and revisions has finally made it into the hands of readers.

Like Margaret, Mabel had a learning disability and had spent much of her childhood, and adult life, in a long-stay institution (St Lawrence's Hospital in Caterham, Surrey). Mabel was a passionate campaigner for the rights of people with learning disabilities, and over the years spoke at many Mencap events. Listening to Mabel tell her life story was an incredible experience, and I feel privileged to have heard her speak first-hand. No one who listened to her voice will ever forget the stories and recollections she shared with them. She was a brilliant storyteller – engaging, inspiring and brutally honest. For Mabel, stories were important historical documents and instruments for change and, in 1997, her memoir was included as part of *Forgotten Lives: Exploring the History of Learning Disability*. This book brought her international recognition as a published author, taking her all over the world, from London to Australia. During her lifetime, she used her platform to ensure that her voice, and the voices of those with learning disabilities, did not go unheard, and that their experiences of living in institutions would never be forgotten.

In 2010, Mabel was awarded an honorary Master's degree at the Barbican in London. She died of cancer in 2013, aged 68.

Margaret Small is, of course, a fictional character, yet many of the events she describes draw from real life experiences and perspectives of individuals like Mabel, who were 'vanished' to long-stay institutions, hidden away because of their disability. A huge amount of research went into the book, and I am grateful to the London Metropolitan Archives where, back in 2010 (yes – that long ago!), I was able to pore through archived documents from St Lawrence's Hospital, everything from medical records and inspections to summer fete programmes and photographs. Special mention must be made here to the work of Dorothy Atkinson, Mark Jackson and Jan Walmsley in *Forgotten Lives: Exploring the History of Learning Disability* (BILD Publications, 1997) and *'A Fit Person to Be Removed': Personal Accounts of Life in a Mental Deficiency Institution* by Maggie Potts and Rebecca Fido (Northcote House Publishers, 1991).

As well as the various online articles and websites I visited as part of my research, the following were extremely useful: *What's It All About?* by Cilla Black; *Austerity Britain, 1945–1951* and *Family Britain, 1951–57* by David Kynaston; *All About Us! The story of people with a learning disability and Mencap*, by Brian Rix; *Fabulous Fanny Cradock* by Clive Ellis, *Fanny Cradock's Common Market Cookery – France* by Fanny Cradock, *White Heat: A History of Britain in the Swinging Sixties* by Dominic Sandbrook; various online Cilla Black obituaries (the *Guardian*, BBC Online). In addition, both of these websites provided inspiration for the fictional Lady Oak Lodge: www.motherandbabyhomes.com and www.movementforanadoptionapology.org.

About Neil Alexander

Neil is a graduate of the Faber Academy 'Writing a Novel' course, taught by Esther Freud and Tim Lott. Originally from Northern Ireland, he now lives in the seaside town of Whitstable in Kent. Neil, who has a Masters degree in English Literature from the University of Kent at Canterbury, began his career working in health journalism and, for many years, worked as part of the PR team for UK learning disability charity Mencap. He currently teaches English part-time at a secondary school in Kent and is working on his second novel.

About Embla Books

Embla Books is a digital-first publisher of standout commercial adult fiction. Passionate about storytelling, the team at Embla publish books that will make you 'laugh, love, look over your shoulder and lose sleep'. Launched by Bonnier Books UK in 2021, the imprint is named after the first woman from the creation myth in Norse mythology, who was carved by the gods from a tree trunk found on the seashore – an image of the kind of creative work and crafting that writers do, and a symbol of how stories shape our lives.

Find out about some of our other books and stay in touch:

Twitter, Facebook, Instagram: @emblabooks
Newsletter: https://bit.ly/emblanewsletter